Praise for LICK

"The stuff my rock-star dreams are made of. A thrill ride. I felt every stomach-dip in the process. And I want to turn right around and ride it again. Every girl who's ever had a rock-star crush, this would be the ultimate fantasy." —*Maryse's Book Blog*

"This book rocked my world!! *Lick* is an addictive blend of heartwarming passion and lighthearted fun. It's a story you can lose yourself in. The perfect rock-star romance!" —*Aestas Book Blog*

"An engrossing, sexy, and emotional read." —*Dear Author*

"Scrumptious and delicious. Firmly in my top ten best books this year!" —*The Book Pushers*

"Fun with great characters, a rocker story line, good angst, and plenty of sexy times. I would strongly recommend this book to anyone looking for something sexy and heartwarming."
—*Fiction Vixen*

"A nice start to a rock 'n' roll series. Very much looking forward to the next one." —*Smexy Books*

"This story is so hot, sexy, steamy, and everything in between!"
—*A Diary of a Book Addict*

"Hot, Hot, Hot! I wouldn't hesitate to get my hands on this one."
—*A Tale of Many Reviews*

"*Lick* made me laugh, broke my heart, and even made me swoon. Those are signs of a great book." —*Under the Covers*

Kylie Scott

🦁 ST. MARTIN'S GRIFFIN ❧ NEW YORK

www.stmartins.com

Designed by Steven Seighman

The Library of Congress Cataloging-in-Publication Data is available upon request.

ISBN 978-1-250-05236-0 (trade paperback)
ISBN 978-1-4668-5240-8 (e-book)

Originally published in Australia by Momentum, an imprint of Pan Macmillan Australia in July 2013 as *Lick: Stage Dive #1*

First published in the United States as an e-book by St. Martin's Griffin in November 2013

St. Martin's Griffin books may be purchased for educational, business, or promotional use. For information on bulk purchases, please contact Macmillan Corporate and Premium Sales Department at 1-800-221-7945, extension 5442, or write specialmarkets@macmillan.com

First St. Martin's Griffin Paperback Edition: May 2014

10 9 8 7 6 5 4 3 2

For Hugh.

And also for Mish, who wanted something without zombies.

ACKNOWLEDGMENTS

First up, all lyrics (with the exception of the final song) are used courtesy of Soviet X-Ray Record Club. You can learn more about the band at www.sovietxrayrecordclub.com. The term "topless cuddles" comes courtesy of the writer Daniel Dalton.

Much love to my family, who suffered as always while I wandered around in a story daze working on this. Your patience is legendary, thank you so much. To my invaluable friends who give me feedback and support (in no particular order because you are all Queens in my eyes): Tracey O'Hara, Kendall Ryan, Mel Teshco, Joanna Wylde, Kylie Griffin, and Babette. A big thank-you to all book bloggers for doing what you do, especially my friends Angie from *Twinsie Talk*, Cath from *Book Chatter Cath*, Maryse from *Maryse's Book Blog*, and Katrina from *Page Flipperz*. Thanks to Joel, Anne, and Mark at Momentum for being so supportive. And special thanks to my editor, Sarah JH Fletcher.

Last but not least, to the lovely folk who chat with me on Twitter and Facebook, and send me e-mails saying kind things about my books. To the people who enjoy my stories and take the time to write a review, THANK YOU.

Lick

CHAPTER ONE

I woke up on the bathroom floor. Everything hurt. My mouth felt like garbage and tasted worse. What the hell had happened last night? The last thing I remembered was the countdown to midnight and the thrill of turning twenty-one— legal, at last. I'd been dancing with Lauren and talking to some guy. Then BANG!

Tequila.

A whole line of shot glasses with lemon and salt on the side.

Everything I'd heard about Vegas was true. Bad things happened here, terrible things. I just wanted to crawl into a ball and die. Sweet baby Jesus, what had I been thinking to drink so much? I groaned, and even that made my head pound. This pain had not been part of the plan.

"You okay?" a voice inquired, male, deep, and nice. Really nice. A shiver went through me despite my pain. My poor broken body stirred in the strangest of places.

"Are you going to be sick again?" he asked.

Oh, no.

I opened my eyes and sat up, pushing my greasy blond hair aside. His blurry face loomed closer. I slapped a hand over my mouth because my breath had to be hideous.

"Hi," I mumbled.

Slowly, he swam into focus. He was built and beautiful and strangely familiar. Impossible. I'd never met anyone like him.

He looked to be in his mid to late twenties—a man, not a boy. He had long, dark hair falling past his shoulders and sideburns. His eyes were the darkest blue. They couldn't be real. Frankly, those eyes were overkill. I'd have swooned perfectly fine without them. Even with the tired red tinge, they were a thing of beauty. Tattoos covered the entirety of one arm and half his bare chest. A black bird had been inked into the side of his neck, the tip of its wing reaching up behind his ear. I still had on the pretty, dirty white dress Lauren had talked me into. It had been a daring choice for me on account of the way it barely contained my abundance of boobage. But this beautiful man easily had me beat for skin on show. He wore just a pair of jeans, scuffed black boots, a couple of small silver earrings, and a loose white bandage on his forearm.

Those jeans . . . he wore them well. They sat invitingly low on his hips and fit in all the right ways. Even my monster hangover couldn't detract from the view.

"Aspirin?" he asked.

And I was ogling him. My gaze darted to his face and he gave me a sly, knowing smile. Wonderful. "Yes. Please."

He grabbed a battered black leather jacket off the floor, the one I'd apparently been using as a pillow. Thank God I hadn't puked on it. Clearly, this beautiful half-naked man had seen me in all my glory, hurling multiple times. I could have drowned in the shame.

One by one he emptied the contents of his pockets out onto the cold white tiles. A credit card, guitar picks, a phone, and a string of condoms. The condoms gave me pause, but I was soon distracted by what emerged next. A multitude of paper scraps tumbled out onto the floor. All had names and numbers scrawled across them. This guy was Mr. Popularity. Hey, I could definitely see why. But what on earth was he doing here with me?

Finally, he produced a small bottle of painkillers. Sweet relief. I loved him, whoever he was and whatever he'd seen.

"You need water," he said, and got busy filling a glass from the sink behind him.

The bathroom was tiny. We both barely fit. Given Lauren's and my money situation, the hotel had been the best we could afford. She'd been determined to celebrate my birthday in style. My goal had been a bit different. Despite the presence of my hot new friend, I was pretty sure I'd failed. The pertinent parts of my anatomy felt fine. I'd heard things hurt after the first couple of times. They sure as hell had after the first. But my vagina might have been the only part of my body not giving me grief.

Still, I took a quick peek down the front of my dress. The corner of a foil package could still be seen, tucked into the side of my bra. Because if it was sitting there, strapped to me, no way would I be caught unprepared. The condom remained whole and hearty. How disappointing. Or maybe not. Finally plucking up the courage to get back on the horse, so to speak, and then not remembering it would have been horrible.

The man handed me the glass of water and placed two pills into my hand. He then sat back on his haunches to watch me. He had an intensity to him that I was in no condition to deal with.

"Thanks," I said, then swallowed the aspirin. Noisy rumbles rose from my belly. Nice, very ladylike.

"Are you sure you're okay?" he asked. His glorious mouth twitched into a smile as if we shared a private joke between us.

The joke being me.

All I could do was stare. Given my current condition, he was just too much. The hair, face, body, ink, all of it. Someone needed to invent a word superlative enough to describe him.

After a long moment it dawned on me that he expected an answer to his question. I nodded, still unwilling to unleash my morning breath, and gave him a grim smile. The best I could do.

"Okay. That's good," he said.

He was certainly attentive. I didn't know what I'd done to deserve such kindness. If I'd picked up the poor guy with promises of sex and then proceeded to spend the night with my head in the toilet, by rights he should be a bit disgruntled. Maybe he hoped I'd make good on the offer this morning. It seemed the only plausible explanation for why he'd linger.

Under normal conditions, he was light-years out of my league and (for the sake of my pride) worlds away from my type. I liked clean-cut. Clean-cut was nice. Bad boys were highly overrated. God knows, I'd watched enough girls throw themselves at my brother over the years. He'd taken what they'd offered if it suited him, and then moved on. Bad boys weren't the stuff serious relationships were made of. Not that I'd been chasing forever last night, just a positive sexual experience. Something not involving Tommy Byrnes being mad at me for getting a smear of blood on the backseat of his parents' car. God, what a horrible memory. The next day the douche had dumped me for a girl on the track team half my size. He then added insult to injury by spreading rumors about me. I hadn't been made bitter or twisted by this event at all.

What had happened last night? My head remained a tangled, throbbing mess, the details hazy, incomplete.

"We should get something into you," he said. "You want me to order some dry toast or something?"

"No." The thought of food was not fun. Not even coffee appealed, and coffee always appealed. I was half tempted to check myself for a pulse, just in case. Instead, I pushed my hand through my crappy hair, getting it out of my eyes. "No . . . ow!" Strands caught on something, tugging hard at my scalp. "Crap."

"Hang on." He reached out and carefully disentangled my messy do from whatever was causing the trouble. "There we go."

"Thanks." Something winked at me from my left hand, snagging my attention. A ring, but not just any ring. An amazing ring, a stupendous one.

"Holy shit," I whispered.

It couldn't be real. It was so big it bordered on obscene. A stone that size would cost a fortune. I stared, bemused, turning my hand to catch the light. The band beneath was thick, solid, and the rock sure shone and sparkled like the real deal.

As if.

"Ah, yeah. About that . . ." he said, dark brows drawn down. He looked vaguely embarrassed by the ice rink on my finger. "If you still wanna change it for something smaller, that's okay with me. It is kinda big. I do get your point about that."

I couldn't shake the feeling I knew him from somewhere. Somewhere that wasn't last night or this morning or anything to do with the ridiculous beautiful ring on my finger.

"You bought me this?" I asked.

He nodded. "Last night at Cartier."

"Cartier?" My voice dropped to a whisper. "Huh."

For a long moment he just stared at me. "You don't remember?"

I really didn't want to answer that. "What is that, even? Two, three carats?"

"Five."

"Five? Wow."

"What do you remember?" he asked, voice hardening just a little.

"Well . . . it's hazy."

"No." His frown increased until it owned his handsome face. "You have got to be fucking kidding me. You seriously don't know?"

What to say? My mouth hung open, useless. There was a lot I didn't know. To my knowledge, however, Cartier didn't do costume jewelry. My head swam. Bad feelings unfurled within my stomach and bile burnt the back of my throat. Worse even than before.

I was not puking in front of this guy.

Not again.

He took a deep breath, nostrils flaring. "I didn't realize you'd had that much to drink. I mean, I knew you'd had a bit, but . . . shit. Seriously? You don't remember us going on the gondolas at the Venetian?"

"We went on gondolas?"

"Fuck. Ah, how about when you bought me a burger? Do you remember that?"

"Sorry."

"Wait a minute," he said, watching me through narrowed eyes. "You're just messing with me, aren't you?"

"I'm so sorry."

He physically recoiled from me. "Let me get this straight, you don't remember anything?"

"No," I said, swallowing hard. "What did we do last night?"

"We got fucking married," he growled.

This time, I didn't make it to the toilet.

I decided on divorce while I brushed my teeth, practiced what I would say to him as I washed my hair. But you couldn't rush these things. Unlike last night, when I'd apparently rushed into marriage. Rushing again would be wrong, foolish. That, or I was a coward taking the world's longest shower. Odds were on the latter.

Holy, holy hell. What a mess. I couldn't even begin to get my head wrapped around it. Married. Me. My lungs wouldn't work. Panic waited right around the corner.

No way could my desire for this disaster to go away come as a surprise to him. Puking on the floor had to have been a huge hint. I groaned and covered my face with my hands at the memory. His look of disgust would haunt me all my days.

My parents would kill me if they ever found out. I had plans, priorities. I was studying to be an architect like my father. Marriage to anyone at this stage didn't fit into those plans. In another ten, fifteen years, maybe. But marriage at twenty-one? Hell no. I hadn't even been on a second date in years and now I had a ring on my finger. No way did that make sense. I was doomed. This crazy wedding caper wasn't something I could hide from.

Or could I?

Unless my parents could not find out. Ever. Over the years I had made something of a habit of not involving them in things that might be seen as unsavory, unnecessary, or just plain stupid. This marriage quite possibly fell under all three categories.

Actually, maybe no one need know. If I didn't tell, how would they find out? They wouldn't. The answer was awe-inspiring in its simplicity.

"Yes!" I hissed and punched the air, clipping the shower head with the side of my fist. Water sprayed everywhere, including straight in my eyes, blinding me. Never mind, I had the answer.

Denial. I'd take the secret to my grave. No one would ever know of my extreme drunken idiocy.

I smiled with relief, my panic attack receding enough so that I could breathe. Oh, thank goodness. Everything would be okay. I had a new plan to get me back on track with the old one. Brilliant. I'd brave up, go and face him, and set things straight. Twenty-one-year-olds with grand life plans didn't marry complete strangers in Vegas, no matter how beautiful those strangers happened to be. It would be fine. He'd understand. In all likelihood, he sat out there right now, working out the most efficient method to dump and run.

The diamond still glittered on my hand. I couldn't bring myself to take it off just yet. It was like Christmas on my finger, so big, bright, and shiny. Though, upon reflection, my temporary husband didn't exactly appear to be rich. His jacket and jeans were both well-worn. The man was a mystery.

Wait. What if he was into something illegal? Maybe I'd married a criminal. Panic rushed back in with a vengeance. My stomach churned and my head throbbed. I knew nothing about the person waiting in the next room. Absolutely not a damn thing. I'd shoved him out the bathroom door without even getting his name.

A knock on the door sent my shoulders sky-high.

"Evelyn?" he called out, proving he at least knew my name.

"Just a second."

I turned off the taps and stepped out, wrapping a towel around myself. The width of it was barely sufficient to cover my curves, but my dress had puke on it. Putting it back on was out of the question.

"Hi," I said, opening the bathroom door a hand's length. He stood almost half a head taller than me, and I wasn't short by any means. Dressed in only a towel, I found him rather intimidating. However much he'd had to drink the previous night, he still looked gorgeous, as opposed to me—pale, pasty, and sopping wet. The aspirins hadn't done nearly as much as they should have.

Of course, I'd thrown them up.

"Hey." He didn't meet my eyes. "Look, I'm going to get this taken care of, okay?"

"Taken care of?"

"Yeah," he said, still avoiding all eye contact. Apparently the hideous green motel carpeting was beyond enticing. "My lawyers will deal with all this."

"You have lawyers?" Criminals had lawyers. Shit. I had to get myself divorced from this guy now.

"Yeah, I have lawyers. You don't need to worry about anything. They'll send you the paperwork or whatever. However this works." He gave me an irritated glance, lips a tight line, and pulled on his leather jacket over his bare chest. His T-shirt still hung drying over the edge of the tub. Sometime during the night I must have puked on it too. How gruesome. If I were him, I'd divorce me and never look back.

"This was a mistake," he said, echoing my thoughts.

"Oh."

"What?" His gaze jumped to my face. "You disagree?"

"No," I said quickly.

"Didn't think so. Pity it made sense last night, yeah?" He shoved a hand through his hair and made for the door. "Take care."

"Wait!" The stupid, amazing ring wouldn't come off my finger. I tugged and turned it, trying to wrestle it into submission. Finally it budged, grazing my knuckle raw in the process. Blood welled to the surface. One more stain in this whole sordid affair. "Here."

"For fuck's sake." He scowled at the rock sparkling in the palm of my hand as if it had personally offended him. "Keep it."

"I can't. It must have cost a fortune."

He shrugged.

"Please." I held it out, hand jiggling, impatient to be rid of the evidence of my drunken stupidity. "It belongs to you. You have to take it."

"No. I don't."

"But—"

Without another word, the man stormed out, slamming the door shut behind him. The thin walls vibrated with the force of it.

Whoa. My hand fell back to my side. He sure had a temper. Not that I hadn't given him provocation, but still. I wish I remembered what had gone on between us. Any inkling would be good.

Meanwhile my left butt cheek felt sore. I winced, carefully rubbing the area. My dignity wasn't the only casualty, it seemed. I must have scratched my behind at some stage, bumped into some furniture or taken a dive in my fancy new heels. The pricey ones Lauren had insisted went with the dress, the ones whose current whereabouts were a mystery. I hoped I hadn't lost them. Given my recent nuptials, nothing would surprise me.

I wandered back into the bathroom with a vague memory of a buzzing noise and laughter ringing in my ear, of him whispering to me. It made no sense.

I turned and raised the edge of my towel, going up on tippy-toes to inspect my ample ass in the mirror. Black ink and hot pink skin.

All the air left my body in a rush.
There was a word on my left butt cheek, a name:
David
I spun and dry-heaved into the sink.

CHAPTER TWO

Lauren sat beside me on the plane, fiddling with my iPhone. "I don't understand how your taste in music can be so bad. We've been friends for years. Have I taught you nothing?"

"To not drink tequila."

She rolled her eyes.

Above our heads the seat belt sign flashed on. A polite voice advised us to return our seats to the upright position as we'd be landing in a few minutes. I swallowed the dregs of my shitty plane coffee with a wince. Fact was, no amount of caffeine could help me today. Quality didn't even come into it.

"I am deadly serious," I said. "I'm also never setting foot in Nevada ever again so long as I live."

"Now, there's an overreaction."

"Not even a little, lady."

Lauren had stumbled back to the motel a bare two hours before our flight was due to leave. I'd spent the time repacking my small bag over and over in an attempt to get my life back into some semblance of order. It was good to see Lauren smiling, though getting to the airport in time had been a race. Apparently she and the cute waiter she'd met would be keeping in touch. Lauren had always been great with guys, while I was more closely related to your standard garden-variety wallflower. My plan to get laid in Vegas had been a deliberate attempt to get out of that rut. So much for that idea.

Lauren was studying economics, and she was gorgeous, inside and out. I was more kind of unwieldy. It was why I made a habit of walking everywhere I could in Portland and trying not to sample the contents of the cake display case at the café where I worked. It kept me manageable, waist-wise. Though my mom still saw fit to give me lectures on the subject because God forbid I dare put sugar in my coffee. My thighs would no doubt explode or something.

Lauren had three older brothers and knew what to say to guys. Nothing intimidated her. The girl oozed charm. I had one older brother, but we no longer interacted outside of major family holidays. Not since he moved out of our parents' home four years back leaving only a note. Nathan had a temper and a gift for getting into trouble. He'd been the bad boy in high school, always getting into fights and skipping classes. Though blaming my lack of success with guys on my nonexistent relationship with my brother was wrong. I could own my deficiencies with the opposite sex. Mostly.

"Listen to this." Lauren plugged my earphones into her phone, and the whine of electric guitars exploded inside my skull. The pain was exquisite. My headache roared back to sudden, horrific life. Nothing remained of my brain but bloody red mush. Of this I was certain.

I ripped out the earphones. "Don't. Please."

"But that's Stage Dive."

"And they're lovely. But, you know, another time maybe."

"I worry about you sometimes. I just want you to know that."

"There is nothing wrong with country music played softly."

Lauren snorted and fluffed up her dark hair. "There is nothing right with country music played at any volume. So what did you get up to last night? Apart from spending quality time heaving?"

"Actually, that about sums it up." The less said the better. How could I ever explain? Still, guilt slid through me and I squirmed in my seat. The tattoo throbbed in protest.

I hadn't told Lauren about my grand having-good-sex plan for the night. She'd have wanted to help. Honestly, sex didn't strike me as the sort of thing you should have help with. Apart from what was required from the sexual partner in question, of course. Lauren's assistance would have involved foisting me on every hottie in the room with promises of my immediate leg-open availability.

I loved Lauren, and her loyalty was above question, but she didn't have a subtle bone in her body. She'd punched a girl in the nose in fifth grade for teasing me about my weight, and we'd been friends ever since. With Lauren, you always knew exactly where you stood. Something I appreciated the bulk of the time, just not when discretion was called for.

Happily, my sore stomach survived the bumpy landing. As soon as those wheels hit the tarmac, I let out a sigh of relief. I was back in my hometown. Beautiful Oregon, lovely Portland, never again would I stray. With mountains in the distance and trees in the city, she was a singular delight. To limit myself to the one city for life might indeed be going overboard. But it was great to be home. I had an all-important internship starting next week that my father had pulled strings to get for me. There were also next semester's classes to start planning for.

Everything would be fine. I'd learned my lesson. Normally, I didn't go past three drinks. Three drinks were good. Three got me happy without tripping me face-first into disaster. Never again would I cross the line. I was back to being the good old organized, boring me. Adventures were not cool, and I was done with them.

We stood and grabbed our bags out of the overhead lockers. Everyone pushed forward in a rush to disembark. The hostesses gave us practiced smiles as we tramped up the aisle and out into the connecting tunnel. Next came security, and then we poured out into the baggage claim. Fortunately we only had carry-on, so no delays there. I couldn't wait to get home.

I heard shouting up ahead. Lights were flashing. Someone famous must have been on the plane. People ahead of us turned and stared. I looked back too but saw no familiar faces.

"What's going on?" Lauren asked, scanning the crowd.

"I don't know," I said, standing on tippy-toes, getting excited by all the commotion.

Then I heard it, my name being called out over and over. Lauren's mouth pursed in surprise. Mine fell open.

"When's the baby due?"

"Evelyn, is David with you?"

"Will there be another wedding?"

"When will you be moving to LA?"

"Is David coming to meet your parents?"

"Evelyn, is this the end for Stage Dive?"

"Is it true that you got tattoos of each other's names?"

"How long have you and David been seeing each other?"

"What do you say to accusations that you've broken up the band?"

My name and his, over and over, mixed into a barrage of endless questions. All of which merged into chaos. A wall of noise I could barely comprehend. I stood gaping in disbelief as flashbulbs blinded me and people pressed in. My heart hammered. I'd never been great with crowds, and there was no escape that I could see.

Lauren snapped out of it first.

She shoved her sunglasses onto my face and then grabbed my hand. With liberal use of her elbows, she dragged me through the mob. The world became a blur, thanks to her prescription lenses. I was lucky not to fall on my ass. We ran through the busy airport and out to a waiting taxi, jumping the queue. People started yelling. We ignored them.

The paparazzi were close behind.

The motherfucking paparazzi. It would have been surreal if it wasn't so frantic and in my face.

Lauren pushed me into the backseat of the cab. I scrambled across, then slumped down, doing my best to hide. Wishing I could disappear entirely.

"Go! Hurry!" she shouted at the driver.

The driver took her at her word. He shot out of the place, sending us sliding across the cracked vinyl seating. My forehead bounced off the back of the (luckily padded) passenger seat. Lauren pulled my seat belt over me and jammed it into the clasp. My hands didn't seem to be working. Everything jumped and jittered.

"Talk to me," she said.

"Ah . . ." No words came out. I pushed her sunglasses up on top of my head and stared into space. My ribs hurt, and my heart still pounded so hard.

"Ev?" With a small smile, Lauren patted my knee. "Did you somehow happen to get married while we were away?"

"I . . . yeah. I, uh, I did. I think."

"Wow."

And then it just all blurted out of me. "God, Lauren. I screwed up so badly and I barely even remember any of it. I just woke up and he was there and then he was so pissed at me and I don't even blame him. I didn't know how to tell you. I was just going to pretend it never happened."

"I don't think that's going to work now."

"No."

"Okay. No big deal. So you're married." Lauren nodded, her face freakily calm. No anger, no blame. Meanwhile, I felt terrible I hadn't confided in her. We shared everything.

"I'm sorry," I said. "I should have told you."

"Yes, you should have. But never mind." She straightened out her skirt like we were sitting down to tea. "So, who did you marry?"

"D-David. His name is David."

"David Ferris, by any chance?"

The name sounded familiar. "Maybe?"

"Where we going?" asked the cabdriver, never taking his eyes off the traffic. He wove in and out among the cars with supernatural speed. If I'd been up to feeling anything, I might have felt fear and more nausea. Blind terror, perhaps. But I had nothing.

"Ev?" Lauren turned in her seat, checking out the cars behind us. "We haven't lost them. Where do you want to go?"

"Home," I said, the first safe place to come to mind. "My parents' place, I mean."

"Good call. They've got a fence." Without pausing for breath, Lauren rattled off the address to the driver. She frowned and pushed the sunglasses back down over my face. "Keep them on."

I gave a rough laugh as the world outside turned back into a smudge. "You really think it'll help, now?"

"No," she said, flicking back her long hair. "But people in these situations always wear sunglasses. Trust me."

"You watch too much TV." I closed my eyes. The sunglasses weren't helping my hangover. Nor was the rest of it. All my own damn fault. "I'm sorry I didn't say something. I didn't mean to get married. I don't even remember what happened exactly. This is such a . . ."

"Clusterfuck?"

"That word works."

Lauren sighed and rested her head on my shoulder. "You're right. You really shouldn't drink tequila ever again."

"No," I agreed.

"Do me a favor?" she asked.

"Mm?"

"Don't break up my favorite band."

"Ohmygod." I shoved the sunglasses back up, frowning hard enough to make my head throb. "Guitarist. He's the guitarist. That's where I know him from."

"Yes. He's the guitarist for Stage Dive. Well spotted."

The David Ferris. He'd been on Lauren's bedroom wall for years. Granted, he had to be the last person I'd expect to wake up with, on a bathroom floor or otherwise. But how the hell could I not have recognized him? "That's how he could afford the ring."

"What ring?"

Shuffling farther down in the seat, I fished the monster out of my jeans pocket and brushed off the lint and fluff. The diamond glittered accusingly in the bright light of day.

Lauren started shaking beside me, muffled laughter escaping her lips. "Mother of God, it's huuuuge!"

"I know."

"No, seriously."

"I know."

"Fuck me. I think I'm about to pee myself," she squealed,

fanning her face and bouncing up and down on the car seat. "Look at it!"

"Lauren, stop. We can't both be freaking out. That won't work."

"Right. Sorry." She cleared her throat, visibly struggling to get herself back under control. "How much is that even worth?"

"I really don't want to guess."

"That. Is. Insane."

We both stared at my bling in awed silence.

Suddenly Lauren started bopping up and down in her seat again like a kid riding a sugar high. "I know! Let's sell it and go backpacking in Europe. Hell, we could probably circle the globe a couple of times on that sucker. Imagine it."

"We can't," I said, as tempting as it sounded. "I've got to get it back to him somehow. I can't keep this."

"Pity." She grinned. "So, congratulations. You're married to a rock star."

I tucked the ring back in my pocket. "Thanks. What the hell am I going to do?"

"I honestly don't know." She shook her head at me, her eyes full of wonder. "You've exceeded all of my expectations. I wanted you to let your hair down a little. Get a life and give mankind another chance. But this is a whole new level of crazy you've ascended to. Do you really have a tattoo?"

"Yes."

"Of his name?"

I sighed and nodded.

"Where, might I inquire?"

I shut my eyes tight. "My left butt cheek."

Lauren lost it, laughing so hard that tears started streaming down her face.

Perfect.

CHAPTER THREE

Dad's cell rang just before midnight. My own had long since been switched off. When the home phone wouldn't stop ringing, we'd unplugged it from the wall. Twice the police had been by to clear people out of the front yard. Mom had finally taken a sleeping pill and gone to bed. Having her neat, ordered world shot to hell hadn't gone down so well. Surprisingly, after an initial outburst, Dad had been dealing all right with the situation. I was suitably apologetic and wanted a divorce. He was willing to chalk this one up to hormones or the like. But that all changed when he looked at the screen of his cell.

"Leyton?" He answered the call, his eyes drilling into me from across the room. My stomach sank accordingly. Only a parent could train you so well. I had disappointed him. We both knew it. There was only one Leyton and only one reason why he'd be calling at this hour on this day.

"Yes," my father said. "It's an unfortunate situation." The lines around his mouth deepened, turning into crevices. "Understandably. Yes. Good night, then."

His fingers tightened around the cell and then he tossed it onto the dining room table. "Your internship has been canceled."

All of the air rushed out of me as my lungs constricted to the size of pennies.

"Leyton rightly feels that given your present situation . . ." My father's voice trailed away to nothing. He'd called in years-old favors to get me the internship with one of Portland's most prestigious architectural firms. It'd had taken only a thirty-second phone call, however, to make it disappear.

Someone banged on the door. Neither of us reacted. People had been hammering on it for hours.

Dad started pacing back and forth across the living room. I just watched in a daze.

Throughout my childhood, times such as this had always followed a certain pattern. Nathan got into a fight at school. The school called our mother. Our mother had a meltdown. Nate retreated to his room or, worse, disappeared for days. Dad got home and paced. And there I'd be among it all, trying to play mediator, the expert at not making waves. So what the hell was I doing standing in the middle of a fucking tsunami?

As kids went, I'd always been pretty low maintenance. I'd gotten good grades in high school and had gone on to the same local college as my father. I might have lacked his natural talent at design, but I put in the hours and effort to get the grades I needed to pass. I had been working part-time in the same coffee shop since I was fifteen. Moving in with Lauren had been my one grand rebellion. I was, all in all, fantastically boring. My parents had wanted me to stay home and save money. Anything else I'd achieved had been done through subterfuge so my parents could sleep soundly at night. Not that I'd gotten up to much. The odd party. The Tommy episode four years back. There'd been nothing to prepare me for this.

Apart from the press, there were people crying on the front lawn and holding signs proclaiming their love for David. One man was holding an old-style boom box high in the air, blasting out music. A song called "San Pedro" was their favorite. The yelling would reach a crescendo every time the singer made it to the chorus, "But the sun was low and we'd no place to go . . ."

Apparently, later they were planning on burning me in effigy.

Which was fine, I wanted to die.

My big brother Nathan had been over to collect Lauren and take her back to his place. We hadn't seen each other since Christmas, but desperate times and desperate measures. The apartment Lauren and I shared was likewise surrounded. Going there was out of the question, and Lauren didn't want to get her family or other friends involved. To say Nathan enjoyed my predicament would be unkind. Not untrue, but definitely unkind. He'd always been the one in trouble. This time, however, it was all on me. Nathan had never gotten accidentally married and inked in Vegas.

Because of course some asshat reporter had asked my mother how she felt about the tattoo, so that secret was out. Apparently now no decent boy from a good family would ever marry me. Previously, I'd been unlikely to land a man due to my various lumps and bumps. But now it was all on the tattoo. I'd decided to forgo pointing out to her that I was already married.

More banging on the front door. Dad just looked at me. I shrugged.

"Ms. Thomas?" a big voice boomed. "David sent me."

Yeah, right. "I'm calling the cops."

"Wait. Please," the big voice said. "I've got him on the phone. Just open the door enough so I can hand it in to you."

"No."

Muffled noises. "He said to ask you about his T-shirt."

The one he'd left behind in Vegas. It was in my bag, still damp. Huh. Maybe. But I still wasn't convinced. "What else?"

More talking. "He said he still didn't want the . . . excuse me, miss . . . 'fucking ring' back."

I opened the door but kept the chain on. A man who resembled a bulldog in a black suit handed me a cell phone.

"Hello?"

Loud music played in the background and there were lots of voices. Apparently this marriage incident hadn't slowed down David at all.

"Ev?"

"Yes."

He paused. "Listen, you probably want to lie low for a while until this all dies down, okay? Sam will get you out of there. He's part of my security team."

Sam gave me a polite smile. I'd seen mountains smaller than this guy.

"Where would I go?" I asked.

"He'll, ah . . . he'll bring you to me. We'll sort something out."

"To you?"

"Yeah, there'll be the divorce papers and shit to sign, so you may as well come here."

I wanted to say no. But taking this away from my parents' front doorstep was wildly tempting. Ditto with getting out of there before Mom woke up and heard about the internship. Still, with good reason or not, I couldn't forget the way David had slammed his way out of my life that morning. I had a vague backup plan taking shape. With the internship gone, I could return to work at the café. Ruby would be delighted to have me full-time for the summer and I loved being there. Turning up with this horde on my heels, however, would be a disaster.

My options were few and none of them appealed, but still I hedged. "I don't know . . ."

He gave a particularly pained-sounding sigh. "What else are you gonna do? Huh?"

Good question.

Out past Sam, the insanity continued. Lights flashed and people yelled. It didn't seem real. If this was what David's everyday life was like, I had no idea how he handled it.

"Look. You need to get the fuck out of there," he said, words brisk, brittle. "It'll calm down in a while."

My dad stood beside me, wringing his hands. David was right. Whatever happened, I had to get this away from the people I loved. I could do that much at least.

"Ev?"

"Sorry. Yes, I'd like to take you up on that offer," I said. "Thank you."

"Hand the phone back to Sam."

I did as asked, also opening the door fully so the big man could come inside. He wasn't overly tall, but he was built. The guy took up serious space. Sam nodded and said some "yes, sirs." Then he hung up. "Ms. Thomas, the car is waiting."

"No," said Dad.

"Dad—"

"You cannot trust that man. Look at everything that's happened."

"It's hardly all his fault. I played my part in this." The whole situation embarrassed me. But running and hiding was not the answer. "I need to fix it."

"No," he repeated, laying down the law.

The problem was, I wasn't a little girl anymore. And this wasn't about me not believing that our backyard was too small for a pony. "I'm sorry, Dad. But I've made my decision."

His face pinked, eyes incredulous. Previously, on the rare occasions he'd taken a hard stance, I'd buckled (or quietly gone about my business behind his back). But this time . . . I was not convinced. For once my father seemed old to me, unsure. More than that, this problem was mine, all mine.

"Please, trust me," I said.

"Ev, honey, you don't have to do this," said Dad, trying a different tack. "We can figure something out on our own."

"I know we could. But he's got lawyers on the job already. This is for the best."

"Won't you need your own lawyer?" he asked. There were new lines on his face, as if just this one day had aged him. Guilt slunk through me.

"I'll ask around, find someone suitable for you. I don't want you being taken advantage of here," he continued. "Someone must know a decent divorce lawyer."

"Dad, it's not like I have any money to protect. We're going to make this as straightforward as possible," I said with a forced smile. "It's okay. We'll take care of it, and then I'll be back."

"We? Honey, you barely know this guy. You cannot trust him."

"The whole world is apparently watching. What's the worst that can happen?" I sent a silent prayer to the heavens that I'd never find out the answer to that.

"This is a mistake . . ." Dad sighed. "I know you're as disappointed over the internship as I am. But we need to stop and think here."

"I have thought about it. I need to get this circus away from you and Mom."

Dad's gaze went to the darkened hallway heading toward where Mom lay in her drug-induced slumber. The last thing I wanted was for my father to feel torn between the two of us.

"It'll be okay," I said, willing it to be true. "Really."

He hung his head at last. "I think you're doing the wrong

thing. But call me if you need anything. If you want to come home, I'll organize a flight for you right away."

I nodded.

"I'm serious. You call me if you need anything."

"Yes. I will." I wouldn't.

I picked up my backpack, still fresh from Vegas. No chance to refresh my wardrobe. All of my clothes were at the apartment. I smoothed back my hair, tucking it neatly behind my ears, trying to make myself look a little less like a train wreck.

"You were always my good girl," Dad said, sounding wistful.

I didn't know what to say.

He patted me on the arm. "Call me."

"Yeah," I said, my throat tight. "Say bye to Mom for me. I'll talk to you soon."

Sam stepped forward. "Your daughter is in safe hands, sir."

I didn't wait to hear Dad's reply. For the first time in hours I stepped outside. Pandemonium erupted. The instinct to turn tail, run, and hide was huge. But with Sam's big body beside me it wasn't quite so crazy frightening as before. He put an arm loosely around my shoulder and hustled me out of there, down the garden path, and toward the waiting crowd. Another man in a sharp black suit came toward us, making a way through the mob from the other side. The noise level skyrocketed. A woman yelled that she hated me and called me a cunt. Someone else wanted me to tell David that he loved him. Mostly, though, it was more questions. Cameras were shoved in my face, the flashbulbs glaring. Before I could stumble, Sam was there. My feet barely touched the ground as he and his friend hurried me into the waiting car. Not a limousine. Lauren would be disappointed. It was a fancy new sedan with an all-leather interior. The door slammed shut behind me and Sam and his friend climbed in. The driver nodded to me in the rearview mirror, then carefully accelerated. People banged on the windows and ran alongside. I huddled down in the middle of the seat. Soon we left them behind.

I was on my way back to David.

My husband.

CHAPTER FOUR

I slept on the short flight to LA, curled up in a super-comfortable chair in a corner of the private jet. It was a level of luxury above anything I'd ever imagined. If you had to turn your life upside down, you might as well enjoy the opulence while you were at it. Sam had offered me champagne and I'd politely declined. The idea of alcohol still turned me inside out. It was entirely possible I'd never drink again.

My career path had been temporarily shot to hell, but never mind, I had a new plan. Get divorced. It was breathtakingly simple. I loved it. I was back in control of my own destiny. One day, when I got married, if I got married, it would not be to a stranger in Vegas. It would not be a terrible mistake.

When I woke up, we were landing. Another sleek sedan stood waiting. I'd never been to LA. It looked every bit as wide-awake as Vegas, though less glam. Plenty of people were still out and about despite the hour of night.

I had to brave turning on my phone sometime. Lauren would be worried. I pushed the little black button and the screen flashed bright lights at me, coming to life. A hundred and fifty-eight text messages and ninety-seven missed calls. I blinked stupidly at the screen but the number didn't change. Holy hell.

Apparently everyone I knew had heard the news, along with quite a few people I did not.

My phone pinged.

Lauren: You okay? Where r u???

Me: LA. Going to him till things calm down. You all right?

Lauren: I'm fine. LA? Living the dream.

Me: Private jet was amazing. Though his fans are crazy.

Lauren: Your brother is crazy.

Me: Sorry about that.

Lauren: I can handle him. Whatever happens, do not break up the band!!!

Me: Got it.

Lauren: But break his heart. He wrote San Pedro after what's-her-face cheated on him. That album was BRIL-LIANT!

Me: Promise to leave him a broken quivering mess.

Lauren: That's the spirit.

Me: xx

It was after three in the morning by the time we reached the massive 1920s-era Spanish-style mansion in Laurel Canyon. It was lovely. Though Dad would not have been impressed—he preferred clean, contemporary lines with minimal fuss. Four-bedroom, two-bathroom houses for Portland's well-to-do. But I don't know, there was something beautiful and romantic about such extravagance. The decorative black wrought iron against the bare white walls.

A gaggle of girls and the obligatory pack of press milled about outside. News of our marriage had apparently stirred things up. Or maybe they always camped here. Ornate iron gates swung slowly open at our approach. Palm trees lined the long, winding driveway, large fronds waving in the wind as we drove by. The place looked like something out of a movie. Stage Dive were big business, I knew that much. Their last two albums had spawned numerous hit songs. Lauren had driven all over the countryside last summer, attending three of their shows in the space of a week. All of them had been in stadiums.

Still, that was a damn big house.

Nerves wound me tight. I wore the same jeans and blue top I'd had on all day. Dressing for the occasion wasn't an option. The best I could do was finger-brush my hair and spray on some perfume I had in my handbag. I might be lacking in glamour, but at least I'd smell all right.

Every light in the house blazed bright, and rock music boomed out into the warm night air. The big double doors stood open, and people spilled out of the house and onto the steps. It seemed the party to end all others was taking place.

Sam opened the car door for me and I hesitantly climbed out.

"I'll walk you in, Ms. Thomas."

"Thank you," I said.

I didn't move. After a moment Sam got the message. He forged ahead and I followed. A couple of girls were making out just inside the door, mouths all over each other. They were both slender and beyond gorgeous, dressed in tiny, sparkly dresses that barely hit their thighs. More people milled about drinking and dancing. A chandelier hung overhead and a grand staircase wound around an interior wall. The place was a Hollywood palace.

Thankfully, no one seemed to notice me. I could gawk to my heart's content.

Sam stopped to talk to a young man slouched against a wall, a bottle of beer to his lips. Long, blond hair stuck out every which way and his nose was pierced with a silver ring. Lots of tattoos. In ripped black jeans and a faded T-shirt, he had the same über-cool air as David. Maybe rock stars brought their clothes artfully aged. People with money were a pack apart.

The man gave me an obvious looking-over. I steadfastly resisted the urge to shrink back. Not happening. When he met my eyes, his gaze seemed curious but not unfriendly. The tension inside me eased.

"Hey," he said.

"Hi." I braved a smile.

"It's all good," he said to Sam. Then he tipped his chin at me. "Come on. He's out this way. I'm Mal."

"Hi," I said again, stupidly. "I'm Ev."

"Are you all right, Ms. Thomas?" asked Sam in a low voice.

"Yes, Sam. Thank you very much."

He gave me a polite nod and headed back the way we'd come. His broad shoulders and bald head soon disappeared among the crowd. Running after him and asking to be taken home wouldn't help, but my feet itched to do so. No, enough with the pity party. Time to pull up my big-girl panties and get on with things.

Hundreds of people had been packed into the place. The only thing in my experience that came close was my senior prom, and it paled significantly. None of the dresses here tonight compared. I could almost smell the money. Lauren was the dedicated celeb-watcher, but even I recognized a few of the faces. One of last year's Oscar winners and a lingerie model I'd seen on billboards back home. A teen pop queen who shouldn't have been swilling from a bottle of vodka, let alone sitting on the lap of a silver-haired member of . . . damn, what was that band's name?

Anyway.

I shut my mouth before someone noticed I had stars in my eyes. Lauren would have loved all this. It was amazing.

When a woman who most closely resembled a half-dressed Amazonian goddess sideswiped me, Mal stopped and frowned after her. "Some people, no manners. Come on."

The sluggish beat of the music moved through me, reawakening the dregs of my headache and putting a taint on the glitter. We weaved our way through a big room filled with plush velvet lounges and the people draped over them. Next came a space cluttered with guitars, amps, and other rock 'n' roll paraphernalia. Inside the house the air was smoky and humid, despite all the open windows and doors. My top clung beneath my arms. We moved outside onto the balcony, where a light breeze was blowing. I raised my face to it gratefully.

And there he was, leaning against a decorative iron railing. The strong lines of his face were in profile. Holy shit, how could I have forgotten? There was no explaining the full effect of David in real life. He fit in with the beautiful people just fine. He was one of them. I, on the other hand, belonged in the kitchen with the waitstaff.

My husband was busy talking to the leggy, enhanced-breasted brunette beside him. Perhaps he was a tit man and that's how we'd wound up wed. It was as good a guess as any. Dressed in only a teeny white bikini, the girl clung to him like she'd been surgically attached. Her hair was artfully messed in a way that suggested a minimum of two hours at a top-notch salon. She was beautiful and I hated her just a little. A trickle of sweat ran down my spine.

"Hey, Dave," Mal called out. "Company."

David turned, then saw me and frowned. In this light, his eyes looked dark and distinctly unhappy. "Ev."

"Hi."

Mal started to laugh. "That's about the only word I've been able to get out of her. Seriously, man, does your wife even speak?"

"She speaks." His tone of voice made it obvious he wished I wouldn't, ever again. Or at least not within his hearing.

I didn't know what to say. Generally, I wasn't after universal love and acceptance. Open hostility, however, was still kind of new to me.

The brunette tittered and rubbed her bountiful boobs against David's arm as if she was marking him. Sadly for her, he didn't seem to notice. She gave me a foul look, red mouth puckered. Charming. Though the fact that she saw me as competition was a huge boost to my ego. I stood taller and looked my husband in the eye.

Big mistake.

David's dark hair had been tied back in a little ponytail with strands falling around his face. What should have reeked of scummy drug dealer worked on him. Of course it did. He could probably make a dirty back alleyway seem like the honeymoon suite. A gray T-shirt molded to his thick shoulders and faded blue jeans covered his long legs. His black army-style boots were crossed at the ankles, easy as you please, because he belonged here. I didn't.

"You mind finding her a room?" David asked his friend.

Mal snorted. "Do I look like your fucking butler? You'll show your own wife to a room. Don't be an asshole."

"She's not my wife," David growled.

"Every news channel in the country would disagree with you there." Mal ruffled my hair with a big hand, making me feel all of eight years old. "Check you later, child bride. Nice to meet you."

"Child bride?" I asked, feeling clueless.

Mal stopped and grinned. "You haven't heard what they're saying?"

I shook my head.

"Probably for the best." With a last laugh, he wandered off.

David disentangled himself from the brunette. Her plump lips pursed in displeasure, but he wasn't looking. "Come on."

He put his hand out to usher me on, and there, spread across the length of his forearm, was his tattoo:

Evelyn

I froze. Holy shit. The man sure had chosen a conspicuous place to put my name. I didn't know how I felt about that.

"What?" His brows drew down and his forehead wrinkled. "Ah, yeah. Come on."

"Hurry back, David," cooed Bikini Girl, primping her hair. I had nothing against bikinis. I owned several despite my mom believing I was too big boned for such things. (I'd never actually worn them, but that was beside the point.) No, what I minded were the sneers and snarly looks Bikini Girl shot me when she thought David wasn't looking.

Little did she know he didn't care.

With a hand to the small of my back, he ushered me through the party toward the stairs. People called out and women preened, but he never slowed. I got the distinct feeling he was embarrassed to be seen with me. Being with David, I sure caught some scrutiny. Any money, I didn't fit the bill of a rock star's wife. People stopped and stared. Someone called out, asking if he could introduce us. No comment from my husband as he hurried me through the crowd.

Hallways spread out in both directions up on the second floor. We went left, down to the end. He threw open a door and there my bag sat, waiting on a big king-size bed. Everything in the sumptuous room had been done in white: the bed, walls, and carpets. An antique white love seat sat in the corner. It was beautiful, pristine. Nothing like my small, cramped room back at the apartment I shared with Lauren, where between the double bed and my desk, you had just enough room to get the cupboard door open, no more. This place went on and on, a sea of perfection.

"I'd better not touch anything," I mumbled, hands tucked into my back pockets.

"What?"

"It's lovely."

David looked around the room with nil interest. "Yeah."

I wandered over to the windows. A luxurious pool sat below, well lit and surrounded by palm trees and perfect gardens. Two people were in the water, making out. The woman's head fell back and her breasts bobbed on the surface. Oh, no, my mistake. They were having sex. I could feel the heat creep up my neck. I didn't think I was a prude, but still. I turned away.

"Listen, some people are going to come to talk to you about the divorce papers. They'll be here at ten," he said, hovering in the doorway. His fingers tapped out a beat on the doorframe. He kept casting longing looks down the hall, clearly impatient to be gone.

"Some people?"

"My lawyer and my manager," he told his feet. "They're rushing things, so . . . it'll all be, ah, dealt with as fast as it can."

"All right."

David sucked in his cheeks and nodded. He had killer cheekbones. I'd seen men in fashion magazines that couldn't have compared. But pretty or not, the frown never lifted. Not while I was around. It would have been nice to see him smile, just once.

"You need anything?" he asked.

"No. Thank you for all this. For flying me down here and letting me stay. It's very kind of you."

"No worries." He took a step back and started closing the door after him. "Night."

"David, shouldn't we talk or something? About last night?"

He paused, half hidden behind the door. "Seriously, Ev. Why fucking bother?"

And he was gone.

Again.

No door slam this time. I counted that as a step forward in our relationship. Being surprised was stupid. But disappointment held me still, staring around the room, seeing nothing. It wasn't that I suddenly wanted him to fall at my feet. But antipathy sucked.

Eventually I wandered back over to the window. The lovers were gone, the pool now empty. Another couple stumbled along the lit garden path, beneath the huge swaying palm trees. They headed toward what had to be the pool house. The man was David, and Bikini Girl hung off him, swishing her long hair and swaying her hips, working it to the nth degree. They looked good together. They fit. David reached out and tugged on the tie of her bikini top, undoing the neat bow and baring her from the waist up. Bikini Girl laughed soundlessly, not bothering to cover herself.

I swallowed hard, trying to dislodge the rock in my throat. Jealousy felt every bit as bad as antipathy. And I had no damn right to be jealous.

At the door to the pool house, David paused and looked back over his shoulder. His eyes met mine. Oh, shit. I ducked behind the curtain and idiotically held my breath. Caught spying—the shame of it. When I checked a moment later, they were gone. Light peeked out from the sides of the curtains in the pool house. I should have brazened it out. I wished I had. It wasn't like I was doing anything wrong.

The immaculate grandeur of the white room spread out before me. Inside and out, I felt a mess. The reality of my situation had apparently sunk in, and what a clusterfuck it was. Lauren had been right on with the word choice.

"David can do what he wants." My voice echoed through the room, startlingly loud even over the thumping of the music downstairs. I straightened my shoulders. Tomorrow I would meet with his people and the divorce would be sorted. "David can do what he wants and so can I."

But what did I want to do? I had no idea. So I unpacked my few items of clothing, settling in for the night. I hung David's T-shirt over a towel rail to finish drying. It was probably going to be needed for sleepwear. Organizing myself took five minutes, max. You could refold a couple of tank tops only so many ways before you just looked pathetic.

What now?

I hadn't been invited to the party downstairs. No way did I want to think about what might be happening in the pool house. Doubtless David was giving Bikini Girl everything I'd wanted in Vegas. No sex for me. Instead, he had sent me to my room like a naughty child.

What a room it was. The adjoining bathroom had a tub larger than my bedroom back home. Plenty of space to splash around. It was tempting. But I never had been much good at getting sent to my room. On the few occasions it happened at home, I used to climb out the window and sit outside with a book. As rebellions went, it lacked a lot, but I'd been satisfied. There was a lot to be said for being a quiet achiever.

Screw staying in the room of splendor. I couldn't do it.

No one noticed me as I crept back down the stairs. I slunk into the closest corner and settled in to watch the beautiful people at play. It was fascinating. Bodies writhed on an impromptu dance floor in the middle of the room. Someone lit up a cigar nearby, filling the air with a rich, spicy scent. Puffs of smoke billowed up toward the ceiling, a good twenty feet above. Diamonds glittered and teeth sparkled, and that was just some of the men. Open opulence fought grunge among the mixed crowd. You couldn't get better people-watching if you tried. No sign of Mal, sadly. At least he'd been friendly.

"You're new," a voice said from beside me, startling the crap out of me. I jumped a mile, or at least a few inches.

A man in a black suit lounged against the wall, sipping a glass of amber liquor. This slick black suit was something else. In all likelihood Sam's had come off the rack, but not this one. I'd never understood the appeal of a suit and tie before, but this man wore them incredibly well. He looked to be about David's age and he had short dark hair. Handsome, of course. Like David, he had the whole divine cheekbones thing going on.

"You know, if you move another foot over you'll disappear entirely behind that palm." He took another sip of his drink. "Then no one would see you."

"I'll give it some thought." I didn't bother denying I was in hiding. Apparently it was already obvious to all.

He smiled, flashing a dimple. Tommy Byrnes had dimples. He'd inured me to their power. The man leaned closer, so as to be heard more easily over the music, most likely. The fact that he backed it up by taking a decent-sized step toward me seemed unnecessary. Personal space was a wonderful thing. Something about this guy gave me the creeps, despite the swanky suit.

"I'm Jimmy."

"Ev."

He pursed his lips, staring at me. "Nope, I definitely don't know you. Why don't I know you?"

"You know everyone else?" I surveyed the room, highly dubious. "There are a lot of people here."

"There are," he agreed, "And I know them all. Everyone except you."

"David invited me." I didn't want to drop David's name, but I was being pushed into a corner, figuratively and literally as Jimmy closed in on me.

"Did he now?" His eyes looked wrong, the pupils pinpricks. Something was up with this guy. He stared down at the small amount of cleavage I had on display like he intended to plant his face there.

"Yeah. He did."

Jimmy didn't exactly seem pleased by the news. He threw back his drink, finishing it off in one large mouthful. "So, David invited you to the party."

"He invited me to stay for a few days," I said, which was not a lie. Happily, hopefully, he had somehow missed the news about David and me. Or maybe he was just too stoned to put two and two together. Either way, I wasn't filling him in.

"Really? That was nice of him."

"Yes, it was."

"What room did he put you in?" He stood in front of me and dropped his empty glass into the potted plant with a careless hand. His grin looked manic. My need to get away from him gained immediate urgency.

"The white one," I said, looking for a way around him. "Speaking of which, I'd better get back."

"The white room? My, my, aren't you special."

"Aren't I just? Excuse me." I pushed past him, giving up on social niceties.

He mustn't have expected it because he stumbled back a step. "Hey. Hold up."

"Jimmy." David appeared, earning my instant gratitude. "There a problem here?"

"Not at all," said Jimmy. "Just getting to know . . . Ev."

"Yeah, well, you don't need to know . . . Ev."

The guy's smile was expansive. "Come on. You know how I like pretty new things."

"Let's go," David said to me.

"It's not like you to cockblock, Davie," said Jimmy. "Didn't I see the lovely Kaetrin with you earlier out on the balcony? Why don't you go find her, get her to do what she's so damn good at? Me and Ev are busy here."

"Actually, no, we're not," I said. And why was David back so soon from his playtime with Bikini Girl? He couldn't possibly have been concerned about his little wife's well-being, surely.

Neither of them appeared to have heard me.

"So you invited her to stay in my house," said Jimmy.

"I was under the impression Adrian rented the place for all of us while we're working on the album. Something changed I don't know about?"

Jimmy laughed. "I like the place. Decided to buy it."

"Great. Let me know when the deal's going through and I'll be sure to get out. In the meantime, my guests are none of your business."

Jimmy looked at me, face alight with malicious glee. "It's her, isn't it? The one you married, you stupid son of a bitch."

"Come on." David grabbed my hand and dragged me toward the staircase. His jaw was clenched tight enough to make a muscle pop out on the side.

"I could have had her against a wall at a fucking party and you married her?"

Bullshit he could have.

David's fingers squeezed my hand tight.

Jimmy chortled like the cretin he was. "She is nothing, you sorry fuck. Look at her. Just look at her. Tell me this marriage didn't come courtesy of vodka and cocaine."

It wasn't anything I hadn't heard before. Well, apart from the marriage reference. But his words still bit. Before I could tell Jimmy what I thought of him, however, the iron-hard hold on my hand disappeared. David charged back to him, grabbing hold of his lapels. They were pretty evenly matched. Both were tall, well built. Neither looked ready to back down. The room hushed, all conversation stopping, though the music thumped on.

"Go for it, little brother," hissed Jimmy. "Show me who the star of this show really is."

David's shoulders went rigid beneath the thin cotton of his T-shirt. Then with a snarl he released Jimmy, shoving him back a step. "You're as bad as Mom. Look at you, you're a fucking mess."

I stared at the two of them, stunned. These two were the brothers in the band. Same dark hair and handsome faces. I clearly hadn't married into the happiest of families. Jimmy looked almost shamefaced.

My husband marched back past me, collecting my arm along the way. Every eye was on us. An elegant brunette took a step forward, hand outstretched. Distress lined her lovely face. "You know he doesn't mean it."

"Stay out of it, Martha," said my husband, not slowing down at all.

The woman shot me a look of distaste. Worse yet, of blame. With the way David was acting, I had a bad feeling that was going around.

Up the steps he dragged me, then down the hallway toward my room. We said nothing. Maybe this time he'd lock me in. Jam a chair under the door handle, perhaps. I could understand him being mad at Jimmy. That guy was a dick of epic proportions. But what had I done? Apart from escaping my plush prison, of course.

Halfway along the long hallway I liberated my limb from his tender care. I had to do something before he cut off the blood supply to my fingers.

"I know the way," I said.

"Still wanna get some, huh? You should have said something, I'd be more than happy to oblige," he said with a false smile. "And hey, you're not even shit-faced tonight. Chances are you'd remember."

"Ouch."

"Something I said untrue?"

"No. But I still think it's fair to say you're being an ass."

He stopped dead and looked at me, eyes wide, startled, if anything. "I'm being an ass? Fucking hell, you're my wife!"

"No, I'm not. You said so yourself. Right before you went off to play in the pool house with your friend," I said. Though he hadn't stayed long in the pool house, obviously. Five, six minutes maybe? I almost felt bad for Bikini Girl. That wasn't service with a smile.

Dark brows descended like thunderclouds. He was less than impressed. Bad luck. My feelings toward him were likewise at an all-time low.

"You're right. My bad. Should I take you back to my brother?"

he asked, cracking his knuckles like a Neanderthal and staring back down the hallway from where we'd come.

"No, thank you."

"That was real nice, making fuck-me eyes at him, by the way. Out of everyone down there, you had to be flirting with Jimmy," he sneered. "Classy, Ev."

"That's honestly what you think was happening?"

"What with you and him getting all fucking cozy in the corner?"

"Seriously?"

"I know Jimmy and I know girls around Jimmy. That's definitely what it looked like, baby." He held his arms out wide. "Prove me wrong."

I wasn't even certain I knew how to make fuck-me eyes. But I definitely hadn't been making them at that tool downstairs. No wonder so many marriages ended in divorce. Marriage sucked and husbands were the worst. My shoulders were caving in on me. I didn't think I'd ever felt so small.

"I think your brother issues might be even worse than your wife issues, and that's saying something." Slowly, I shook my head. "Thank you for offering me the opportunity to defend myself. I really appreciate it. But you know what, David? I'm just not convinced your good opinion is worth it."

He flinched.

I walked away before I said something worse. Forget anything amicable. The sooner we were divorced, the better.

CHAPTER FIVE

Sunlight poured in through the windows when I woke the next morning. Someone was hammering on the door, turning the handle, trying to get in. I'd locked it after the scene with David last night. Just in case he was tempted to return to trade some more insults with me. It had taken me hours to get to sleep with the music thrumming through the floor and my emotions running wild. But exhaustion won out in the end.

"Evelyn! Hello?" a female voice yelled from out in the hallway. "Are you in there?" I crawled across the ginormous bed, tugging on the hem of David's T-shirt. Whatever he'd used to wash it in Vegas, it didn't smell of puke. The man had laundry skills. Fortunate for me, because apart from my dirty party dress and a couple of tops, I had nothing else to wear

"Who is it?" I asked, yawning loudly.

"Martha. I'm David's PA."

I cracked open the door and peered out. The elegant brunette from last night stared back at me, unimpressed. From being made to wait or the sight of my bed hair, I didn't know. Did everyone in this house look like they'd just slunk off the cover of *Vogue*? Her eyes turned into slits at the sight of David's shirt.

"His representatives are here to meet with you. You might want to get your ass into gear." The woman spun on her heel and strode off down the hallway, heels clacking furiously against the terra-cotta tiled floor.

"Thanks."

She didn't acknowledge me, but, then, I didn't expect her to. This part of LA was clearly a colony for ill-mannered douches. I rushed through a shower, pulled on my jeans and a clean T-shirt. It was the best I could do.

The house stayed silent as I rushed down the hallway. There were no signs of life on the second level. I'd slapped on a little mascara, tied my wet hair back in a ponytail, but that was it. I could either hold people up or go without makeup. Politeness won. If coffee had been in the offering, however, I'd have left David's representatives hanging for at least two cups. Running on zero caffeine seemed suicidal given the stressful circumstances. I hurried down the stairs.

"Ms. Thomas," a man called, stepping out of a room to the left. He wore jeans and a white polo shirt. Around his neck hung a thick, gold chain. So who was this? Another of David's entourage?

"Sorry I'm late."

"It's fine." He smiled, but I didn't quite believe him despite the big white teeth. Nature had clearly played no part in his teeth or tan. "I'm Adrian."

"Ev. Hello."

He swept me into the room. Three men in suits sat waiting at an impressively long dining table. Overhead, another crystal chandelier sparkled in the morning light. On the walls were beautiful, colorful paintings. Originals, obviously.

"Gentlemen, this is Ms. Thomas," Adrian announced. "Scott Baker, Bill Preston, and Ted Vaughan are David's legal representatives. Why don't you sit here, Ev?"

Adrian spoke slowly, as if I were a feeble-minded child. He

pulled a chair out from the table for me directly opposite the team of legal eagles, then walked around to sit on their side. Wow, that sure told me. The lines had been drawn.

I rubbed my sweaty palms on the sides of my jeans and sat up straight, doing my best not to wilt beneath their hostile gazes. I could definitely do this. How hard could it be to get a divorce, after all?

"Ms. Thomas," the one Adrian had identified as Ted started. He pushed a black leather folder full of papers toward me. "Mr. Ferris asked us to draw up annulment papers. They'll cover all issues, including details of your settlement from Mr. Ferris."

The size of the stack of papers before me was daunting. These people worked fast. "My settlement?"

"Yes," Ted said. "Rest assured Mr. Ferris has been very generous."

I shook my head in confusion. "I'm sorry. Wha—"

"We'll deal with that last," Ted rushed on. "You'll notice here that the document covers all conditions to be met by yourself. The main issues include your not speaking to any member of the press with regard to this matter. This is nonnegotiable, I'm afraid. This condition remains in force until your death. Do you fully understand the requirement, Ms. Thomas? Under no circumstances may you talk to any member of the press regarding Mr. Ferris in any way while you're alive."

"So I can talk to them after I die?" I asked with a weak little laugh. Ted was getting on my nerves. I guess I hadn't gotten enough sleep after all.

Ted showed me his teeth. They weren't quite as impressive as Adrian's. "This is a very serious matter, Ms. Thomas."

"Ev," I said. "My name is Ev and I do realize the seriousness of this issue, Ted. I apologize for being flippant. But if we could get back to the part about the settlement? I'm a little confused."

"Very well." Ted looked down his nose at me and tapped a thick, gold pen on the paperwork in front of me. "As I said, Mr. Ferris has been very generous."

"No," I said, not looking at the papers, "you don't understand."

Ted cleared his throat and looked down at me over the top of his glasses. "It would be unwise of you to try and press for more given the circumstances, Ms. Thomas. A six-hour marriage in Las Vegas entered into while you were both heavily under the influence of alcohol? Textbook grounds for annulment."

Ted's cronies tittered and I felt my face fire up. My need to accidentally kick the prick under the table grew and grew.

"My client will not be making another offer."

"I don't want him to make another offer," I said, my voice rising.

"The annulment will go ahead, Ms. Thomas," said Ted. "There is no question of that. There will be no reconciliation."

"No, that's not what I meant."

Ted sighed. "We need to finalize this today, Ms. Thomas."

"I'm not trying to hold anything up, Ted."

The other two lawyers watched me with distaste, backing up Ted with sleazy, knowing smiles. Nothing pissed me off faster than a bunch of people trying to intimidate someone. Bullies had made my life hell back in high school. And really, that's all these people were.

Adrian gave me a big-toothed, faux-fatherly grin. "I'm sure Ev can see how kind David's being. There are not going to be any delays here, are there?"

These people, they blew my mind. Speaking of which, I had

to wonder where my darling husband was. Too busy banging bikini models to turn up to his own divorce, the poor guy. I pushed back my fringe, trying to figure out the right thing to say. Trying to get my anger managed. "Wait—"

"We all just want what's best for you given the unfortunate situation," Adrian continued, obviously lying through his big, bright teeth.

"Great," I said, fingers fidgeting beneath the table. "That's . . . that's really great of you."

"Please, Ms. Thomas." Ted tapped his pen imperiously alongside a figure on the paperwork and I dutifully looked, though I didn't want to. There were lots of zeros. I mean, really a lot. It was insane. In two lifetimes I couldn't earn that kind of money. David must have wanted me gone something fierce. My stomach rumbled nervously but my puking days were over. The whole scene felt horrific, like something out of a bad B movie or soap opera. Girl from the wrong side of the tracks hijacks hot, rich guy and tricks him into marriage. Now all that was left was for him to use his people to chase me off into the sunset.

Well, he won.

"This was all just a mistake," said Adrian. "I'm sure Ev is every bit as keen to put it behind her as David is. And with this generous financial settlement she can move forward to a bright future."

"You'll also never attempt to make contact with Mr. Ferris ever again, in any manner. Any attempt on your part to do so will see you in breach of contract." Ted withdrew his pen, sitting back in his seat with a false smile and his hands crossed over his belly. "Is that clear?"

"No," I said, scrubbing my face with my hands. They actually thought I'd fall over myself to get at that money. Money

I'd done nothing to earn, no matter how tempting accepting it was. Of course, they also thought I'd sell my story to the press and harass David every spare moment I got for the rest of my life. They thought I was cheap, trashy scum. "I think I can honestly say that nothing about this is clear."

"Ev, please." Adrian gave me a disappointed look. "Let's be reasonable."

"I'll tell you what . . ." I stood and retrieved the ring from my jeans pocket, throwing it onto the sea of paperwork. "You give this back to David and tell him I don't want any of it. None of this." I gestured at them, the table, the papers, and the entire damn house. The lawyers looked nervously among themselves as if they'd need more paperwork before they could allow me to go waving my arms about in such a disorderly fashion.

"Ev . . ."

"I don't want to sell his story, or stalk him, or whatever else you have buried in subclause 98.2. I don't want his money."

Adrian coughed out a laugh. Fuck him. The phony bastard could think what he liked.

Ted frowned at my big sparkly ring lying innocently among the mess. "Mr. Ferris didn't mention a ring."

"No? Well. Why don't you tell Mr. Ferris he can shove it wherever he feels it might best fit, Ted."

"Ms. Thomas!" Ted stood, his puffy face outraged. "That is unnecessary."

"Going to have to disagree with you there, Ted." I bolted out of the dining room of death and made straight for the front door as fast as my feet could carry me. Immediate escape was the only answer. If I could just get the hell away from them long enough to catch my breath, I could come up with a new plan to deal with this ridiculous situation. I'd be fine.

A brand new-black Jeep pulled up as I tore down the front steps.

The window lowered to show my guide from last night, Mal, sitting in the driver's seat. He smirked from behind black sunglasses. "Hey there, child bride."

I flipped him the finger and jogged down the long, winding driveway toward the front gates. Toward liberty and freedom and my old life, or whatever remained of it. If only I'd never gone to Vegas. If only I'd tried harder to convince Lauren that a party at home would be fine, none of this would have happened. God, I was such an idiot. Why had I drunk so much?

"Ev. Hold up." Mal pulled up alongside me in his Jeep. "What's wrong? Where're you going?"

I didn't answer. I was done with all of them. That and I had the worst feeling I was about to cry, damn it. My eyes felt hot, horrible.

"Stop." He pulled the brake and climbed out of the Jeep, running after me. "Hey, I'm sorry."

I said nothing. I had nothing to say to any of them.

His hand wrapped around my arm gently, but I didn't care. I swung at him. I'd never hit anyone in my life. Apparently, I wasn't about to start now. He dodged my flying fist with ease.

"Whoa! Okay." Mal danced back a step, giving me a wary look over the top of his shades. "You're mad. I get it."

Hands on hips, he looked back toward the house. Ted and Adrian stood on the front steps, staring after us. Even from this distance the dynamic duo did not appear happy. Evil bastards.

Mal hissed out a breath. "You're fucking joking. He sicced that ball sucker Ted onto you?"

I nodded, blinking, trying to get myself under control.

"Did you have anyone with you?" he asked.

"No."

He cocked his head. "Are you going to cry?"

"No!"

"Fuck. Come on." He held out his hand to me and I stared at in disbelief. "Ev, think. There're photographers and shit waiting out front. Even if you get past them, where are you going to go?"

He was right. I had to go back, get my bag. So stupid of me not to have thought of it. Just as soon as I had myself under control I'd go in and retrieve it, then get the hell out of here. I fanned my face with my hands, took a big breath. All good.

Meanwhile, his hand hovered, waiting. There were a couple of small blisters on it, situated in the join between thumb and finger. Curious.

"Are you the drummer?" I asked with a sniff.

For some reason he cracked up laughing, almost doubling over, clutching at his belly. Maybe he was on drugs or something. Or maybe he was just one more lunatic in this gigantic asylum. Batman would have had a hard time keeping this place in check.

"What is your problem?" I asked, taking a step away from him. Just in case.

His snazzy sunglasses fell off, clattering on the asphalt. He swiped them up and shoved them back on his face. "Nothing. Nothing at all. Let's get out of here. I've got a house at the beach. We'll hide out there. Come on, it'll be fun."

I hesitated, giving the jerks on the front steps a lethal look. "Why would you help me?"

"Because you're worth helping."

"Oh, really? Why would you think that?"

"You wouldn't like my answer."

"I haven't liked a single answer I've had all morning, why stop now?"

He smiled. "Fair enough. I'm David's oldest friend. We've gotten drunk and out of control more times than I can remember. He's had girls angling to snare him for years, even before we had money. He never was the slightest bit interested in marriage. It was never even on his radar before. So the fact that he married you, well, that suggests to me you're worth helping. Come on, Ev. Stop worrying."

Easy for him to say, his life hadn't been skewered by a rock star.

"I need to get my stuff."

"And get cornered by them? Worry about it later." He held his hand out, fingers beckoning for mine. "Let's get out of here."

I put my hand in his and we went.

CHAPTER SIX

"So, hang on, this song isn't about his dog dying or something?"

"You're not funny." I laughed.

"I so am." Mal sniggered at the opposite end of the couch as Tim McGraw let rip about his kind of rain on the flat-screen TV taking up the opposite wall. "Why do they all wear such big hats, do you think? I have a theory."

"Shush."

The way these people lived blew my tiny little mind. Mal, short for Malcolm, lived in a place at the beach that was mostly a three-story architectural feat of steel and glass. It was amazing. Not ridiculously huge like the place in the hills, but awe-inspiring just the same. My dad would have been in raptures over the minimalism of it, the cleanliness of the lines, or some such. I just appreciated having a friend in my time of need.

Mal's house was clearly a bachelor pad–slash–den of iniquity. I'd had a vague notion to make lunch to thank him for taking me in, but there wasn't a single speck of food in the house. Beer filled the fridge and vodka the freezer. Oh, no, there was a bag of oranges used as wedges to go with shots of vodka, apparently. He'd ruled out touching those. His super-slick coffee machine, however, made everything right. He even had decent beans. I wowed him by busting out a few of my barista moves. After drinking three cups in the space of an hour, I felt a lot more like my old well-planned, caffeinated self.

Mal dialed for pizza and we watched TV late into the night. Mostly he found his joy in mocking my taste in pretty much everything: movies, music, the lot. At least he did it good-naturedly. We couldn't go outside because a couple of photographers were waiting on the beach. I felt bad about it but he'd just shrugged it off.

"What about this song?" he asked. "You like this?"

Miranda Lambert strode on screen in a cool '50s frock and I grinned. "Miranda is mighty."

"I've met her."

I sat up straight. "Really?"

More sniggering from Mal. "You're impressed I've met Miranda Lambert but you didn't even know who I was. Honestly, woman, you are hard on the ego."

"I saw the gold and platinum records lining the hallway, buddy. I'm thinking you can take it."

He snorted.

"You know, you remind me a lot of my brother." I almost managed to duck the bottle cap he flicked at me. It bounced off my forehead. "What was that for?"

"Can't you at least pretend to worship me?"

"No. Sorry."

With total disregard for my Lambert love, Mal started surfing the channels. Home shopping, football, *Gone with the Wind*, and me. Me on TV.

"Wait," I said.

He groaned. "Not a good idea."

First my school pictures paraded past, followed by one of Lauren and me at our senior prom. They even had a reporter standing across the road from Ruby's, prattling on about my life before being elevated to the almighty status of David's wife. And then there was the man himself in some concert footage, guitar in his hands as he sang backup. The lyrics were your typical my-woman-is-mean, "She's my one and only, she's got me on my knees . . ." I wondered if he'd write songs about me. If so, odds were they'd be highly uncomplimentary. "Shit," I hugged a couch cushion tight to my chest.

Mal leaned over and fluffed my hair. "David's the favorite, darlin'. He's pretty, plays guitar, and writes the songs. Girlies faint when he walks by. Team that with your being a young 'un and you've got the news of the week."

"I'm twenty-one."

"And he's twenty-six. It's enough of a difference if they hype it just right." Mal sighed. "Face it, child bride. You got married in Vegas by an Elvis impersonator to one of rock 'n' roll's favorite sons. It was always bound to cause a shitstorm. Given there's also been some crap going on with the band lately . . . what with Jimmy partying like it's 1999 and Dave losing his music-writing mojo. Well, you get the picture. But next week, someone else will do something wacky and all the attention will move on."

"I guess so."

"I know so. People are constantly fucking up. It's a glorious thing." He sat back with his hands behind his head. "Go on, smile for Uncle Mal. You know you want to."

I smiled halfheartedly.

"That's a bullshit smile and I'm ashamed of you. You're not going to fool anyone with that. Try again."

I tried harder, smiling till my cheeks hurt.

"Damn. Now you just look like you're in pain."

Banging on the front door interrupted our merriment.

Mal raised his brows at me. "Wondered how long he'd take."

"What?" I trailed him to the front door, lurking behind a divider just in case it was more press.

He opened the door and David charged in, face tight and furious. "You piece of shit. You better not have touched her. Where is she?"

"The child bride is otherwise occupied." Mal cocked his head, taking David in with a cool glance. "Why the fuck do you even care?"

"Don't start with me. Where is she?"

Quietly, Mal shut the door, facing off against his friend. I hesitated, hanging back. All right, so I skulked in a cowardly fashion. Whatever.

Mal crossed his arms. "You left her to face Adrian and three lawyers on her own. You, my friend, are most definitely the piece of shit in this particular scenario."

"I didn't know Adrian would go at her with all that."

"You didn't want to know," said Mal. "Lie to everyone else out there, Dave. Not me. And sure as fuck not to yourself."

"Back off."

"You need some serious life advice, friend."

"Who are you, Oprah?"

Coughing out a laugh, Mal slumped against the wall. "Hell, yeah. Soon I'm gonna be giving out cars, so stick around."

"What did she say?"

"Who, Oprah?"

David just scowled at him. He didn't even notice me spying. Sad to say, even a scowling David was a thing of rare beauty. He did things to me. Complicated things. My heart tripped about in my chest. The anger and emotion in his voice couldn't be concern for me. That made no sense, not after last night and this morning. I had to be projecting, and it sucked that I even wanted him to care. My head made no sense. Getting away from this guy was the safest option all round.

"Dave, she was so upset she took a swing at me."

"Bullshit."

"I kid you not. She was nearly in tears when I found her," said Mal.

I banged my forehead in silent agony against the wall. Why the hell did Mal have to tell him that?

My husband hung his head. "I didn't mean for that to happen."

"Seems you didn't mean for a shitload to happen." Mal shook his head and tutted. "Did you even mean to marry her, dude? Seriously?"

David's face screwed up, his brow doing the wrinkly James Dean thing again. "I don't know anymore, okay? Fuck. I went to Vegas because I was so sick of all this shit, and I met her. She was different. She seemed different that night. I just . . . I wanted something outside of all this fucking idiocy for a change."

"Poor Davey. Did being a rock god get old?"

"Where is she?"

"I feel your manpain, bro. Really, I do. I mean, all you wanted was a girl who wouldn't kiss your ass for once and now you're pissed at her for the same damn reason. It's complicated, right?"

"Fuck you. Leave it alone, Mal. It's done." My husband huffed out a breath. "Anyway, she's the one who wanted the fucking divorce. Why aren't you giving her the third degree, huh?"

With a dramatic sigh, Mal flung out his arms. "Because she's really busy hiding around the corner, listening. I can't disturb her now."

David's body stilled and his blue eyes found me. "Evelyn."

Huh. Busted.

I stepped away from the wall and tried to put on a happy face. It didn't work. "Hi."

"She says that so well." Mal turned to me and winked. "So did you really ask the mighty David Ferris for a divorce?"

"She threw up on me when I told her we were married," my husband reported.

"What?" Mal dissolved into laughter, tears leaking from his eyes. "Are you serious? Fucking hell, that is fantastic. Oh, man, I wish I'd been there."

I gave David what I hoped to be the meanest look in all of time and space. He stared back, unimpressed.

"It was the floor," I clarified. "I didn't throw up on him."

"That time," said David.

"Please keep going," said Mal, laughing harder than ever. "This just gets better and better."

David didn't. Thank God.

"Seriously, I fucking love your wife, man. She's awesome. Can I have her?"

The look I got from David spoke of a much more reluctant affection. With the line between his brows, it was closer to out-right irritation. I blew him a kiss. He looked away, hands fisted like he was barely holding himself back from throttling me. The feeling was entirely mutual.

Ah, marital bliss.

"You two are just the best." A chiming sound came from Mal's pocket and he pulled out a cell phone. Whatever he saw on the screen stopped his laughter dead. "You know, you should take her to your house, Dave."

"I don't think that's a good idea." David's mouth pulled wide in a truly pained expression.

I didn't think it was a good idea either. I'd happily go

through life without setting foot inside the house of horrors ever again. Maybe if I asked Mal nicely he'd fetch my stuff for me. Imposing on him further didn't appeal, but I was running low on options.

"Whoa." With a grim face, Mal shoved his cell at David.

"Fuck," David mumbled. He wrapped his hand around the back of his neck and squeezed. The worried glance he gave me from beneath his dark brows set every alarm ringing inside my head. Whatever was on that screen was bad.

Really bad.

"What is it?" I asked.

"Oh, you, ah . . . you don't need to worry about it." His gaze dropped to the phone again, then he passed it back to Mal. "My place would be cool, actually. We should do that. Fun. Yeah."

"No." For David to be so nice to me it had to be something truly bad. I held out my hand, fingers twitching from impatience or nerves or a bit of both. "Show me."

After a reluctant nod from David, Mal handed it over.

There could be no doubting what it was, even on the small screen. There was a lot of skin on account of my being bare from the waist down. My naked butt sat front and center in all its pale, dimpled glory. God, it looked huge. Had they used a wide lens camera or something? The party dress had been pushed up and I stood, bent over a table while a tattoo artist worked hard inking my rear. My panties had been cinched down, barely covering the basics. Shit. Talk about a compromising position. Taking part in a porn shoot was definitely not part of the plan.

At the other end of the frame, our faces were close together and David was smiling. Huh. So that was what he looked like when he smiled.

I remembered it then, the buzz of the needle, and him talking to me, holding my hands. At first, that needle had stung. "You were pretending to bite my fingers. The tattoo artist got mad at us for messing around."

David tipped his chin. "Yeah. You were s'posed to be keeping still."

I nodded, trying to remember more but coming up empty.

People would see this picture. People had seen this. People I knew and strangers both. Anyone and everyone. My head spun woozily, the same as it had then. Only alcohol wasn't at fault this time.

"How did they get it?" I asked, my voice wavering and my heart at my toes. Or maybe that was just what remained of my tattered dignity.

David gave me sad eyes. "I don't know. We were in a private room. This should never have happened, but people get offered a lot of money for this sort of thing."

I nodded and handed Mal back his phone. My hand shook. "Right. Well . . ."

They both just looked at me, faces tense, waiting for me to burst into tears or something. Not happening.

"It's okay," I said, doing my best to believe it.

"Sure," said Mal.

David shoved his hands into his pockets. "It's not even that clear a picture."

"No, it's not," I agreed. The pity in his eyes was more than I could take. "Excuse me a minute."

Fortunately, the closest bathroom was only a short dash away. I locked the door and sat on the edge of the Jacuzzi, trying to slow my breathing, trying to be calm. There was nothing I could do. The picture was already out there. This was no death and dismemberment. It was a stupid picture of me in a compromising position showing more skin than I liked. But so what? Big deal. Accept it and move on. Despite the fact that everyone I knew would likely see it. Worse things had happened in the history of the world. I just needed to put it in context and stay calm.

"Ev?" David tapped lightly on the door. "Are you okay?"

"Yep." No. Not really.

"Let me in?"

I gave the door a pained look.

"Please."

Slowly, I stood and flicked the lock. David wandered in and shut the door behind him. No ponytail today. His dark hair hung down, framing his face. He had three small silver earrings in one ear playing peekaboo behind his hair. I stared at them because meeting his eyes was out of the question. I was not going to cry. Not about this. What the hell was even wrong with my eyes lately? Letting him in had been dumb.

With a heavy frown he stared down at me. "I'm sorry."

"It's not your fault."

"Yeah, it is. I should have looked after you better."

"No, David." I swallowed hard. "We were both drunk. God, this is all so horrifically, embarrassingly stupid."

He just stared at me.

"Sorry."

"Hey, you're allowed to be upset. That was a private moment. It shouldn't be out there."

"No," I agreed. "I . . . actually, I'd like to be alone for a minute."

He made a growly noise and suddenly his arms wrapped around me, pulling me in against him. He caught me off guard and I stumbled, my nose bumping into his chest. It hurt. But he smelled good. Clean, male, and good. Familiar. Some part of me remembered being this close to him and it was comforting. Something in my mind said "safe." But I couldn't remember how or why.

A hand moved restlessly over my back.

"I'm sorry," he said, "so fucking sorry."

The kindness was too much. Stupid tears flowed. "I'd hardly even shown anyone my ass and now it's all over the Internet."

"I know, baby."

He rested his head against the top of mine, holding on tight as I blubbered into his T-shirt. Having someone to hold on to helped. It would be okay. Deep down I knew it would be. But right then I couldn't see my way clear. Standing there with his arms around me felt right.

I don't know when we started swaying. David rocked me gently from side to side as if we were dancing to some slow song. The overwhelming temptation to stay like that with my face pressed into his shirt was what made me step back, pull myself together. His hands sat lightly on my hips, the connection not quite broken.

"Thanks," I said.

"S'okay." The front of his shirt had a damp patch, thanks to me.

"Your shirt's all wet."

He shrugged.

I ugly-cried. It was a gift of mine. The mirror confirmed it, demon-red eyes and flushed fluoro-pink cheeks. With an awkward smile I stepped away from him, and his hands fell back to his sides. I splashed my face with water and dried it on a towel while he stood idly by, frowning.

"Let's go for a drive," he said.

"Really?" I gave him a dubious look. David and me alone?

Given the marriage situation and our previous sober encounters, it didn't seem the wisest plan.

"Yeah." He rubbed his hands together, getting all enthused. "Just you and me. We'll get out of here for a while."

"David, like you said out there, I don't think that's a good idea."

"You want to stay in LA?" he scoffed.

"Look, you've been really sweet since you stepped through that door. Well, apart from telling Mal about me puking on you. That was unnecessary. But in the preceding twenty-four hours you dumped me alone in a room, went off with a groupie, accused me of trying to get it on with your brother, and sicced your posse of lawyers onto me."

He said nothing.

"Not that you going off with a groupie is any of my business. Of course."

He turned on his heel and paced to the other end of the bathroom, his movements tight, angry. Despite it being five times the size of the one back home, it still didn't leave enough room for a showdown like this. And he was between me and the door. Because suddenly exiting seemed a smart move.

"I just asked them to sort out the paperwork," he said.

"And they sure did." I put my hands on my hips, standing my ground. "I don't want any of your money."

"I heard." His face was carefully blank. My statement prompted in him none of the disbelief or mockery it had in the suited bullies. Lucky for him. I doubt he believed me, but at least he was willing to pretend. "They're drawing up new papers."

"Good." I stared him down. "You don't have to pay me off. Don't make assumptions like that. If you want to know something, ask. And I was never going to sell the story to the press. I wouldn't do that."

"Okay." He slumped against the wall, leaning his head back to stare up at nothing. "Sorry," he told the ceiling. I'm sure the plasterwork appreciated it immensely.

When I made no response, his gaze eventually found me. It had to be wrong, or at the very least immoral, to be so pretty. Normal people didn't stand a chance. My heart took a dive every time I looked at him. No, a dive didn't cover it. It plummeted.

Where was Lauren to tell me I was being melodramatic when I needed her most?

"I'm sorry, Ev," he repeated. "I know the last twenty-four hours have been shit. Offering to get out of here for a while was my way of trying to make things better."

"Thank you," I said. "And also for coming in here to check on me."

"No problem." He stared at me, eyes unguarded for once. And the honesty in his gaze changed things for me, the brief flash of something more. Sadness or loneliness, I don't know. A kind of weariness that was there and gone before I could understand. But it left its mark. There was a lot more to this man than a pretty face and a big name. I needed to remember that and not make my own assumptions.

"You really want to go?" I asked. "Really?"

His eyes were bright with amusement. "Why not?"

I gave him a cautious smile.

"We can talk over whatever we need to, just you and me. I need to make a couple of calls, then we'll head off, okay?"

"Thank you. I'd like that."

With a parting nod he opened the door and strode back out. He and Mal talked quietly about something in the lounge room. I took the opportunity to wash my face once more and finger-brush my hair for luck. The time had come to take control. Actually, it was well overdue. What was I doing, bouncing from one disaster to the next? That wasn't me. I liked being in control, having a plan. Time to stop worrying about what I couldn't change and take decisive action on what I could. I had money saved up. One of these days my poor old car would die and I'd been planning accordingly. Because once winter hit, and things turned cold, gray, and wet, walking wouldn't always appeal. The thought of using my savings didn't fill me with glee, but emergency measures and all that.

David's lawyers would draw up papers minus the money and I would sign them. No point worrying about that side of things. However, getting out of the public eye for a couple of weeks was well within my capabilities. I just needed to stop and think for a change instead of reacting. I was a big girl and I could take care of myself. The time had come to prove it. I'd go for the drive with him, sort out the basics, and get gone, first on a hideaway holiday, and then back to my very ordinary, well-ordered life devoid of any rock-star interventions.

Yes.

"Give me the keys to the Jeep," said David, squaring off against Mal in the lounge.

Mal winced. "I was joking about giving away cars."

"Come on. Quit bitching. I rode over on the bike and I don't have a helmet for her."

"Fine." With a sour face, Mal dropped his car keys into David's outstretched hand. "But only 'cause I like your wife. Not a scratch, you hear me?"

"Yeah, yeah." David turned and saw me. A hint of a smile curled his lips.

Except for that first day on the bathroom floor, I'd never

seen him smile, never even seen him come close. This bare trace of one made me light up inside. My knees wobbled. That couldn't be normal. I shouldn't be feeling all warm and happy just because he was. I couldn't afford to have any feelings for him at all. Not if I wanted to get out of this in one piece.

"Thanks for putting up with me today, Mal," I said.

"The pleasure was all mine," he drawled. "Sure you wanna go with him, child bride? Fucktard here made you cry. I make you laugh."

David's smile disappeared and he strode to my side. His hand sat lightly against the base of my spine, warm even through the layer of clothing. "We're out of here."

Mal grinned and winked at me.

"Where are we going?" I asked David.

"Does it matter? Let's just drive."

CHAPTER SEVEN

My neck had seized up. Pain shot through me as I slowly straightened and blinked the sleep from my eyes. I rubbed at the offending muscles, trying to get them to unlock. "Ow."

David took one hand off the steering wheel and reached out, rubbing the back of my neck with strong fingers. "You okay?"

"Yeah. I must have slept funny." I shuffled up in the seat, taking in our surroundings, trying not to enjoy the neck rub too much. Because of course he was crazy good with his hands. Mr. Magic Fingers cajoled my muscles back into some semblance of order with seemingly little effort. I couldn't be expected to resist. Impossible. So instead I moaned loudly and let him have his way with me.

Being barely awake was my only excuse.

The sun was just rising. Tall, shadowy trees rushed by outside. Trying to get out of LA, we'd gotten caught in a traffic jam the likes of which this Portland girl had never seen. For all my good intentions, we hadn't really talked. We'd stopped and gotten food and gas. The rest of the time, Johnny Cash had played on the stereo and I'd practiced speeches in my head. None of the words made it out of my mouth. For some reason, I was reluctant to call a halt to our adventure and go off on my own. It had nothing to do with pulling up my big-girl panties and everything to do with how comfortable I'd begun to feel with him. The silence wasn't awkward. It was peaceful. Refreshing, even, given the last day's worth of drama. Being with him on the open road . . . there was something freeing about it. At around two in the morning, I'd fallen asleep.

"David, where are we?"

He gave me a sidelong look, his hand still massaging my muscles. "Well . . ."

A sign flew past outside. "We're going to Monterey?"

"That's where my place is," he said. "Stop tensing up."

"Monterey?"

"Yeah. What've you got against Monterey, hmm? Have a bad time at a music festival?"

"No." I backpedaled fast, not wanting to appear ungrateful. "It's just a surprise. I didn't realize we were, umm . . . Monterey. Okay."

David sighed and pulled off the road. Dust flew and stones pinged off the Jeep. (Mal wouldn't be pleased.) He turned to face me, resting an elbow on the top of the passenger seat, boxing me in.

"Talk to me, friend," he said.

I opened my mouth and let it all tumble out. "I have a plan. I have some money put away. I was going to go someplace quiet for a couple of weeks until this blew over. You didn't have to put yourself out like this. I just need to get my stuff from back at the mansion and I can be out of your hair."

"All right." He nodded. "Well, we're here now and I'd like to go check out my place for a couple of days. So why don't you come with me? Just as friends. No big deal. It's Friday now, the lawyers said they'd have the new papers sent to us Monday. We'll sign them. I've got a show early next week back in LA.

If you want, you can lie low at the house for a few weeks till things calm down. Sound like a plan? We spend the weekend together, then go our separate ways. All sorted."

It did sound like a solid idea. But still, I deliberated for a second. Apparently, it was a second too long.

"You worried about spending the weekend with me or something? Am I that scary?" His gaze held mine, our faces a bare hand's breadth apart. Dark hair fell around his perfect face. For a moment I almost forgot to breathe. I didn't move. I couldn't. Outside a motorcycle roared past then all fell quiet again.

Was he scary? The man had no idea.

"No," I lied, throwing in some scoff for good measure.

I don't think he believed me. "Listen, I'm sorry about acting like a creep back in LA."

"It's okay, really, David. This situation would do anyone's head in."

"Tell me something," he said in a low voice. "You remembered about getting the tat. Anything else come back to you?"

Reliving my drunken rampage wasn't somewhere I wanted to go. Not with him. Not with anyone. I was paying the consequences by having my life upended and splashed about on the Internet. Ridiculous, given nothing in my past was even mildly sordid. Well, apart from the backseat of Tommy's parents' car. "Does this even matter? I mean, isn't it a bit late to be having this conversation?"

"Guess so." He shifted back in his seat and put a hand on the wheel. "You need to stretch your legs or anything?"

"A restroom would be great."

"No worries."

We pulled back out onto the road, and silence ensued for several minutes. He'd turned off the stereo sometime while I slept. The quiet was awkward now and it was all my doing. Guilt sucked first thing in the morning. It probably didn't improve later in the day, but first up, without even a drop of caffeine to fortify me, it was horrible. He'd been nice to me, trying to talk, and I'd shut him down.

"Most of that night is still a blur," I said.

He lifted a couple of fingers off the steering wheel in a little wave. Such was the sum total of his response.

I took a deep breath, fortifying myself to go further. "I remember doing shots at midnight. After that, it's hazy. I remember the sound of the needle at the tattoo parlor, us laughing, but that's about it. I've never blacked out in my life. It's scary."

"Yeah," he said quietly.

"How did we meet?"

He exhaled hard. "Ah, me and a group of people were leaving to go to another club. One of the girls wasn't looking where she was going, bumped into a cocktail waitress. Apparently the waitress was new or something and she crashed her tray. Luckily, it was only a couple of empty beer bottles."

"How did I get involved?"

He darted me a glance, taking his eyes off the road for a moment. "Some of them started giving the poor waitress shit, telling her they were going to get her fired. You just swooped in and handed them their asses."

"I did?"

"Oh, yeah." He licked his lips, the corner of his mouth curling. "Told them they were evil, pretentious, overpriced assholes who should watch where they were walking. You helped the girl pick up the beer bottles and then you insulted my friends some more. It was pretty fucking classic, actually. I can't remember everything you said. You got pretty creative with the insults by the end."

"Huh. And you liked me for that?"

He shut his mouth and said nothing. A whole wide world of nothing. Nothing could actually cover a lot of ground when you put that much effort into it.

"What happened next?" I asked.

"Security came over to throw you out. Not like they were gonna argue with the rich kids."

"No. I guess not."

"You looked panicky, so I got you out of there."

"You left your friends for me?" I watched him in amazement. He did a one-shoulder shrug. As if it meant nil.

"What then?"

"We took off and had a drink in another bar."

"I'm surprised you stuck with me." Stunned was closer.

"Why wouldn't I?" he asked. "You treated me like a normal person. We just talked about everyday stuff. You weren't angling to get anything out of me. You didn't act like I was a different fucking species. When you looked at me it felt . . ."

"What?"

He cleared his throat. "I dunno. Doesn't matter."

"Yes, you do. And it does."

He groaned.

"Please?"

"Fuck's sake," he muttered, shifting around in the driver's seat all uncomfortable-like. "It felt real, okay? It felt right. I don't know how else to explain it."

I sat in stunned silence for a moment. "That's a good way to explain it."

Suddenly, he got decidedly smirky. "Plus, I'd never been propositioned quite like that."

"Yeeeah. Okay, stop now." I covered my face with my hands, and he laughed.

"Relax," he said. "You were very sweet."

"Sweet?"

"Sweet is not a bad thing."

He pulled the Jeep into a gas station, stopping in front of a pump. "Look at me."

I lowered my fingers.

David stared back at me, beautiful face grinning. "You said that you thought I was a really nice guy. And that it would be great if we could go up to your room and have sex and just hang out for a while, if maybe that was something I'd be interested in doing."

"Ha. I have all the moves." I laughed. There might have been more embarrassing conversations in my life. Doubtful, though. Oh, good God, the thought of me trying out my smooth seduction routine on David. He who had groupies and glamour models throwing themselves at him on a daily basis. If there'd been enough room under the car seat, I'd have hid down there. "What did you say?"

"What do you think I said?" Without taking his gaze off me, he popped the glove box and pulled out a baseball cap. "Looks like the restrooms are around the side."

"This is so mortifying. Why couldn't you have forgotten too?"

He just looked at me. The smirk was long gone. For a long moment he held my gaze captive, unsmiling. The air in the car seemed to drop by about fifty degrees.

"I'll be right back," I said, fingers fumbling with the seat belt.

"Sure."

I finally managed to unbuckle the stupid thing, heart galloping inside my chest. The conversation had gotten crazy heavy toward the end. It had caught me unawares. Knowing he'd stood up for me in Las Vegas, that he'd chosen me over his friends . . . it changed things. And it made me wonder what else I needed to know about that night.

"Wait." He rifled among the collection of sunglasses, pulled out a pair of designer aviator shades, and handed them to me. "You're famous now too, remember?"

"My butt is."

He almost smiled. He fit the baseball cap to his head and rested an arm on the steering wheel. The tattoo of my name was right there, in all its glory. It was pink around the edges and some of the letters had small scabs on them. I wasn't the only one permanently marked by this.

"See you in a bit," he said.

"Right." I opened the door and slowly climbed out of the car. Tripping and landing on my ass in front of him must be avoided at all costs.

I saw to the necessities, then washed my hands. The girl in the restroom mirror looked wild-eyed and then some. I splashed water on my face and did a little damage control on my hair. What a joke. This adventure I was on was undoing any and all attempts at keeping control. Me, my life, all of it seemed to be in a state of flux. That shouldn't have felt as strangely good as it did.

When I got back he was standing by the Jeep, signing an autograph for a couple of guys, one of whom was busy doing an enthusiastic air guitar performance. David laughed and clapped him on the back and they talked for a couple of minutes more. He was kind, gracious. He stood smiling, chatting with them, until he noticed me hovering nearby. "Thanks, guys. If you could keep this quiet for a couple of days I'd appreciate it, hey? We could do with a break from the fuss."

"No worries." One of the guys turned and grinned at me. "Congratulations. You're way prettier in person than in your pictures."

"Thanks." I waved a hand at them, not quite knowing what else to do.

David winked at me and opened the passenger door for me to hop in.

The other man pulled out a cell phone and started snapping pictures. David ignored him and jogged around to the other side of the vehicle. He didn't speak till we were back out on the road.

"It's not far now," he said. "We still going to Monterey?"

"Absolutely."

"Cool."

Hearing David talk about our first meeting had put a new spin on things. That conversation had aroused my curiosity. That he'd chosen me to some degree that night . . . I don't think the possibility had occurred to me before. I'd figured we'd both let tequila do the thinking and somehow fallen into this mess together. I was wrong. There was more to the story. Much more. David's reluctance to answer certain questions made me wonder.

I wanted answers. But I needed to tread carefully.

"Is it always like that for you?" I asked. "Being recognized? Having people approach you all the time?"

"They were fine. The crazies are a worry, but you handle it. It's part of my job. People like the music, so . . ."

A bad feeling crept through me. "You did tell me who you were that night, didn't you?"

"Yeah, of course I did." He gave me a snarky look, his brows bunched up.

My bad feeling crept away, only to be replaced by shame. "Sorry."

"Ev, I wanted you to know what the fuck you were getting into. You said you really liked me, but you weren't that keen on my band." He fiddled with the stereo, another half smile on his face. Soon some rock song I didn't know played quietly over the speakers. "You felt pretty bad about it, actually. You kept apologizing over and over. Insisted on buying me a burger and shake to make up for it."

"I just prefer country."

"Believe me, I know. And stop apologizing. You're allowed to like whatever the hell you want.

"Was it a good burger and shake?"

He gave me a one-shoulder shrug. "It was fine."

"I wish I remembered."

He snorted. "There's a first."

I don't know what exactly came over me. Maybe I just wanted to see if I could make him smile. With a knee beneath me I pulled out a length of seat belt, raised myself up, and kissed him quick on the cheek. A surprise attack. His skin was warm and smooth against my lips. The man smelled so much better than he had any right to.

"What was that for?" he asked, shooting me a look out of the corners of his eyes.

"For getting me out of Portland and then LA. For talking to me about that night." I shrugged, trying to play it off. "For lots of things."

A little line appeared above the bridge of his nose. When he spoke, his voice was gruff. "Right. No problem."

His mouth stayed shut and his hand went to his cheek, touching where I'd been. The frown-faced side-on looks continued for quite some time. Each one made me wonder a bit more if David Ferris was just as scared of me as I was of him. This reaction was even better than a smile.

The log-and-stone house rose out of the trees, perched on the edge of a cliff. The place was awe-inspiring on a whole different level from the mansion back in LA. Below, the ocean went about its business of being spectacular.

David climbed out of the car and walked up to the house, fiddling with a set of keys from his pocket. He opened the front door, then stopped to punch numbers into a security system.

"You coming?" he yelled.

I lingered beside the car, looking up at the magnificent house. Him and me alone. Inside there. Hmm. Waves crashed on the rocks nearby. I swore I could hear the swell of an orchestral accompaniment not too far off in the distance. The place was decidedly atmospheric. And that atmosphere was pure romance.

"What's the problem?" David came back down the stone path toward me.

"Nothing . . . I was just—"

"Good." He didn't stop. I didn't know what was going on until I found myself hanging upside down over his shoulder in a fireman's hold.

"Shit. David!"

"Relax."

"You're going to drop me!"

"I'm not going to drop you. Stop squirming," he said, his arm pressing against the back of my legs. "Show some trust."

"What are you doing?" I battered my hands against the ass of his jeans.

"It's traditional to carry the bride across the threshold."

"Not like this."

He patted my butt cheek, the one with his name on it. "Why would we wanna start being conventional now, huh?"

"I thought we were just being friends."

"This is friendly. You should probably stop feeling my ass, though, or I'm gonna get the wrong idea about us. Especially after that kiss in the car."

"I'm not feeling your ass," I grumbled, and stopped using his butt cheeks for a handhold. Like it was my fault the position left me no alternative but to hold on to his firm butt.

"Please, you're all over me. It's disgusting."

I laughed despite myself. "You put me over your shoulder, you idiot. Of course I'm all over you."

Up the steps we went, then onto the wide wooden patio and into the house. Hardwood floors in a rich brown and moving boxes, lots and lots of moving boxes. I couldn't see much else.

"This could be a problem," he said.

"What could be?" I asked, still upside down, my hair obscuring my view.

"Hang on." Carefully, he righted me, setting my feet on the floor. All the blood rushed from my head and I staggered. He grabbed my elbows, holding me upright.

"Okay?" he asked.

"Yeah. What's the problem?"

"I thought there'd be more furniture," he said.

"You've never been here before?"

"I've been busy."

Apart from boxes there were more boxes. They were everywhere. We stood in a large central room with a huge stone fireplace set in the far wall. You could roast a whole cow in the thing if you were so inclined. Stairs led to a second floor above and another level below this one. A dining room and open-plan kitchen came next. The place was a combination of floor-to-ceiling glass, neat lines of logs, and gray stonework. The perfect mix of old and new design techniques. It was stunning. But then all the places he lived in seemed to be.

I wondered what he'd make of my and Lauren's tiny be-draggled apartment. A silly thought. As if he'd ever see it.

"At least they got a fridge." He pulled one of the large stainless steel doors open. Every inch of space inside had been packed with food and beverages. "Excellent."

"Who are 'they'?"

"Ah, the people that look after the place for me. Friends of mine. They used to look after it for the previous owner too. I rang them, asked them to sort some stuff out for us." He pulled out a Corona and popped the lid. "Cheers."

I smiled, amused. "For breakfast?"

"I've been awake for two days. I want a beer, then I want a bed. Man, I hope they thought to get a bed." Beer in hand, he ambled back through the lounge and up the stairs. I followed, curious.

He pushed open one bedroom door after another. There were four all up and each had its own bathroom because cool, rich people clearly couldn't share. At the final door at the end of the hall he stopped and sagged with relief. "Thank fuck for that."

A kingdom of a bed made up with clean, white sheets waited within. And a couple more boxes.

"What's with all the boxes?" I asked. "Did they only get one bed?"

"Sometimes I buy stuff on my travels. Sometimes people give me stuff. I've just been sending it all here for the last few years. Take a look if you want. And yes, there's only one bed." He took another swig of beer. "You think I'm made of money?"

I huffed out a laugh. "Says the guy who got Cartier to open so I could pick out a ring."

"You remember that?" He smiled around the bottle of beer.

"No, I just assumed given what time of night it must have

been." I wandered over to the wall of windows. Such an amazing view.

"You tried to pick some shitty little thing. I couldn't believe it." He stared at me, but his gaze was distant.

"I threw the ring at the lawyers."

He flinched and studied his shoes. "Yeah, I know."

"I'm sorry. They just made me so mad."

"Lawyers do that." He took another swig of the beer. "Mal said you took a swing at him."

"I missed."

"Probably for the best. He's an idiot but he means well."

"Yeah, he was really kind to me." Crossing my arms, I checked out the rest of his big bedroom, wandering into the bathroom. The Jacuzzi would have made Mal's curl up in shame. The place was sumptuous. Yet again the feeling of not belonging, of not fitting in with the décor, hit me hard.

"That's some heavy frown, friend," he said.

I attempted a smile. "I'm just still trying to figure things out. I mean, is that why you took the plunge in Vegas? Because you're unhappy? And apart from Mal you're surrounded by jerks?"

"Fuck." His let his head fall back. "Do we have to keep talking about that night?"

"I'm just trying to understand."

"No," he said. "It wasn't that, okay?"

"Then what?"

"We were in Vegas, Ev. Shit happens."

I shut my mouth.

"I don't mean . . ." He wiped a hand across his face. "Fuck. Look, don't think it was just all drinking and partying and that's the only reason anything happened. Why we happened. I wouldn't want you to think that."

I flailed. It seemed the only proper response. "But that's what I do think. That's exactly what I think. That's the only way this fits together in my head. When a girl like me wakes up married to a guy like you, what else can she possibly think? God, David, look at you. You're beautiful, rich, and successful. Your brother was right, this makes no sense."

He turned on me, face tight. "Don't do that. Don't run yourself down like that."

I just sighed.

"I'm serious. Don't you ever give what that asshole said another thought, understood? You are not nothing."

"Then give me something. Tell me what it was like between us that night."

He opened his mouth, then snapped it closed. "Nah. I don't want to dredge it all up, you know, water under the bridge or whatever. I just don't want you thinking that the whole night was some alcohol-fueled frenzy or something, that's all. Honestly, you didn't even seem that drunk most of it."

"David, you're hedging. Come on. It's not fair that you remember and I don't."

"No," he said, his voice hard, cold, in a way I hadn't heard it. He loomed over me, jaw set. "It's not fair that I remember and you don't, Evelyn."

I didn't know what to say.

"I'm going out." True to his word, he stormed out the door. Heavy footsteps thumped along the hallway and back down the stairs. I stood staring after him.

I gave him awhile to cool off, then followed him out onto the beach. The morning light was blinding, clear blue skies all the way. It was beautiful. Salty sea air cleared my head a little.

David's words raised more questions than they answered. Puzzling that night out consumed my thoughts. I'd reached two conclusions. Both worried me. The first was that the night in Vegas was special to him. My prying or trivializing the experience upset him. The second was, I suspected, he hadn't been all that drunk. It sounded like he knew exactly what he was doing. In which case, how the hell must he have felt the next morning? I'd rejected him and our marriage out of hand. He must have been heartsore, humiliated.

There'd been good reasons for my behavior. I'd still, however, been incredibly thoughtless. I didn't know David then. But I was beginning to now. And the more we talked, the more I liked him.

David sat on the rocks with a beer in hand, staring out to sea. A cool ocean wind tossed his long hair about. The fabric of his T-shirt was drawn tight across his broad back. He had his knees drawn up with an arm wrapped around them. It made him seem younger than he was, more vulnerable.

"Hi," I said, squatting beside him.

"Hey." Eyes squinted against the sun, he looked up at me, face guarded.

"I'm sorry for pushing."

He nodded, stared back out at the water. "S'okay."

"I didn't mean to upset you."

"Don't worry about it."

"Are we still friends?"

He huffed out a laugh. "Sure."

I sat down next to him, trying to figure out what to say next, what would set things right between us. Nothing I could think of saying was going to make up for Vegas. I needed more time with him. The ticking clock of the annulment papers grew louder by the minute. It unnerved me, thinking our time would be cut short. That it would soon all be over and I wouldn't see or talk to him again. That I wouldn't get to figure out the puzzle that was us. My skin grew goose pimples from more than the wind.

"Shit. You're cold," he said, wrapping an arm around my shoulders, pulling me in closer against him.

And I got closer, happily. "Thanks."

He put down the beer bottle, wrapping both arms around me. "Should probably get you inside."

"In a bit." My thumbs rubbed over my fingers, fidgeting. "Thank you for bringing me here. It's a lovely place."

"Mm."

"David, really, I'm so sorry."

"Hey." He put a finger beneath my chin, raising it. The anger and hurt were gone, replaced by kindness. He gave me one of his little shrugs. "Let's just let it go."

The idea actually sent me into a panic. I didn't want to let go of him. The knowledge was startling. I stared up at him, letting it sink in. "I don't want to."

He blinked. "All right. You want to make it up to me?"

I doubted we were talking about the same thing, but I nodded anyway.

"I've got an idea."

"Shoot."

"Different things can jog your memory, right?"

"I guess so," I said.

"So if I kiss you, you might remember what we were like together."

I stopped breathing. "You want to kiss me?"

"You don't want me to kiss you?"

"No," I said quickly. "I'm okay with you kissing me."

He bit back a smile. "That's very kind of you."

"And this kiss is for the purposes of scientific research?"

"Yep. You want to know what happened that night and I don't really want to talk about it. So, I figure, easier all around if you can maybe remember some of it yourself."

"That makes sense."

"Excellent."

"How far did we go that night?"

His gaze dropped to the neck of my tank top and the curves of my breasts. "Second base."

"Shirt on?"

"Off. We were both topless. Topless cuddles are best." He watched as I absorbed the information, his face close to mine.

"Bra?"

"Absolutely not."

"Oh." I licked my lips, breathing hard. "So, you really think we should do this?"

"You're overthinking it."

"Sorry."

"And stop apologizing."

My mouth opened to repeat the sentiment but I snapped it shut.

"S'okay. You'll get the hang of it."

My brain stuttered and I stared at his mouth. He had the most beautiful mouth, with full lips that pulled up slightly at the edges. Stunning.

"Tell me what you're thinking," he said.

"You said not to think. And honestly, I'm not."

"Good," he said, leaning even closer. "That's good."

His lips brushed against mine, easing me into it. Soft but firm, with no hesitation. His teeth toyed with my bottom lip. Then he sucked on it. He didn't kiss like the boys I knew, though I couldn't exactly define the difference. It was just better and . . . more.

Infinitely more. His mouth pressed against mine and his tongue slipped into my mouth, rubbing against mine. God, he tasted good. My fingers slid into his hair as if they'd always wanted to. He kissed me until I couldn't remember anything that had come before. None of it mattered.

His hand slid around the nape of my neck, holding me in place. The kiss went on and on. He lit me up from top to toe. I never wanted it to end.

He kissed me till my head spun, and I hung on for dear life. Then he pulled back, panting, and set his forehead against mine once again.

"Why did you stop?" I asked when I could form a coherent sentence. My hands pulled at him, trying to bring him back to my mouth.

"Shh. Relax." He took a deep breath. "Did you remember something? Anything about that familiar to you?"

My kiss-addled mind came up blank. Damn it. "No. I don't think so."

"That's a pity." A ridge appeared between his brows. The dark smudges beneath his beautiful blue eyes seemed to have darkened. I'd disappointed him again. My heart sank.

"You look tired," I said.

"Yeah. Might be time to get some shut-eye." He planted a quick kiss on my forehead. Was it a friend's kiss, or more? I couldn't tell. Maybe it too was just for scientific purposes.

"We tried, huh?" he said.

"Yeah. We did."

He rose to his feet, collecting his beer bottle. Without him to warm me, the breeze blew straight through me, shaking my bones. It was the kiss, though, that had really shaken me. It had blown my ever-lovin' mind. To think I'd had a night of kisses like that and forgotten it. I needed a brain transplant at the earliest convenience.

"Do you mind if I come with you?" I asked.

"Not at all." He held out a hand to help me to my feet.

Together, we wandered back up to the house, up the stairs into the master bedroom. I tugged off my shoes as David dealt with his own footwear. We lay down on the mattress, not touching. Both of us staring at the ceiling like there might be answers there.

I kept quiet. For all of about a minute. My mind was wide awake and babbling at me. "I think I understand a little better now how we ended up married."

"Do you?" He turned his head to face me.

"Yes." I'd never been kissed like that before. "I do."

"C'mere." A strong arm encircled my waist, dragging me into the center of the bed.

"David." I reached for him with a nervous smile. More than ready for more kisses. More of him.

"Lie on your side," he said, his hands maneuvering me until he lay behind me. One arm slipped beneath my neck and the other was slung over my waist, pulling me in closer against him. His hips fit against my butt perfectly.

"What are we doing?" I asked, bewildered.

"Spooning. We did it that night for a while. Until you felt sick."

"We spooned?"

"Yep," he said. "Stage two in the memory rehab process, spooning. Now go to sleep."

"I only woke up an hour ago."

He pressed his face into my hair and even threw a leg over mine for good measure, pinning me down. "Bad luck. I'm tired and I wanna spoon. With you. And the way I figure it, you owe me. So we're spooning."

"Got it."

His breath warmed the side of my neck, sending shivers down my spine.

"Relax. You're all tense." His arms tightened around me.

After a moment, I picked up his left hand, running the pads of my fingers over his calluses. Using him for my fidget toy. The tips of his fingers were hard. There was also a ridge down his thumb and another slight one along the bottom of his fingers where they joined the palm of his hand. He obviously spent a lot of time holding guitars. On the back of his fingers the word *Free* had been tattooed. On his right hand was the word *Live*. I couldn't help but wonder if marriage would impinge on that freedom. Japanese-style waves and a serpentine dragon covered his arm, the colors and detail impressive.

"Tell me about your major," he said. "You're doin' architecture, right?"

"Yes," I said, a little surprised he knew. I'd obviously told him in Vegas. "My dad's one."

He meshed his fingers with mine, putting the kibosh on my fidgeting.

"Did you always want to play guitar?" I asked, trying not to get too distracted by the way he was wrapped around me.

"Yeah. Music's the only thing that ever really made sense to me. Can't imagine doing anything else."

"Huh." It must be nice, having something to be so passionate about. I liked the idea of being an architect. Many of my childhood games had involved building blocks or drawing. But I didn't feel driven to do it, exactly. "I'm pretty much tone deaf."

"That explains a lot." He chuckled.

"Be nice. I was never particularly good at sports either. I

like drawing and reading and watching movies. And I like to travel, not that I've done much of it."

"Yeah?"

"Mm."

He shifted behind me, getting comfortable. "When I travel, it's always about the shows. Doesn't leave much time for looking around."

"That's a pity."

"And being recognized can be a pain in the ass sometimes. Now and then, it gets ugly. There's a fair bit of pressure on us, and I can't always do what I want. Truth is, I'm kind of ready to slow things down, hang out at home more."

I said nothing, turning his words over inside my head.

"The parties get old after a while. Having people around all the damn time."

"I bet." And yet, back in LA he'd still had a groupie hanging off him, cooing at his every word. Obviously parts of the lifestyle still appealed. Parts that I wasn't certain I could compete with even if I wanted to. "Won't you miss some of it?"

"Honestly, it's all I've done for so long, I don't know."

"Well, you have a gorgeous home to hang out in."

"Hmm." He was quiet for a moment. "Ev?"

"Yeah?"

"Was being an architect your idea or your dad's?"

"I don't remember," I admitted. "We've always talked about it. My brother was never interested in taking up the mantle. He was always getting into fights and skipping class."

"You said you had a tough time at high school too."

"Doesn't everyone?" I wriggled around, turned over so I could see his face. "I don't usually talk about that with other people."

"We talked about it. You said you got picked on because of

your size. I figured that's what set you off with my friends. The fact that they were bullying that girl like a pack of fucking schoolkids."

"I guess that would do it." The teasing wasn't a subject I liked to raise. Too easily, it bought back all of the crappy feelings associated with it. David's arms didn't allow for any of that to slip through, however. "Most of the teachers just ignored it. Like it was an extra hassle they didn't need. But there was this one teacher, Miss Hall. Anytime they started in on me or one of the other kids, she'd intercede. She was great."

"She sounds great. But you didn't really answer my question. Do you want to be an architect?"

"Well, it's what I've always planned to do. And I, ah, I like the idea of designing someone's home. I don't know that being an architect is my divine calling, like music is for you, but I think I could be good at it."

"I'm not doubting that, baby," he said, his voice soft but definite.

I tried not to let the endearment reduce me to a soggy mess on the mattress. Subtlety was the key. I'd hurt him in Vegas. If I was serious about this, about wanting him to give us another go, I needed to be careful. Give him good memories to replace the bad. Memories we could both share this time.

"Ev, is it what you want to do with your life?"

I stopped. Having already trotted out the standard responses, extra thought was required. The plan had been around for so long I didn't tend to question it. There was safety and comfort to be had there. But David wanted more and I wanted to give it to him. Maybe this was why I'd spilled my secrets to him in Vegas. Something about this man drew me in, and I didn't want to fight it. "Honestly, I'm not sure."

"That's okay, you know." His gaze never shifted from mine. "You're only twenty-one."

"But I'm supposed to be an adult now, taking responsibility for myself. I'm supposed to know these things."

"You've been living with your friend for a few years, yeah? Paying your own bills and doing your classes and all that?"

"Yes."

"Then how are you not taking responsibility for yourself?" He tucked his long dark hair behind an ear, getting it out of his face. "So you start out in architecture and see how you go."

"You make it sound so simple."

"It is. You either stick with that or try something else, see how it works for you. It's your life. Your call."

"Do you only play guitar?" I asked, wanting to know more about him. Wanting the topic of conversation to be off me. The knot of tension building inside me was not pleasant.

"No." A smile tugged at the corner of his mouth—he knew exactly what I was about. "Bass and drums too. Of course."

"Of course?"

"Anyone passable at guitar can play bass if they put their mind to it. And anyone who can pick up two sticks at the same time can play drums. Be sure to tell Mal I said that next time you see him, yeah? He'll get a kick out of that."

"You got it."

"And I sing."

"You do?" I asked, getting excited. "Will you sing something for me? Please?"

He made a noncommittal noise.

"Did you sing to me that night?"

He gave me a small pained smile. "Yeah, I did."

"So it might bring back a memory."

"You're going to use that now, aren't you? Anytime you want something you're going to throw it at me."

"Hey, you started it. You wanted to kiss me for scientific purposes."

"It was for scientific purposes. A kiss between friends for reasons of pure logic."

"It was a very friendly kiss, David."

A lazy smile lit his face. "Yes, it was."

"Please sing me something?"

"Okay," he huffed. "Turn back around, then. We were in spoon position for this."

I snuggled back down against him and he shuffled closer. Being David's cuddle toy was a wonderful thing. I couldn't imagine anything better. Pity he was sticking with the scientific rationale. Not that I could blame him. If I were him, I'd be wary of me.

His voice washed over me, deep, rough in the best way possible as he sang the ballad.

I've got this feeling that comes and goes
Ten broken fingers and one broken nose
Dark waters very cold
I know I'll make it home
This sorry sun has burned the sky
She's out of touch and she's very high
Her bed was made of stone
I know I'll break her throne
These aching bones won't hold me up
My swollen shoes they have had enough
These smokestacks burn them down
This ocean let it drown

When he finished I was quiet. He gave me a squeeze, probably checking I was still alive. I squeezed his arms right back, not turning over so he couldn't see the tears in my eyes. The combination of his voice and the moody ballad had undone me. I was always making a mess of myself around him, crying or puking. Why he wanted anything to do with me, I had no idea.

"Thank you," I said.

"Anytime."

I lay there, trying to decipher the lyrics. What it might mean that he'd chosen that song to sing to me. "What's it called?"

" 'Homesick.' I wrote it for the last album." He rose up on one elbow, leaning over to check out my face. "Shit, I made you sad. I'm sorry."

"No. It was beautiful. Your voice is amazing."

He frowned but lay back down, pressed his chest against my spine. "I'll sing you something happy next time."

"If you like." I pressed my lips to the back of his hand, to the veins tracing across, and the dusting of dark hair. "David?"

"Hmm?"

"Why don't you sing in the band? You have such a great voice."

"I do backup. Jimmy loves the limelight. It was always more his thing." His fingers twined with mine. "He wasn't always the asshole he is now. I'm sorry he hassled you in LA. I could have killed him for saying that shit."

"It's okay."

"No, it's not. He was off his face. He didn't have a fucking clue what he was talking about." His thumb moved restlessly over my hand. "You're gorgeous. You don't need to change a thing."

I didn't know what to say at first. Jimmy had said some

horrible things and it had stayed with me. Funny how the bad stuff always did.

"I've both puked and cried on you. Are you entirely sure about that?" I joked, finally.

"Yes," he said simply. "I like you the way you are, blurting out whatever shit crosses your mind. Not trying to play me, or use me. You're just . . . being with me. I like you."

I lay there speechless for a moment, taken aback. "Thank you."

"You're welcome. Anytime, Evelyn. Anytime at all."

"I like you too."

His lips brushed against the back of my neck. Shivers raced across my skin. "Do you?"

"Yes. Very much."

"Thanks, baby."

It took a long time for his breathing to even out. His limbs got heavier and he stilled, asleep against my back. My foot went fuzzy with pins and needles, but never mind. I hadn't slept with anyone before, apart from the occasional platonic bed-sharing episode with Lauren. Apparently, sleeping was all I'd be doing today.

In all honesty, it felt good, lying next to him.

It felt right.

CHAPTER EIGHT

"Hey." David padded down the stairs seven hours later, wearing a towel wrapped around his waist. He'd slicked his wet hair back and his tattoos were displayed to perfection, defining his lean torso and muscular arms. There was a lot of skin on show. The man was a visual feast. I made a conscious effort to keep my tongue inside my head. Keeping the welcoming grin off my face was beyond my abilities. I'd planned to play it cool so as not to spook him. That plan had failed.

"Whatcha doin'?" he asked.

"Nothing much. There was a delivery for you." I pointed to the bags and boxes waiting by the door. All day I'd pondered the problem of us. The only thing I'd come up with was that I didn't want our time to end. I didn't want to sign those annulment papers. Not yet. The idea made me want to start puking all over again. I wanted David. I wanted to be with him. I needed a new plan.

The pad of my thumb rubbed over my bottom lip, back and forth, back and forth. I'd gone for a long walk up the beach earlier, watching the waves crash on the shore and reliving that kiss. Over and over again, I'd played it inside my mind. The same went for our conversations. In fact, I'd picked apart every moment of our time together, explored every nuance. Every moment I could remember, anyway, and I'd tried damn hard to remember all of it.

"A delivery?" He crouched down beside the closest package and started tearing at the wrapping. I averted my eyes before I caught a glimpse up his towel, despite being wildly curious.

"Would you mind if I used your phone?" I asked.

"Ev, you don't need to ask. Help yourself to whatever."

"Thanks." Lauren and my folks were probably freaking out, wondering what was going on. It was time to brave up to the butt-picture repercussions. I groaned on the inside.

"This one's for you." He handed me a thick brown-paper parcel done up with string, followed by a shopping bag with some brand I'd never heard of printed on the side. "Ah, this one too, by the look."

"It is?"

"Yeah. I asked Martha to order some stuff for us."

"Oh."

"Oh? No." David shook his head. Then he kneeled down in front of me and tore into the brown package in my hands. "No 'oh.' We need clothes. It's really simple."

"That's very kind of you, David, but I'm fine."

He wasn't listening. Instead he held up a red dress the same thigh-baring length as those girls at the mansion had worn. "What the fuck? You're not wearing this." The designer dress went flying, and he ripped into the shopping bag at my feet.

"David, you can't just throw it on the ground."

"Sure I can. Here, this is a little better."

A black tank top fell into my lap. At least this one looked the right size. The thigh-high red dress had been a size-four joke. Quite possibly a mean one, given Martha's dislike of me back in LA. No matter.

A tag dangled from the tank. The price. Shit. They couldn't be serious.

"Whoa. I could pay my rent for weeks with this top."

In lieu of a response he threw a pair of skinny black jeans at me. "Here, they're okay too."

I put the jeans aside. "It's a plain cotton tank top. How can this possibly cost two hundred dollars?"

"What do you think of this?" A length of silky blue fabric dangled from his hand. "Nice, huh?"

"Do they sew the seams with gold thread? Is that it?"

"What are you talking about?" He held up the blue dress, turning it this way and that. "Hell no, it's backless. The top of your ass will probably show in that." It joined the red dress on the floor. My hands itched to rescue them, fold them away nicely. But David just ripped into the next box. "What were you saying?"

"I'm talking about the price of this top."

"Shit, no. We're not talking about the price of that top because we're not talking about money. It's an issue for you, and I'm not going there." A micromini denim skirt came next. "What the fuck was Martha thinking ordering you this sort of stuff?"

"Well, to be fair, you do normally have girls in bikinis hanging off you. In comparison, the backless dress is quite sedate."

"You're different. You're my friend, aren't you?"

"Yes." I didn't entirely believe the tone of my own voice.

His forehead wrinkled up with disdain. "Damn it. Look at the length of this. I can't even tell if it's meant to be a skirt or a fucking belt."

Laughter burst out of me and he gave me a hurt look, big blue puppy-dog eyes of extreme sadness and displeasure. Clearly, I had hurt his heart.

"I'm sorry," I said. "But you sound like my father."

He shoved the micromini back into its bag. At least it wasn't on the floor. "Yeah? Your dad and I should meet. I think we'd get along great."

"You want to meet my father?"

"Depends. Would he shoot me on sight?"

"No." Probably not.

He just gave me a curious look and burrowed into the next box. "That's better. Here."

He passed me a couple of sedate T-shirts, one black and one blue.

"I don't think you should be selecting nun's clothing for me, friend," I said, amused at his behavior. "It's vaguely hypo-critical."

"They're not nun's clothes. They just cover the essentials. Is that too much to ask?" The next bulging bag was passed to me in its entirety. "Here."

"You do admit it's just a tiny bit hypocritical, though, right?"

"Admit nothing. Adrian taught me that a long time ago. Look in the bag."

I did so and he burst out laughing, whatever expression I wore being apparently hilarious.

"What is this?" I asked, feeling all wide-eyed with wonder. It might have been a thong if the makers had seen fit to invest just a little more material into it.

"I'm dressing you like a nun."

"La Perla." I read the tag, then turned it over to check out the price.

"Shit. Will you not look at the price, please, Ev?" David dived at me and I lay back, trying to make out the figures on the crazily swaying tag that was bigger than the scrap of lace.

His larger hand closed over mine, engulfing the thong. "Don't. For fuck's sake."

The back of my head hit the edge of a step and I winced, my eyes filling with tears. "Ow."

"You all right?" His body stretched out above mine. A hand rubbed carefully at the back of my skull.

"Um, yeah." The scent of his soap and shampoo was pure heaven. Lord help me. But there was something more than that. His cologne. It wasn't heavy. Just a light scent of spice. There was something really familiar about it.

The tag hanging down in front of my face momentarily distracted me however. "Three hundred dollars?"

"It's worth it."

"Holy shit. No, it's not."

He hung the thong from the tip of a finger, a crazy cool smile on his face. "Trust me. I'd have paid ten times that amount for this. No questions asked."

"David, I could get the exact same thing for less than a tenth of that price in a normal store. That's insane."

"No, you couldn't." He balanced his weight on an elbow set on the step beside my head and started reading from the tag. "See, this exquisite lace is handmade by local artists in a small region of northern Italy famous for just such craftsmanship. It's made from only the finest of silks. You can't get that at Walmart, baby."

"No, I guess not."

He made a pleased humming sound and looked at me with eyes soft and hazy. Then his smile faded. He pulled back and scrunched the thong up in his hand. "Anyway."

"Wait." My fingers curled around his biceps, keeping him in place.

"What's up?" he asked, his voice tightening.

"Just, let me . . ." I lifted my face to his neck. The scent was strongest there. I breathed him deep, letting myself get high off the scent of him. I shut my eyes and remembered.

"Evelyn?" The muscles in his arms flexed and hardened. "I'm not sure this is a good idea."

"We were in the gondolas at the Venetian. You said you couldn't swim, that I'd have to save you if we capsized."

His Adam's apple jumped. "Yeah."

"I was terrified for you."

"I know. You hung on to me so tight I could barely breathe."

I drew back so I could see his face.

"Why do you think we stayed on them for so long?" he asked. "You were practically sitting in my lap."

"Can you swim?"

He laughed quietly. "Of course I can swim. I don't even think the water was that deep."

"It was all a ruse. You're tricky, David Ferris."

"And you're funny, Evelyn Thomas." His face relaxed, his eyes softening again. "You remembered something."

"Yes."

"That's great. Anything else?"

I gave him a sad smile. "No, sorry."

He looked away, disappointed, I think, but trying not to let it show.

"David?"

"Mm?"

I leaned forward to press my lips to his, wanting to kiss him, needing to. He pulled back again. My hopes dived. "Sorry. I'm sorry."

"Ev. What are you doing?"

"Kissing you?"

He said nothing. Jaw rigid, he looked away.

"You're allowed to kiss me and cuddle me and buy me insanely priced lingerie and I can't kiss you back?" My hands slid down to his and he held them. At least he wasn't rejecting me totally.

"Why do you wanna kiss me?" he asked, his voice stern.

I studied our entwined fingers for a moment, getting my thoughts in order. "David, I'm probably not ever going to remember everything about that night in Vegas. But I thought we could maybe make some new good memories this weekend. Something we can both share."

"Just this weekend?"

My heart filled my throat. "No. I don't know. It just . . . it feels like there's meant to be more between us."

"More than friends?" He watched me, eyes intent.

"Yes. I like you. You're kind and sweet and beautiful and you're easy to talk to. When we're not always arguing about Vegas. I feel like . . ."

"What?"

"Like this weekend is a second chance. I don't want to just let it slip by. I think I'd regret that for a long time."

He nodded, cocked his head. "So what was your plan? Just kiss me and see what happened?"

"My plan?"

"I know about you and your plans. You told me all about how anal you are."

"I told you that?" I was an idiot.

"Yeah. You did. You especially told me about the big plan." He stared down at me, eyes intense. "You know . . . finish school then spend three to five years establishing yourself at midrange firm before moving up the ranks somewhere more prestigious and starting your own small consultancy business by thirty-five. Then there'd maybe time to get a relationship and those pesky 2.4 kids out of the way."

My throat was suddenly a dry, barren place. "I was really chatty that night."

"Mm. But what was interesting was the way you didn't talk about that plan like it was a good thing. You talked about it like it was a cage and you were rattling the bars."

I had nothing.

"So, come on," he said softly, taunting me. "What's the plan here, Ev? How were you going to convince me?"

"Oh. Well, I was um . . . I was going to seduce you, I guess. And see what happened. Yeah . . ."

"How? By complaining about me buying you stuff?"

"No. That was just an added bonus. You're welcome."

He licked his lips, but I saw the smile. "Right. Come on, then, show me your moves."

"My moves?"

"Your seduction techniques. Come on, time's a-wasting." I hesitated and he clicked his tongue, impatient. "I'm only wearing a towel, baby. How hard can this be?"

"Fine, fine." I held his fingers tight, refusing to let go. "So, David?"

"Yes, Evelyn?"

"I was thinking . . ."

"Hmm?"

I was so hopelessly outclassed with him. I gave him the only thing I could think of. The only thing that I knew had a track record of working. "I think you're a really nice guy and I was wondering if you'd maybe like to come up to my room and have sex with me and maybe hang out for a while. If that's maybe something you'd be interested in doing . . ."

His eyes darkened, accusing and unhappy. He started to pull back again. "Now you're just being funny."

"No." I slipped my hand around the back of his neck, beneath his damp hair, trying to bring him back to me. "No, I'm very, very serious."

Jaw tensed, he stared at me.

"You asked me this morning in the car if I thought you were scary. The answer is yes. You scare me shitless. I don't know what I'm doing here. But I hate the thought of leaving you."

His gaze searched my face, but still he said nothing. He was going to turn me down. I knew it. I'd asked for too much, pushed him too far. He'd walk away from me, and who could blame him after everything?

"It's okay," I said, gathering what remained of my pride up off the floor.

"Ah, man." He sighed. "You're kinda terrifying too."

"I am?"

"Yeah, you are. And wipe that smile off your face."

"Sorry."

He angled his head and kissed me, his lips firm and so good. My eyes closed and my mouth opened. The taste of him took me over. The mint of his toothpaste and the slide of his tongue against mine. All of it was beyond perfect. He lay me back against the stairs. The new bruise at the back of my head throbbed in protest when I bumped it yet again. I flinched but didn't stop. David cupped the back of my skull, guarding against further injury.

The weight of his body held me in place, not that I was trying to escape. The edge of the steps pressed into my back and I couldn't care less. I'd have happily lain there for hours with him above me, the warm scent of his skin making me high. His hips held my legs wide open. If not for my jeans and his towel, things would get interesting fast. God, I hated cotton just then.

We didn't once break the kiss. My legs wrapped around his waist and my hands curved around his shoulders. Nothing had ever felt this good. My ache for him increased and caught fire, spreading right through me. My legs tightened around him, muscles burning. I couldn't get close enough. Talk about frustrating. His mouth moved over my jaw and down my neck, lighting me up from inside. He bit and licked, finding sensitive spots below my ear and in the crook of my neck. Places I hadn't known I had. The man had magic. He knew things I didn't. Where he'd learned his tricks didn't matter. Not right then.

"Up," he said in a rough voice. Slowly he stood, one hand beneath my ass and the other still protecting my skull.

"David." I scrambled to tighten my hold on his back.

"Hey." He drew back just enough to look into my eyes. His pupils were huge, almost swallowing the blue iris whole. "I am not going to drop you. That's never going to happen."

I took a deep breath. "Okay."

"You trust me?"

"Yes."

"Good." His hand slid down my back. "Now put your arms around my neck."

I did, and my balance immediately felt better. Both of David's hands gripped my butt and I locked my feet behind his back, holding on tight. His face showed no sign of pain or imminent back breakage. Maybe he was strong enough to carry me around after all.

"That's it." He smiled and kissed my chin. "All good?"

I nodded, not trusting myself to speak.

"Bed?"

"Yes."

He chuckled in a way that did bad things to me. "Kiss me," he said.

Without hesitation, I did so, fitting my mouth to his. Sliding my tongue between his lips and getting lost in him all over again. He groaned, his hands holding me hard against him.

Which was when the doorbell rang, making a low, mournful sound that echoed in my heart and groin. "Nooo."

"You're fucking joking." David's face screwed up and he gave the tall double doors the foulest of looks. At least I wasn't alone. I groaned and gave him a tight full-body hug. It would have been funny if it didn't hurt so much.

A hand rubbed at my back, sliding beneath the hem of my tank to stroke the skin beneath. "It's like the universe doesn't want me inside you or something, I swear," he grumbled.

"Make them go away. Please."

He chuckled, clutching me tighter.

"It hurts."

He groaned and kissed my neck. "Let me answer the door and get rid of them, then I'll take care of you, okay?"

"Your towel is on the floor."

"That's a problem. Down you hop."

I reluctantly loosened my hold and put my feet back on firm ground. Again the gonglike sound filled the house. David grabbed a pair of black jeans out of a bag and quickly pulled them on. All I caught was a flash of toned ass. Keeping my eyes mostly averted might have been the hardest thing I'd ever done.

"Hang back just in case it's press." He looked into a small screen embedded beside the door. "Ah, man."

"Trouble?"

"No. Worse. Old friends with food." He gave me a brief glance. "If it makes you feel any better, I'll be hurting too."

"But—"

"Anticipation makes it sweeter. I promise," he said, then

threw open the door. A hand tugged down the front of his T-shirt, trying to cover the obvious bulge beneath his jeans. "Tyler. Pam. Hey, good to see you."

I was going to kill him. Slowly. Strangle him with the overpriced thong. A fitting death for a rock star.

A couple about my parents' age came in, laden down with pots and bottles of wine. The man, Tyler, was tall, thin, and covered in tats. Pam looked to have Native American in her heritage. Beautiful long black hair hung down her back in a braid, thick as my wrist. They both wore wide grins and gave me curious glances. I could feel my face heat when they took in the lingerie and clothing strewn about on the floor. It probably looked like we'd been about to embark on a two-person orgy. Which was the truth, but still.

"How the hell are ya?" Tyler roared in an Australian accent, giving David a one-armed hug on account of the Crock-Pot he held in the other. "And this must be Ev. I have to read about it in the damn paper, Dave? Are you serious?" He gave my husband a stern look, one brow arched high. "Pam was pissed."

"Sorry. It was—ah, it was sudden." David kissed Pam on the cheek and took a casserole dish and a laden bag from her. She patted him on the head in a motherly fashion.

"Introduce me," she said.

"Ev, this is Pam and Tyler, old friends of mine. They've also been taking care of the house for me." He looked relaxed standing between these people. His smile was easy and his eyes were bright. I hadn't seen him looking so happy before. Jealousy reared its ugly head, sinking its teeth in.

"Hello." I put out my hand for shaking, but Tyler engulfed me in a hug.

"She's so pretty. Isn't she pretty, hon?" Tyler stepped aside and Pam came closer, a warm smile on her face.

I was being a jerk. These were nice people. I should be profoundly grateful not every female David knew rubbed her boobs on him. Damn my screaming hormones for making me surly.

"She sure is. Hello, Ev. I'm Pam." The woman's coffee-brown eyes went liquid. She seemed ready to burst into tears. In a rush, she took my hands and squeezed my fingers tight. "I'm just so happy he found a nice girl, finally."

"Oh, thank you." My face felt flammable.

David gave me a wry grin.

"Okay, enough of that," Tyler said. "Let's let these lovebirds have their privacy. We can visit another time."

David stood aside, still holding the casserole dish and bag. When he saw me watching, he winked.

"I'll have to show you the setup downstairs sometime," Tyler said. "You here for long?"

"We're not sure," he said, giving me a glance.

Pam clung to my hands, reluctant to leave. "I made chicken enchiladas and rice. Do you like Mexican? It's David's favorite." Pam's brows wrinkled. "But I didn't think to check if that was all right with you. You might be vegetarian."

"No, I'm not. And I love Mexican," I said, squeezing her fingers back, though not as hard. "Thank you so much."

"Phew." She grinned.

"Hon," called Tyler.

"I'm coming." Pam gave my fingers a parting pat. "If you need anything at all while you're here, you give me a call. Okay?"

David said nothing. It was clearly my decision if they stayed or went. My body was still abuzz with need. That, and we seemed to do better alone. I didn't want to share him because I was shallow and wanted hot sex. I wanted him all to myself.

But it was the right thing to do. And if anticipation made it sweeter, well, maybe this once the right thing to do was also the best thing to do.

"Stay," I said, stammering out the words. "Have dinner with us. You've made so much. We could never possibly finish it all."

David's gaze jumped to me, a smile of approval on his face. He looked almost boyish, trying to contain his excitement. Like I'd just told him his birthday had been brought forward. Whoever these people were, they were important to him. I felt as though I'd just passed some test.

Pam sighed. "Tyler is right, you're newlyweds."

"Stay. Please," I said.

Pam looked to Tyler.

Tyler shrugged but smiled, obviously delighted.

Pam clapped her hands with glee. "Let's eat!"

CHAPTER NINE

Warm hands pushed up my tank top as the sun rose. Next came hot kisses down my back, sending a shiver up my spine. My skin came to immediate goose-pimpled attention, despite the truly horrible time of day.

"Ev, baby, roll over." David whispered in my ear.

"What time is it?"

We'd all gone downstairs to the recording studio after dinner for a "quick look." At midnight Pam had bailed, saying Tyler could call her when they were done. No one anticipated that being anytime soon, since they'd opened a bottle of bourbon. I'd stretched out on the big couch down there while David and Tyler messed around, moving between the control room and the studio. I'd wanted to be close to David, to listen to him play guitar and sing snippets of songs. He had a beautiful voice. What he could do with a six-string in his hands blew my mind. His eyes would take on this faraway look and he was gone. It was like nothing else existed. Sometimes, I actually felt a little lonely, lying there watching him. Then the song would end and he'd shake his head, stretch his fingers, returning to earth. His gaze would find me and he'd smile. He was back.

At some stage I'd dozed off. How I'd gotten up to bed I had

no idea. David must have carried me. One thing was certain: I could smell booze.

"It's almost five in the morning," he said. "Roll over."

"Tired," I mumbled, staying right where I was.

The mattress shifted as he straddled my hips and put an arm either side of my head, bending down over me, covering me.

"Guess what?" he asked.

"What?"

Gently he pushed my hair back off my face. Then he licked my ear. I squirmed, ticklish.

"I wrote two songs," he said, his voice a little slurred, soft around the edges.

"Mm." I smiled without opening my eyes. Hopefully he'd take that as being supportive. I couldn't manage much more on fewer than four hours' sleep. I simply wasn't wired that way. "That's nice."

"No, you don't understand. I haven't written anything in over two years. This is fucking amazing." He nuzzled my neck. "And they're about you."

"Your songs?" I asked, stunned. And still dazed. "Really?"

"Yeah, I just . . ." He breathed deep and nipped my shoulder, making my eyes pop open.

"Hey!"

He leaned over so I could see his face, his dark hair hanging down. "There you are. So, I think of you and suddenly I have something to say. I haven't had anything I wanted to say in a long time. I didn't give a fuck. It was all just more of the same. But you changed things. You fixed me."

"David, I'm glad you got your mojo back, but you're incredibly talented. You were never broken. Maybe you just needed some time off."

"No." From upside down, he frowned at me. "Roll over. I

can't talk to you like this." I hesitated and he slapped my butt. The nontattooed cheek, lucky for him. "Come on, baby."

"Watch it with the biting and spanking, buddy."

"So move already," he growled.

"Okay. Okay."

He climbed off me onto the other side of the mammoth mattress and I sat, drawing my knees up to my chest. The man was shirtless, staring back at me with only a pair of jeans on. How the hell did he keep losing his shirt? The sight of his bare chest brought me to the dribble point. The jeans pushed me right over. No one wore jeans like David. And having caught a glimpse of him without them only made it worse. My imagination went into some sort of sexual berserker rage. The pictures that filled my head . . . I have no idea where they all came from. The images were surprisingly raw and detailed. I was quite certain I wasn't flexible enough to achieve some of them.

All of the air left the room. Truth was, I wanted him. All of him. The good and the bad and the bits in between. I wanted him more than I'd ever wanted anything before in my life.

But not when he'd been drinking. We'd already been there, made that mistake. I didn't know quite what was going on between us, but I didn't want to mess it up.

So, right. No sex. Bad.

I had to stop looking at him. So I took a deep breath and studied my knees. My bare knees. I'd gone to sleep wearing jeans. Now I had only panties and my tank top on. My bra had also mysteriously disappeared. "What happened to the rest of my clothes?"

"They left," he said, face serious.

"You took them?"

He shrugged. "You wouldn't have been comfortable sleeping in them."

"How on earth did you manage to get my bra off without waking me?"

He gave me a sly smile. "I didn't do anything else. I swear. I just . . . removed it for safety reasons. Underwire is dangerous."

"Riiiight."

"I didn't even look."

I narrowed my eyes on him.

"That's a lie," he admitted, rolling his shoulders. "I had to look. But we are still married, so looking is okay."

"It is, huh?" It was pretty much impossible to be mad at him when he looked at me like that. My foolish girl parts got giddy.

No. Sex.

"What are you doing up that end of the bed? That's not going to work," he said, totally unaware of my wakening hormones and distress at same.

Faster than I'd have thought possible given the amount of booze on his breath, he grabbed my feet and dragged me down the bed. My back hit the mattress and my head bounced off the pillow. David sprawled out on top of me before I could attempt any more evasive maneuvers. His weight pressed me into the mattress in the best possible way. Saying no under these conditions was a big ask.

"I don't think we should have sex now," I blurted out.

The side of his mouth kicked up. "Relax. There's no way we're fucking right now."

"No?" Damn it, I actually whined. My patheticness knew no end.

"No. When we do it the first time we'll both be stone-cold sober. Trust me on that. I'm not waking up in the morning again to find you're freaking out because you don't remember or you've changed your mind or something. I'm done being the asshole here."

"I never thought you were an asshole, David." Or at least, not exactly. A jerk maybe, and definitely a bra thief, but not an asshole.

"No?"

"No."

"Not even in Vegas when I started swearing at you and slamming doors?" His fingers slid into my hair, rubbing at my scalp. Impossible not to push into his touch like a happy kitty. He had magic hands. He even made mornings bearable. Though five o'clock was pushing it.

"That wasn't a good morning for either of us," I said.

"How about in LA with that girl hanging off me?"

"You planned that?"

He shut one eye and looked down at me. "Maybe I needed some armor against you."

I didn't know what to say. At first. "It's none of my business who you have hanging off you."

His smile was one of immense self-satisfaction. "You were jealous."

"Do we have to do this right now?" I pushed against his hard body, getting nowhere. "David?"

"Can't own up to it, can you?"

I didn't reply.

"Hey, I couldn't bring myself to touch her. Not with you there."

"You didn't?" I calmed down a lot at that statement. My heart palpitations eased. "I wondered what happened. You came back so fast."

He grunted, got closer. "Seeing you with Jimmy . . ."

"Nothing was going on. I swear."

"No, I know. I'm sorry about that. I was out of line."

My pushing hands turned to petting. Funny that. They slid over his shoulders, around his neck to fiddle with his hair. I just wanted to feel the heat of his skin and keep him near. He made for an emotional landslide, turning me from sleep deprived and cranky to adoring in under eight seconds. "It's great that you wrote some songs."

"Mm. How about when I left you with Adrian and the lawyers? Were you mad at me then?"

I huffed out a breath. "Fine. I might admit to being a bit upset about that."

He nodded slowly, his eyes never leaving mine. "When I got back and they told me what had happened, that you'd taken off with Mal, I lost it. Trashed my favorite guitar, used it to take apart Mal's kit. Still can't believe I did that. I was just so fucking angry and jealous and mad at myself."

I could feel my face scrunch up in disbelief. "You did?"

"Yeah." His eyes were stark, wide. "I did."

"Why are you telling me this now, David?"

"I don't want you hearing it from someone else." He swallowed, making the line of his throat move. "Listen, I'm not like that, Ev. It won't happen again, I promise. I'm just not used to this. You get to me. This whole situation does. I dunno, I'm fucking rambling. Do you understand?"

Later, he mightn't even remember any of this. But right now, he looked so sincere. My heart hurt for him. I looked into his bloodshot eyes and smiled. "I think so. It definitely won't happen again?"

"No. I swear." The relief in his voice was palpable. "We're okay?"

"Yes. Are you going to play the songs for me later?" I asked. "I'd love to hear them."

"They're not done yet. When they're done, I will. I want them perfect for you."

"Okay," I said. He'd written songs about me. How incredible, unless they were the uncomplimentary kind, in which case we needed to talk. "They're not about how much I annoy you sometimes, are they?"

He seesawed his hand in the air. "A little. In a good way, though."

"What?" I cried.

"Trust me."

"Do you actually state what a pain in the ass I am in these songs?"

"Not those words exactly. No." He chuckled, his good humor returned. "You don't want me to lie and say everything's always fucking unicorns and rainbows, do you?"

"Maybe. Yes. People are going to know these are about me. I have a reputation as a constant delight to protect."

He groaned. "Evelyn, look at me."

I did so.

"You are a constant fucking delight. I don't think anyone could ever doubt that."

"You're awful pretty when you lie."

"Am I, now? They're love songs, baby. Love isn't always smooth or straightforward. It can be messy and painful," he said. "Doesn't mean it isn't still the most incredible thing that can ever happen to you. Doesn't mean I'm not crazy about you."

"You are?" I asked, my voice tight with emotion.

"Of course I am."

"I'm crazy about you too. You're beautiful, inside and out, David Ferris."

He lay his forehead against mine, closing his eyes for a moment. "You're so fucking sweet. But, you know, I like that you can bite too. Like you did in Vegas with those assholes. I like that you cared, standing up for that girl. I even kind of like it when you piss me off. Not all the time, though. Shit. I'm rambling again . . ."

"It's okay," I whispered. "I like you rambling."

"So you're not angry at me for losing my temper?"

"No, David. I'm not angry at you."

Without another word, he crawled off me and lay at my side. He pulled me into his arms, arranging an arm beneath me and another over my hip. "Ev?"

"Hmm?"

"Take your shirt off. I wanna be skin to skin," he said. "Please? Nothing more, I promise."

"Okay." I sat up and pulled the tank top off over my head, then snuggled back down against him. Topless had a lot going for it. He tucked me in beneath his chin, and the feel of his warm chest was perfect, thrilling and calming all at once. Every inch of my skin seemed alive with sensation. But being like this with him soothed the savage storm within or something. It never occurred to me to worry about my belly or hips or any of that crap.

Never mind the lingering scent of booze on his skin, I just wanted to be close to him.

"I like sleeping with you," he said, his hand stroking over my back. "Didn't think I'd be able to sleep with someone else in the bed, but with you it's okay."

"You've never slept with anyone before?"

"Not in a long time. I need my space." His fingers toyed with the band on my boy-leg shorts, making me squirm.

"Huh."

"This with you is torture, but it's good torture."

Everything fell quiet for a few minutes and I thought he might have fallen asleep. But he hadn't. "Talk to me, I like hearing your voice."

"All right. I had a nice time with Pam, she's lovely."

"Yeah, she is." His fingers trailed up and down along my spine. "They're good people."

"It was really kind of them to bring us dinner." I didn't know what to say. I wasn't ready to confess I'd been thinking about what he'd said about my becoming an architect. That I'd started questioning the almighty plan. Saying I was scared I'd mess up and somehow ruin things between us didn't seem smart either. Maybe the fates would be listening and screw me over first chance they got. God, I hoped not. So instead I chose to talk trivial. "I love how you can hear the ocean here."

"Mm," he hummed his agreement. "Baby, I don't want to sign those papers on Monday."

I held perfectly still, my heart pounding. "You don't?"

"No." His hand crept up, fingers stroking below my breast, tracing the line of my rib cage. I had to remind myself to breathe. But he didn't even seem to be aware he did it, like he was just doodling on my skin the same way you would on paper. His arms tightened around me. "There's no reason it can't wait. We could spend some time together, see how things went."

Hope rushed through me, hot and thrilling. "David, are you serious about this?"

"Yeah, I am." He sighed. "I know I've been drinking. But I've been thinking it over. I don't . . . shit, I didn't even like having you out of my sight the last few hours, but you looked like you needed to sleep. I don't want us to sign those papers."

I squeezed my eyes tight and sent up a silent prayer. "Then we won't."

"You sure?"

"Yes."

He pulled me in tight against him. "Okay. Okay, that's good."

"We're going to be fine." I sighed happily. The relief made me weak. If I hadn't been lying down I'd have landed on the floor.

Suddenly he sniffed at his shoulder and underarms. "Shit, I stink of bourbon. I'm going to have a shower." He gave me a quick kiss and rolled out of the bed. "Kick me out of bed next time I try to come in smelling like this. Don't let me cuddle up to you."

I loved that he was talking about our being together like it would be an everyday thing. I loved it so much, I didn't even care how bad he smelled.

True love.

CHAPTER TEN

The gong of the doorbell echoed through the house just after ten. David slept on against my back. He didn't stir at all. With a couple more hours' sleep I felt happily half human. I crawled out from beneath his arm, trying not to disturb him. I pulled my top and jeans back on and dashed down the stairs, doing my best not to break my neck in the process. In all likelihood it would be more deliveries.

"Child bride! Let me in!" Mal hollered from the other side of the door. He followed it up with an impressive percussive performance, banging his hands against the solid wood. Definitely the drummer. "Evvie!"

No one called me Evvie. I'd stamped out that nickname years ago. However, it might be better than child bride.

I opened the door and Mal barreled in, Tyler dragging himself along after. Considering Tyler had sat up drinking and playing music with David until the wee small hours, I wasn't really surprised at his condition. The poor man clearly suffered with the hangover from hell. He looked like he'd been punched in both eyes, the bruises from lack of sleep were so bad. An energy drink was attached to his lips.

"Mal. What are you doing here?" I stopped, rubbed the

sleep from my eyes. Wake-up call, it wasn't even my house. "Sorry, that was rude. It's just a surprise to see you. Hi, Tyler."

I'd been hoping to have my husband to myself today, but apparently it wasn't to be.

Mal dropped my backpack at my feet. He was so busy looking around the place he didn't even seem to have heard my question, rude or not.

"David is still asleep," I said, and rifled through the contents of my bag. Oh, my stuff. My wonderful stuff. My purse and phone in particular were a delight to lay eyes on. Many text messages from Lauren, plus a few from my dad. I hadn't even known he could text. "Thank you for bringing this."

"Dave called me at four in the morning and told me he'd written some new stuff. Figured I'd come up and see what was going on. Thought you'd like your gear." Hands on hips, Mal stood before the wall of windows pondering the magnificence of nature. "Man, check out that view."

"Nice, huh?" said Tyler from behind his drink. "Wait till you see the studio."

Mal cupped his hands around his mouth. "Hipster King. Get down here!"

"Hi, sweetie." Pam wandered in, twirling a set of keys on her finger. "I tried to make them leave it a few more hours, but as you can see, I lost. Sorry."

"Never mind," I said. I'm not much of a hugger normally. We didn't do a lot of it in my family. My parents preferred a more hands-free method. But Pam was so nice that I hugged her back when she threw her arms around me.

We'd talked for hours the night before down in the recording studio. It had been illuminating. Married to a popular session player and producer, she'd lived the lifestyle for over twenty years. Touring, recording, groupies . . . she'd experienced the whole rock 'n' roll shebang. She and Tyler had attended a music festival and fallen in love with Monterey with its jagged coastline and sweeping ocean views.

"The lounge and another couple of beds are on their way, should be here soon. Mal, Tyler, help move the boxes. We'll stack them against the fireplace." Suddenly Pam stopped, giving me a cautious smile. "Hang on. You're the woman of the house. You give the orders here."

"Oh, against the fireplace sounds great, thanks," I said.

"You heard her, boys. Get moving."

Tyler grumbled but put down his can and lumbered toward a box, dragging his feet like the walking dead.

"Hold up." Mal smacked his lips at Pam and me. "I haven't gotten my hello kisses yet." He caught Pam up in a bear hug, lifting her off her feet and twirling her around until she laughed. Arms wide, he stepped toward me next. "Come to daddy, bedhead girl."

I put a hand out to halt him, laughing. "That's actually really disturbing, Mal."

"Leave her be," said David from the top of the stairs, yawning and rubbing the sleep from his eyes. Still wearing just the jeans. He was my kryptonite. All the strength of my convictions to be careful disappeared. My legs actually wobbled. I hated that.

Were we married or not today? He'd had a hell of a lot to drink last night. Drunk people and promises did not go well together—we'd both learned that the hard way. I could only hope he remembered our conversation and still felt the same way.

"What the fuck are you doing here?" growled my husband.

"I want to hear the new stuff, asswipe. Deal with it." Mal stared up at him, his jaw set in a hard line. "I should beat the living crap out of you. Fuck, man. That was my favorite kit!"

Body rigid, David started down the stairs. "I said I'm sorry. I meant it."

"Maybe. But it's still time to pay, you dickwad."

For a moment David didn't reply. Tension lined his face but there was a look of inevitability in his weary eyes. "All right. What?"

"It's gotta hurt. Bad."

"Worse than you turning up when Ev and me are having time alone?"

Mal actually looked a little shamefaced.

David stopped at the foot of the steps, waiting. "You wanna take this outside?"

Pam and Tyler said nothing, just watched the byplay. I got the feeling this wasn't the first time these two had faced off. Boys will be boys and all that. But I stood beside Mal, every muscle tensed. If he took one step toward David, I'd jump him. Pull his hair or something. I didn't know how, but I'd stop him.

Mal gave him a measuring look. "I'm not hitting you. I don't want to mess up my hands when we've got work to do."

"What, then?"

"You already trashed your favorite guitar. So it's going to have to be something else." Mal rubbed his hands together. "Something money can't buy."

"What?" asked David, his eyes suddenly wary.

"Hi, Evvie." Mal grinned, and slung an arm around my shoulder, pulling me in against him.

"Hey," I protested.

In the next moment his mouth covered mine, entirely unwelcome. David shouted a protest. An arm wrapped around my back and Mal dipped me, kissing me hard, bruising my lips. I grabbed at his shoulders, afraid I'd hit the floor. When he tried to put his tongue in my mouth, however, I didn't hesitate to bite him.

The idiot howled.

Take that.

Just as fast as he'd dipped me, he set me to rights. My head spun. I put a hand to the wall to stop from stumbling. I rubbed at my mouth, trying to get rid of the taste of him, while Mal gave me a wounded look.

"Damn it. That hurt." He carefully touched his tongue, searching for damage. "I'm bleeding!"

"Good."

Pam and Tyler chuckled, highly amused.

Arms wrapped around me from behind and David whispered in my ear, "Nice work."

"Did you know he was going to do that?" I asked, sounding distinctly pissy.

"Fuck no." He rubbed his face against the side of my head, mussing my bed hair. "I don't want anyone else touching you."

It was the right answer. My anger melted away. I put my hands on top of his, and the grip on me tightened.

"You want me to beat the shit out of him?" asked David. "Just say the word."

I pretended to consider it for a moment while Mal watched us with interest. We obviously looked a lot friendlier than we had in LA. But it was nobody's business. Not his friend's, not the press's, nobody's.

"No," I whispered back, my belly doing backflips. I was falling so fast for him it scared me. "I guess you'd better not."

David turned me in his arms and I fit myself against him, wrapping my arms around his waist. It felt natural and right. The scent of his skin made me high. I could have stood there breathing him in for hours. It felt like maybe we were together, but I no longer trusted my own judgment, if I ever had to be-gin with.

"Malcolm is joining you on your honeymoon?" Pam's voice was heavy with disbelief.

David chuckled. "No, this isn't our honeymoon. If we have a honeymoon it'll be somewhere far away from everyone. Sure as hell, he won't be there."

"If?" she asked.

I really did love Pam.

"When," he corrected, holding me tight.

"This is all real cute, but I came to make music," Mal an-nounced.

"Then you're just going to have to fucking wait," said David. "Ev and I have plans this morning."

"We've been waiting two years to come up with something new."

"Tough shit. You can wait a few more hours." David took my hand and led me back toward the stairs. Excitement ran rife through me. He'd chosen me and it felt wonderful.

"Evvie, sorry about the mouth mauling," Mal said, sitting himself down on the nearest box.

"You're forgiven," I said with a queenly wave, feeling mag-nanimous as we headed up the stairs.

"You going to apologize for biting me?" Mal asked.

"Nope."

"Well, that's not very nice," he called out after us.

David sniggered.

"Okay, people, we need to move boxes." I heard Pam say.

David rushed us down the hallway, then closed and locked the bedroom door behind us.

"You put your clothes back on," he said. "Get them off."

He didn't wait for me to do it, grabbing the hem of my shirt and lifting it up over my head and raised arms.

"I didn't think answering the door mostly naked was a good idea."

"Fair enough," he murmured, pulling me in against him and backing me up against the door. "You looked worried about something downstairs. What was it?"

"It was nothing."

"Evelyn." There was something about the way he said my name. It made me a quivering mess. Also the way he cornered me, pressing his body against mine. I put my hands flat on his hard chest. Not pushing him away, just needing to touch him.

"I was wondering," I said. "After our talk this morning, when we, um, discussed signing the papers on Monday."

"What about it?" he asked, staring straight at me. I couldn't have looked away if I'd tried.

"Well, I wasn't sure if you still felt the same way. About not signing them, I mean. You'd had a lot to drink."

"I haven't changed my mind." His pelvis aligned with mine and his hands swept up my sides. "You changed yours?"

"No."

"Good." His warm hands cupped my breasts, and I lost all ability to think straight.

"You okay with this?" He gave his hands a pointed a look.

I nodded. Talking had gone with thinking, apparently.

"Then here's the plan. Because I know how you like your plans. We're going to stay in this room until we're both satisfied we're on the same page when it comes to us. Agreed?"

I nodded again. Without a doubt, the plan had my full support.

"Good." He placed the palm of one hand between my breasts, flat against my chest. "Your heart's beating real fast."

"David."

"Hmm?"

Nope, I still had no words. So instead, I covered his hand with my own, holding it against my heart. He smiled.

"This is a dramatic reenactment of the night we got married," he announced, looking at me from beneath dark brows. "Hang on. We were sitting on the bed in your motel room. You were straddling me."

"I was?"

"Yeah." He led me to the bed and sat at the edge. "Come on."

I climbed onto his lap, my legs wrapped around him. "Like this?"

"That's it." His hands gripped my waist. "You refused to go back to my suite at the Bellagio. Said I was out of touch with real life and needed to see how the little people lived."

I groaned with embarrassment. "That doesn't sound the least bit arrogant of me."

His mouth curved into a small smile. "It was fun. But also, you were right."

"Better not tell me that too often or it'll go to my head."

His chin rose. "Stop making jokes, baby. I'm being serious. I needed a dose of reality. Someone who'd actually say no to me occasionally and call bullshit on that scene. That's what we do. We push each other out of our comfort zones."

It made sense. "I think you're right . . . Is it enough?"

He held his hand to my heart again and bumped the tip of his nose against mine. "Can you feel what we're doing here? We're building something."

"Yes." I could feel it, the connection between us, the overwhelming need to be with him. Nothing else mattered. There was the physical, the way he went to my head faster than anything I'd ever experienced. How wonderful he smelled all sleep warm first thing in the morning. But I wanted more from him than just that. I wanted to hear his voice, hear him talk about everything and anything.

I felt all lit up inside. Like a potent mix of hormones was racing through me at light speed. His other hand curled around the back of my neck, bringing my mouth to his. Kissing David threw kerosene on the mix within me. He slid his tongue into my mouth to stroke against my own, before teasing over my teeth and lips. I'd never felt anything so fine. Fingers caressed my breast, doing wonderful things and making me gasp. God, the heat of his bare skin. I shuffled forward, seeking more, needing it. His hand left my breast to splay across my back, pressing me against him. He was hard. I could feel him through both layers of denim. The pressure that provided between my legs was heavenly. Amazing.

"That's it," he murmured as I rocked against him, seeking more.

Our kisses were fierce, hungry. His hot mouth moved over my jaw and chin, my neck. Where my neck met my chest, he stopped and sucked. Everything in me drew tight.

"David—"

He pulled back and looked at me, his eyes dilated. Every bit as affected as I was. Thank God I wasn't alone with the panting. A finger traced a slow path between my breasts down to the waistband of my jeans.

"You know what happened next," he said. His hand slipped beneath. "Say it, Ev." When I hesitated, he leaned forward and nipped at my neck. "Go on. Tell me."

Biting had never appealed to me before, neither in thought

nor in action. Not that there'd been much action. But the sensation of David's teeth pressing into my skin turned me inside out. I shut my eyes tight. A bit from the bite and a lot from having to say the words he wanted.

"I've only done this once before."

"You're nervous. Don't be nervous." He kissed me where he'd just bitten. "So, anyway, let's get married."

My eyelids opened and a startled laugh flew out of me. "I bet that's not what you said that night."

"I might have been a little concerned by your inexperience. And we might have had words about it." He gave me a faint smile and kissed the side of my mouth. "But everything worked out fine."

"What words? Tell me what happened."

"We decided to get married. Lie back on the bed for me."

He grasped my hips, helping me climb off him and onto the mattress. My hands slid over the smooth, cool cotton sheet. I lay on my back and he swiftly undid my jeans and disposed of them. The bed shifted beneath me as he knelt above me. I felt ready to implode, my heart hammering, but he seemed perfectly calm and in control. Nice that one of us was. Of course, he'd done this dozens of times.

Probably more, what with groupies and all that. Hundreds? Thousands, even?

I really didn't want to think about it.

His gaze rose to meet mine as he hooked fingers into my panties. In no rush at all, he dragged the last of my clothing down my legs. The urge to cover myself was overwhelming. But I fisted the sheet instead, rubbing the fabric between my fingers.

He undid his jeans. The rustles of his clothing were the only sounds. We didn't break eye contact. Not until he turned to the bedside table and retrieved a condom, discreetly tucking it underneath the pillow next to me.

David naked defied description. Beautiful didn't begin to cover it, all the hard lines of his body and the tattoos covering his skin, but he didn't give me much time to look.

He climbed back onto the bed, lying at my side, raised up on one elbow. His hand curled over my hip. Dark hair fell forward, blocking his face from view. I wanted to see him. He leaned down, kissing me gently this time on my lips, my face. His hair brushed against my skin.

"Where were we?" he asked, his voice a low rumble in my ear.

"We decided to get married."

"Mm, because I'd just had the best night of my life. First time I hadn't felt alone in so fucking long. The thought of not having you with me every other night . . . I couldn't do it." His mouth traveled up my neck. "I couldn't let you go. Especially once I knew you'd only been with one other guy."

"I thought that bothered you?"

"It bothered me, all right," he said, and kissed my chin. "You were obviously ready to give sex another try. If I was stupid enough to let you go, you might have met someone else. I couldn't stand the thought of you fucking anyone but me."

"Oh."

"Oh," he agreed. "Speaking of which, any second thoughts about what we're doing here?"

"No." Lots of nerves but no second thoughts.

The hand on my hip traced over my stomach. It circled my belly button before dipping lower, making me shiver.

"You are so damn pretty," he breathed. "Every piece of you. And when I dared you to put aside your plan and run away with me, you said yes."

"I did?"

"You did."

"Thank God for that."

Fingers stroked over the top of my sex before moving on to my thigh muscles clenched tight together. If I wanted this to go any further I was going to need to open my legs. I knew this. Of course I did. Memories of the pain from last time made me hesitate. My toes were curled and a cramp was threatening to start up in my calf muscle from all of the tensing. Ridiculous. Tommy Byrnes had been a thoughtless prick. David wasn't like that.

"We can go as slow as you want," he said, reading me just fine. "Trust me, Ev."

His warm hand smoothed over my thigh as his tongue traveled the length of my neck. It felt wonderful, but it wasn't enough.

"I need . . ." I turned my face to him, searching for his mouth. He fit his lips to mine, making everything right. Kissing David healed every ill. The knot of tension inside me turned into something sweet at the taste of him, the feel of his body against mine. One arm was trapped underneath me, but the other I made full use of, touching all of him within reach. Kneading his shoulder and feeling the hard, smooth planes of his back.

When I sucked on his tongue, he moaned in the back of his throat and my confidence soared. His hand slipped between my legs. Just the pressure of his palm had me seeing stars. I broke off the kiss, unable to breathe. He touched me gently at first, letting me get used to him. The things his fingers could do.

"Elvis couldn't be with us today," he said.

"What?" I asked, mystified.

He stopped and put two fingers into his mouth, wetting them or tasting me I didn't know. Didn't matter. What was important was him putting his hand back on me, fast.

"I didn't want to share this with anyone." The tip of his finger pushed into me, easing inside just a little. Pulling back before pressing in again. It didn't have the same thrill attached to it that came with him stroking me, but it didn't hurt. Not yet.

"So, no Elvis. I'll have to ask the questions," he said.

I frowned at him, finding it hard to focus on what he was saying. It couldn't be as important as him touching me. The pursuit of pleasure ruled my mind. Maybe he babbled during foreplay. I didn't know. If he wanted, I was more than willing to listen to him later.

His gaze lingered on my breasts until finally he dipped his head, taking one into his mouth. My back bowed, pushing his finger further inside. The way his mouth drew on me erased any discomfort. He stroked me between my legs and the pleasure grew. I tingled in the best way possible. When I did this, it was nice. When David did it, it reached the heights of spectacular, stellar. I knew he was crazy good at guitar, but this had to be where his true talent lay. Honestly.

"God, David." I arched against him when he moved to my other breast. Two fingers worked inside me, a little uncomfortable but nothing I couldn't handle. Not so long as he kept his mouth on me, lavishing my breasts with attention. His thumb rubbed around a sweet spot and my eyes rolled back into my head. So close. The strength of what was building was staggering. Mind-blowing. My body was going to be blown to dust, atoms, when this hit.

If he stopped, I'd cry. Cry, and beg. And maybe kill.

Happily, he didn't stop.

I came, groaning, every muscle drawn taut. It was almost too much. Almost. I floated, my body limp, satiated for all time. Or at least until the next time.

When I opened my eyes again, he was there waiting. He ripped open the condom with his teeth and then put it on. I'd barely caught my breath when he rose over me, moved between my legs.

"Good?" he asked, with a smile of satisfaction.

A nod was the best I could do.

He took the bulk of his weight onto his elbows, his body pressing me into the bed. I'd noticed he enjoyed using his size to the advantage of both of us. It worked. Certainly, there was nothing boring or claustrophobic about the position. I don't know why I'd thought there would be. In the back of Tommy Byrnes's parents' car I'd been cramped and uncomfortable, but this was nothing like that. Lying underneath him, feeling the heat of his skin against mine was perfect. And there could be no doubting how much he wanted this. I lay there, waiting for him to push into me.

Still waiting.

He brushed his lips against mine. "Do you, Evelyn Jennifer Thomas, agree to stay married to me, David Vincent Ferris?"

Oh, that was the Elvis he'd been talking about. The one who'd married us. Huh. I held back his hair, needing to see his eyes. I should have asked him to tie it back. It made it hard to try and gauge his seriousness.

"You really want to do this now?" I asked, a little thrown. I'd been so busy worrying about the sex I hadn't seen this coming.

"Absolutely. We're doing our vows again right now."

"Yes?" I said.

He cocked his head, narrowing his eyes at me. The look on his face was distinctly pained. "Yes? You're not sure?"

"No. I mean, yes," I repeated, more definitely. "Yes. I'm sure. I am."

"Thank fuck for that." His hand rifled under the pillow next to me, returning with the ring of stupendousness sparkling between his fingers. "Hand."

I held my hand between us and he slid the ring on. My cheeks hurt, I was smiling so hard. "Did you say yes too?"

"Yes." He took my mouth in a hard kiss. His hand slid down my side, over my stomach to cup me between my legs. Everything there was still sensitive and no doubt wet. The hunger in his kisses and the way he touched me assured me he certainly didn't mind.

He fit himself to me and pushed in. This was it. And suddenly, shit, I couldn't relax. The memory of pain from the last time I'd attempted this messed with my mind. Wet didn't matter when my muscles wouldn't give. I gasped, my thighs squeezing his hips. David was hard and thick and it hurt.

"Look at me," he said. The blue of his eyes had darkened and his jaw was set. His damp skin gleamed in the low lighting. "Hey."

"Hey." My voice sounded shaky even to my own ears.

"Kiss me." He lowered his face and I did so, pressing my tongue into his mouth, needing him. Carefully, he rocked against me, moving deeper inside me. The pad of his thumb played around my clit, counteracting the hurt. The pain eased, coming closer to being plain old discomfort with an edge of pleasure. No problem. This I could handle.

Fingers wrapped around my leg before sliding down to cup a butt cheek. He pulled me in against him and moved deeper inside me. Rocking against me until I'd taken him all. Which was a problem, because there wasn't enough damn room in me for him.

"It's okay," he groaned.

Easy for him to say.

Shit.

Bodies flush against each another, we lay there, unmoving. My arms were around his head so tight, clinging to him, that I'm not certain how he breathed. Somehow he managed to turn his face enough to kiss my neck, lick the sweat from my skin. Up, over my jaw to my mouth. The death grip I had on him eased when he kissed me.

"That's it," he said. "Try and relax for me."

I nodded jerkily, willing my body to unwind.

"You are so damn beautiful and, God, you feel fucking amazing." His big hand petted my breast, calloused fingers stroking down my side, easing me. My muscles began to relax incrementally, adjusting to his presence. The hurt faded more every time he touched me, whispering words of praise.

"This is good," I said at last, my hands resting on his biceps. "I'm okay."

"No, you're better than okay. You're amazing."

I gave him a giddy smile. He said the best things.

"You mean I can move?" he asked.

"Yes."

He started rocking against me again, moving a little more each time. Gradually gaining momentum as our bodies moved slickly together. We fit, mostly. And we were actually doing it, the deed. Talk about feeling close to someone. You couldn't get physically closer. I was so profoundly glad it was him. It meant everything.

Tommy had lasted two seconds. Long enough to break my hymen and hurt me. David touched me and kissed me and took his time. Slowly, the sweet heat, that sensation of pressure building, came again. He tended to it with care, feeding me long, wet kisses. Stroking himself into me in a way that brought only pleasure. He was incredible, watching me so closely, gauging my reactions to everything he did.

Eventually, I clung onto him and came hard. It felt like the New Year's fireworks display inside me, hot and bright and perfect. So much more with inside and over me, his skin plastered to mine. I stuttered out his name and he pressed hard against me. When he groaned, his whole body shuddered. He buried his face in my neck, his breath heating my skin.

We'd done it.

Huh.

Wow.

Things did ache a little. People were right about that. But nothing like last time.

Carefully, he moved off me, collapsing on the bed at my side.

"We did it," I whispered.

His eyes opened. His chest was still heaving, working to get more air into him. After a moment, he rolled onto his side to face me. There'd never been a better man. Of this I was certain.

"Yeah. You okay?" he asked.

"Yes." I shuffled closer, seeking out the heat of his body. He slid an arm over my waist, drawing me in. Letting me know I was wanted. Our faces were a bare hand's width apart. "It was so much better than last time. I think I like sex after all."

"You have no idea how relieved I am to hear that."

"Were you nervous?"

He chuckled, shuffling closer. "Not as nervous as you were. I'm glad you liked it."

"I loved it. You're a man of many talents."

His smile took on a certain glow.

"You're not going to get all cocky on me now, are you? All puns intended."

"I wouldn't dare. I trust you to keep me grounded, Mrs. Ferris."

"Mrs. Ferris," I said, with no small amount of wonder. "How about that?"

"Hmm." His fingers stroked my face.

I caught his bare hand, inspecting it. "You don't have a ring."

"No, I don't. We'll have to fix that."

"Yes, we will."

He smiled. "Hey, Mrs. Ferris."

"Hey, Mr. Ferris."

There wasn't enough room in me for all the feelings he inspired.

Not even close.

CHAPTER ELEVEN

We spent the afternoon back down in the recording studio with Tyler and Mal. When David wasn't playing, he pulled me onto his lap. When he was busy on guitar, I listened, in awe of his talent. He didn't sing, so I remained in the dark about the lyrics. But the music was beautiful in a raw, rock 'n' roll sort of way. Mal seemed pleased with the new material, bopping his head along in time.

Tyler beamed behind the splendid board of buttons and dials. "Play that lick again, Dave." My husband nodded and his fingers moved over the fretboard, making magic.

Pam had been busy while we'd been upstairs, starting on unpacking the collection of boxes. When she made a move to return to the job in the early evening, I went with her. Asked or not, it wasn't fair that she got lumped with the task on her own. Plus, it pleased my inner need to organize. I snuck back downstairs now and then as the hours passed, stealing kisses, before heading back up to help Pam again. David and company remained immersed in the music. They'd come up seeking food or drink but returned immediately to the studio.

"This is what it's like when they're recording. They lose track of time, get caught up in the music. The number of dinners Tyler has missed because he simply forgot!" said Pam, hands busy unpacking the latest box.

"It's their job, but it's also their first love," she continued, dusting off an Asian-style bowl. "You know that one old girlfriend that's always hanging around the fringes, drunk-dialing them at all hours and asking them to come over?"

I laughed. "How do you deal with never getting to come first?"

"You have to strike a balance. Music's a part of them that you have to accept, hon. Fighting it won't work. Have you ever been really passionate about something?"

"No," I answered in all honesty, eyeing up another stringed instrument I'd never seen the likes of. It had intricate carving encircling the sound hole. "I enjoy college. I love being a barista, it's a great job. I really like the people. But I can't sling coffee for the rest of my life." I stopped, grimaced. "God, those are my father's words. Forget I ever said that."

"You can totally sling coffee for the rest of your life, if you so choose," she said. "But sometimes it takes time to find your thing. There's no rush. I was a born and bred photographer."

"That's great."

Pam smiled, her gaze going distant. "That's how Tyler and I met. I went on tour for a couple of days with the band he was in at the time. I ended up going right around Europe with them. We got married in Venice at the end of the tour and we've been together ever since."

"That's a wonderful story."

"Yeah." Pam sighed. "It was a wonderful time."

"Did you study photography?"

"No, my father taught me. He worked for National Geographic. He put a camera in my hand at age six and I refused to give it back. The next day he brought me an old secondhand one. I carried it everywhere I went. Everything I saw was through its lens. Well, you know what I mean . . . the world made sense when I looked at it that way. Better than that, it made everything beautiful, special." She pulled a couple of books out of a box, adding them to the shelves built into one wall. We'd already managed to half fill them with various books and mementoes.

"You know, David's dated a lot of women over the years. But he's different with you. I don't know . . . the way he watches you, I think it's adorable. It's the first time he's brought anyone here in six years."

"Why was the place empty so long?"

Pam's smile faded and she avoided my eyes. "He wanted it to be his place to come home to, but then things changed. The band was just hitting it big. I guess things got complicated. He could explain it to you best."

"Right," I said, intrigued.

Pam sat back on her haunches, looking around the room. "Listen to me rabbiting on. We've been at this all day. I think we deserve a break."

"I second that."

Nearly half the boxes were open. The contents we couldn't think of an immediate home for were lined up along one wall. A big plush black couch had been delivered. It fit the house and its owner perfectly. With various rugs, pictures, and instruments strewn about, the place had almost begun to look like a home. I wondered if David would approve. Easily, I could picture us spending time here when I wasn't in classes. Or maybe holidays would be spent touring. Our future was a beautiful, dazzling thing, filled with promise.

In the here and now, however, I still hadn't caught up with Lauren. A fact that caused me great guilt. Explaining this situation didn't appeal, nor did confessing my fast-growing feelings for David.

"Come on, let's go grab some food from down the road. The bar does the best ribs you've ever tasted. Tyler goes crazy for them," said Pam.

"That's a brilliant idea. I'll just let him know we're going. Do I need to change?" I had on the black jeans and tank top, a pair of Converses. The only shoes I'd been able to find among Martha's buys that didn't feature four-inch-plus heels. For once, I looked almost rock 'n' roll–associated. Pam wore jeans and a white shirt, a heavy turquoise necklace around her throat. It was casual in theory, but Pam was a striking woman.

"You're dressed fine," she said. "Don't worry. It's very relaxed."

"All right."

The sound of music still drifted up from downstairs. When I went down there, the door was shut and the red light shining. I could see Tyler with headphones on, busy at the console. I'd forgotten to charge my phone with all the recent excitement. But I didn't have David's phone number so I couldn't have texted him anyway. I didn't want to interrupt. In the end, I left a note on the kitchen bench. We wouldn't be gone long. David probably wouldn't even notice.

The bar was a traditional wooden wonderland with a big jukebox and three pool tables. Staff called out "hellos" to Pam as we walked in. No one even blinked at me, which was a relief. The place was packed. It felt good to be back out among people, just part of the crowd. Pam had phoned ahead, but the order wasn't ready yet. Apparently the kitchen was every bit as busy as the bar. We grabbed a couple of drinks and settled in to wait. It was a nice place, very relaxed. There was lots of laughter, and country music blared from the jukebox. My fingers tapped along in time.

"Let's dance," said Pam, grabbing my hand and tugging me out of my chair. She bopped and swayed as I followed her onto the crowded dance floor.

It felt good to let loose. Sugarland turned into Miranda Lambert and I raised my arms, moving to the music. A guy came up behind me and grabbed my hips, but he backed up a step when I shook my head with a smile. He grinned back at me and kept dancing, not moving away. A man spun Pam and she whooped, letting him draw her into a loose hold. They seemed to know each other.

When the guy beside me moved a little closer, I didn't object. He kept his hands to himself and it was all friendly enough. I didn't know the next song, but it had a good beat and we kept right on moving. My skin grew damp with sweat, my hair clinging to my face. Then Dierks Bentley came on. I'd had a terrible crush on him since age twelve, but it was all about his pretty blond hair and nothing to do with his music. My love for him was a shameful thing.

Dude One moved away and another took his place, slipping an arm around my waist and trying to pull me in against him. I planted my hands on his chest and pushed back, giving him the same smile and headshake that had worked on the last. He might have been only about my height, despite the huge hat, but he was built solid. He had a big barrel of a chest and he stank of cigarette smoke.

"No," I said, still trying to push him off me. "Sorry."

"Don't be sorry, darlin'," he yelled in my ear, knocking me in the forehead with the brim of his hat. "Dance with me."

"Let go."

He grinned and his hands slapped down hard on both my butt cheeks. The jerkoff started grinding himself against me.

"Hey!" I pushed against him, getting nowhere. "Get off me."

"Darlin'." The letch leaned in to kiss me, smacking me in the nose with the brim of his hat again. It hurt. Also, I hated him. If I could just wiggle my leg between his and knee the asswipe in the groin, I'd be able to even the playing field. Or leave him writhing on the floor crying for his mommy. An outcome I was fine with.

I shoved my foot between the two of his, getting closer to my objective. Closer . . .

"Let her go." David miraculously appeared out of the crowd beside us, a muscle jumping in his jaw. Oh, shit. He looked ready to kill.

"Wait your turn," the cowboy yelled back, pushing his pelvis into me. God, it was disgusting. Puking could happen. It would be no less than he deserved.

David snarled. Then he grabbed the man's hat and sent it flying off into the crowd. The man's eyes went round as plates and his hands dropped away from me.

I skipped back a step, free at last. "David—"

He looked to me, and in that moment, the cowboy swung. His fist clipped David's jaw. David's head snapped back and he stumbled. The cowboy dove at him. They landed hard, sprawled across the dance floor. Fists flew. Feet kicked. I could barely see who did what. People formed a circle around them, watching. No one doing anything to stop it. Blood spurted, spraying the floor. The pair rolled and pushed, and David came out on top. Then just as fast he fell aside. My pulse pounded behind my ears. The violence was startling. Nathan used to get into fights regularly after school. I'd hated it. The blood and the dirt, the mindless rage.

But I couldn't just stand by, caught in a cold stupor. I wouldn't.

A strong hand grabbed my arm, halting my forward momentum.

"No," said Mal.

Then he and another couple of guys stepped in. Relief poured through me. Mal and Tyler wrestled David off the cowboy. Another pair restrained the bloody-faced fool who bellowed on and on about his hat. Goddamn idiot.

They hustled David out of the bar, dragging him backward. Through the front doors and down the steps they went while his feet kicked out, trying to get back into it. And he kept right on fighting until they threw him up against Mal's big black Jeep.

"Knock it off!" Mal yelled in his face. "It's over."

David slumped against the vehicle. Blood seeped from one nostril. His dark hair hung in his face. Even in the shadows he looked swollen, misshapen. Not half as bad as the other guy, but still.

"Are you okay?" I stepped closer to check the extent of his wounds.

"I'm fine," he said, shoulders still heaving as he stared at the ground. "Let's go."

Moving in slow motion, he turned and opened the passenger-side door, climbing in. With a mumbled good-bye, Pam and Tyler headed for their own car. A couple of people stood on the steps leading into the bar, watching. One guy held a baseball bat as if he expected further trouble.

"Ev. Get in the car." Mal opened the door to the backseat and ushered me in. "Come on. Cops could be coming. Or worse."

Worse was the press. I knew that now. They'd be all over this in no time.

I got in the car.

CHAPTER TWELVE

Mal disappeared as soon as we got home. David stomped up the stairs to our bedroom. Was it really ours? I didn't have a clue. But I followed. He turned and faced me as soon as I entered the room. His expression was fierce, dark brows down and his mouth a hard line. "You call that giving us a chance?"

Whoa. I licked my lips, giving myself a moment. "I call it going out to pick up some food. The kitchen was running late so we got a beer. We liked the music so we decided to get up to dance for a couple of songs. Nothing more."

"He was all over you."

"I was about to knee him in the balls."

"You left without a fucking word!" he shouted.

"Don't yell at me," I said, searching for a calm I didn't have in me just then. "I left you a note in the kitchen."

He shoved his hands through his hair, visibly fighting for calm. "I didn't see it. Why didn't you come talk to me?"

"The red light was on. You were recording and I didn't want to disturb you. We weren't supposed to be gone for long."

Bruised face furious, he walked a few steps away, then turned and marched back. No calmer from what I could tell despite the pacing. But at least he seemed to be trying. His temper was the third person in the room, and it took up all the damn space. "I was worried. You didn't even have your phone on you, I found it on the fucking table. Pam's phone kept ringing out."

"I'm sorry you were worried." I held out my hands, out of excuses for both of us. "I forgot to charge my phone. It happens sometimes. I'll try to be more careful in future. But David, nothing was going on. I'm allowed to leave the house."

"Fuck, I know that. I just . . ."

"You're doing your thing, and that's great."

"This was some sort of fucking punishment?" He forced the hard words out through gritted teeth. "Is that it?"

"No. Of course not." I sighed. Quietly.

"So you weren't trying to get picked up?"

"I'm going to pretend you didn't say that." Slapping him upside the head wasn't out of the question. I kept my clenched fists safely at my sides, resisting the urge.

"Why'd you let him touch you?"

"I didn't. I asked him to move back and he refused. That's when you arrived." I rubbed at my mouth with my fingers, fast running out of patience. "We're just going around in circles here. Maybe we should talk about this later when you've had a chance to calm down."

Hands shaking, I turned toward the door.

"You're leaving? Fucking perfect." He threw himself back onto the bed. Laughter wholly lacking in humor came out of his mouth. "So much for us sticking together."

"What? No. I don't want to fight with you, David. I'm going downstairs before we start saying things we don't mean. That's all."

"Go," he said, his voice harsh. "I fucking knew you would."

"God," I growled, turning back to face him. The desire to scream and shout at him, to try to make some sense of this, boiled over inside of me. "Are you even listening to me? Are you hearing me at all? I'm not leaving you. Where is this coming from?"

He didn't answer, just stared at me, eyes accusing. It made no sense.

I almost tripped getting back to him, my feet fumbling. Landing on my face would be perfect. It was exactly where this was heading. I didn't even understand what we were fighting about anymore, if I ever had.

"Who are you comparing me to here?" I asked, every bit as angry as him now. "Because I am not her."

He kept right on glaring at me.

"Well?"

His lips stayed shut and my frustration and fury skyrocketed. I wanted to grab him and shake him apart. Make him admit to something, anything. Make him tell me what the hell was really going on.

I crawled onto the bed, getting in his face. "David, talk to me!"

Nothing.

Fine.

I pushed back with trembling legs and tried to clamber off the mattress. He grabbed at my arms, trying to hold on. And like fuck he was. I pushed back hard. All brawling limbs, we tumbled off the bed and rolled onto the floor. His back hit the hardwood floor. Immediately, he rolled us again, putting me on the bottom. My blood pounded behind my ears. I kicked and pushed and wrestled him with all the hurt he'd inspired. Before he could get his bearings I rolled us again, regaining the uppermost position. He couldn't stop me, the bastard. Escape was imminent.

But it didn't happen.

David grabbed my face in both hands and mashed his lips to mine, kissing the stuffing out of me. I opened my mouth and his tongue slipped in. The kiss was rough and wet. Breathing was an issue. We both had anger management problems and neither of us entirely refrained from biting. With his bruised mouth, he definitely had the most to lose. It wasn't long before the metallic taste of blood hit my tongue.

He pulled back with a hiss, fresh blood on his swollen top lip. "Fuck."

He grabbed my hands. I didn't make it easy on him, struggling for all I was worth. But he was stronger. He pinned them to the floor above my head with relative ease. The press of his hard-on between my legs felt exquisite, insane. And the more I bucked against him, the better it got. Adrenaline had already been pouring through me, amping me up. The need to have him sat just below the surface, prickling my skin, making me hyperaware of everything.

So this was angry sex. I couldn't bring myself to hurt him, not really. But there were other ways to assert myself in this situation. He came back to my mouth and I nipped him again in warning.

A mad smile appeared on his face. It probably matched my own. We were both panting, fighting for air. Both as stubborn as hell. Without another word, he released my wrists and drew back. Quickly, he grabbed my waist and turned me over, pulling me up onto my elbows and knees. Arranging me how he wanted me. Rough hands tore at the button and zip on my jeans. He yanked down my denim and my crazily overpriced thong, body poised over mine.

His hands smoothed over my ass. Teeth dragged over the sensitive skin of one cheek, just above the tattoo of his name. A hand slipped beneath to cup my sex. The press of his fingers against me had me seeing stars. When they started stroking me, working me higher, I couldn't hold back my moan. He nipped me on the rump, a sharp sting of sensation. Then he pressed kisses up my spine. Stubble from his chin scratched my shoulder.

The lack of words, the absolute silence apart from our heavy breathing made it more. It made it different.

One finger slid inside me. Not nearly enough, damn it. He slid in a second finger, stretching me a little. Once, twice he slowly pumped them into me. I pushed back against his hand, needing more. Next came the sound of the bedside drawer sliding open as he searched for a condom. His fingers slid out of me and the loss was excruciating. I heard his zipper being lowered, the rustle of clothes, and the crinkle of a condom wrapper. Then his cock pressed against me, rubbing over my opening. He pushed in slow and steady, filling me up until there was nothing left that wasn't me and him. For a moment he stopped, letting me adjust.

But not for long.

Hands gripped my hips and he began to move. Each thrust was a little faster and harder than the last. Labored breathing and the slap of skin against skin swallowed the silence. The scent of sex hung heavy in the air. I pushed back against him, meeting him thrust for thrust, spurring him on. It was nothing like the sweet and slow of this morning. Neither of us was tender. My jeans shackled me at the knees, making me slip forward a little with each thrust. His fingers dug into my hips, holding me in place. He stroked over something inside me and I gave a startled gasp. Again and again he concentrated on that spot, making me mindless. I felt superheated. Like fire burned through me. Sweat dripped off my skin. I hung my head, closed my eyes, and held onto the floor with all my might. My voice called out without my consent, saying his name. Damn it. My body wasn't my own. I came hard, awash with sensation. My back bowed, every muscle drawn tight.

David pounded into me, hands slipping over my slick skin. He came a moment later in silence, holding himself deep. His face rested against my back, arms wrapped around my body, which was lucky. I'd lost all traction. Slowly I slid to the floor. If he hadn't been holding me I'd have face-planted. I doubt I'd have even cared.

In silence, he picked me up and carried me into the bathroom, sat me on the sink. Without fuss he dealt with the condom, started running a bath, holding a hand beneath the faucet to check the temperature. He undressed me like I was a child, pulling off my sneakers and socks, my jeans and panties. He tugged off my shirt and unclipped my bra. His own clothes were ripped off with far less care. I felt curiously naked with him now, the way he was treating me. Being so careful with me despite my biting and big-boned unwieldiness. He treated me like I was precious. Like I was a china doll. One he could apparently have rough sex with upon occasion. Once more, he checked the water, then he picked me up again and into the bath we went.

I huddled against him, my skin cooling off fast. My teeth chattered. He held me tighter, resting his cheek against the top of my head.

"I'm sorry if I was too rough," he said finally. "I didn't mean it, accusing you of shit like that. I just . . . fuck. I'm sorry."

"Rough wasn't a problem, but the trust issue . . . we're going to need to talk about it sometime." I rested my head against his shoulder, stared up into his troubled eyes.

His chin jerked as he gave me a tight nod.

"But right now, I'd like to talk about Vegas."

The arms around me tensed. "What about Vegas?"

I stared back at him, still trying to think everything through. Not wanting to get this wrong, whatever this was.

Marriage, that's what it was.

Shit.

"We've covered a lot of ground in the last twenty-four hours," I said.

"Yeah, I guess we have."

I held up my hand, my sparkly ring. The size of the diamond didn't matter. That David had put it on me was what made it important. "We talked about lots of things. We slept together, and we made promises to each other, important ones."

"You regretting any of it?"

My hand slid around the back of his neck. "No. Absolutely not. But if you woke up tomorrow, and you'd somehow forgotten all of this. If it was all gone for you, like it had never happened, I would be furious at you."

His forehead wrinkled.

"I'd hate you for forgetting all this when it's meant everything to me."

He licked his lips and turned off the tap with a foot. Without the water gushing out, the room quieted instantly.

"Yeah," he said. "I was angry."

"I'm not going to let you down like that again."

Beneath me his chest rose and fell heavily. "Okay."

"I know it takes time to learn to trust someone. But in the meantime, I need you to at least give me the benefit of the doubt."

"I know." Wary blue eyes watched me.

I sat up and reached for the washcloth on the edge of the bath. "Let me clean you up a little."

A dark lump sat on his jaw. Blood lingered beneath his nose and near his mouth. He was a mess. A big red mark was on his ribs.

"You should see a doctor," I said.

"Nothing's broken."

Carefully, I wiped the blood from the side of his mouth and beneath his nose. Seeing him in pain was horrible. Knowing I was the cause made my stomach twist and turn. "Tell me if I press too hard."

"You're fine."

"I'm sorry you got hurt. In the bar tonight, and in Vegas. I didn't mean for that to happen."

His eyes softened and his hands slid over me. "I want you to come back to LA with me. I want you with me. I know school will start back eventually and we're gonna have to work something out. But whatever happens, I don't want us apart."

"We're not going to be."

"Promise?"

"Promise."

CHAPTER THIRTEEN

Morning light woke me. I rolled over and stretched, working out the kinks. David lay on his back beside me, fast asleep. He had an arm flung over his face, covering his eyes. With him there, everything was right with my world. But also, everything was on show. He'd kicked off the sheet sometime during the night. So the morning wood thing was true. There you go. Lauren had been right on that count.

Waking up beside him with my wedding ring back on my finger had me grinning like a loon. Of course waking up beside a bare-naked David would have made just about anybody smile. Between my legs felt a little sore from last night's efforts, but nothing too bad. Nothing sufficient to distract me from the view that was my husband.

I shuffled down the bed a bit, checking him out at my leisure for once. He didn't have much of a belly button. It was basically a small indent followed by a fine trail of dark hair leading down across his flat stomach directly to it. And it was hard, thick, and long.

"It" being his penis, of course.

Gah. No, that didn't sound right.

His cock. Yeah, much better.

We'd sat in the warm bath for a while last night at his insistence, soaking. We'd just talked. It had been lovely. There'd been no mention of the woman who'd obviously cheated on him and/or left him at sometime in his past. But I'd felt her presence lurking. Time would kick her out the back door, I was sure of it.

He smelled faintly of soap, a little musky, perhaps. Warm wasn't something I'd ever registered as having a smell before, but that's what David smelled of. Warmth, like he was liquid sunshine or something. Heat and comfort and home.

I quickly checked his face. His eyes were still closed beneath the length of his arm, thank goodness. His chest rose and fell in a steady rhythm. I really didn't need him catching me sniffing at his crotch, no matter how poetic my thoughts. That would be embarrassment on a scale I'd prefer not to experience.

The skin looked super smooth despite the veins, and the head stood out distinctly. He was uncircumcised. Curiosity got the better of me, or maybe it already had. With all of his front half at my disposal, look where I'd wound up. I gently laid the palm of my hand atop him. The skin was soft and warm. Carefully, I wrapped my fingers around him. His cock twitched and I jerked back, startled.

David burst out laughing, loud and long.

Bastard.

Embarrassment was a dam that had burst wide open inside of me. Heat flashed up my neck.

"I'm sorry," he said, reaching for me with his hand. "But you should have seen your face."

"It's not funny."

"Baby, you wouldn't believe how fucking funny it was." He wrapped his fingers around my wrist, dragging me up and onto him. "Come here. Aw, the tips of your ears are all pink."

"No, they're not," I mumbled, lying across his chest.

He stroked my back, still sniggering. "Don't let this scar you for life, though, hey? I like you touching me."

I huffed noncommittally.

"You know, if you play with my dick, things will always happen. I guarantee it."

"I know that." The crook of his neck was handy for burying my hot face in, so I took full advantage. "I just got a surprise."

"You sure did." He squeezed me tight, then slid a hand down to cup my bottom. "How are you feeling?"

"Okay."

"Yeah?"

"A little sore," I admitted. "A lot happy. Though that was before you callously mocked me."

"Poor baby. Let me see," he said, rolling me over onto the mattress until he was on top.

"What?"

He sat up between my legs with a hand holding my knees open. With a practiced eye he checked me over. "You don't look too swollen. Probably just a bit sore inside, yeah?"

"Probably." I tried to pull my legs up, to close them. Because I heartily doubted having him look at me there in that way helped the color of my ear tips.

"I have to be more careful with you."

"I'm fine. Not that breakable, honestly."

"Mm."

"Takes more than a round of rough sex on the hardwood floor to worry me."

"That so? Stay still for me," he said, shuffling back to lie down at the end of the mattress.

This situated him distinctly between my legs, face-to-face with my girl bits, guaranteeing I wouldn't be going anywhere.

I'd heard good things about this, things that made my embarrassment levels redundant. Plus, I was curious.

He brushed his lips against my sex, the warmth of his breath making me shiver. My stomach muscles spasmed in anticipation.

His gaze met mine over the top of my torso. "Okay?"

I gave him a jerky nod, impatient.

"Put the other pillow behind your head too," he instructed. "I want you to be able to watch."

My husband had the best ideas. I did as asked, settling in to watch though my legs were aquiver. He kissed the inside of my thighs, first one, then the other. Everything in me focused on the sensations emanating from there. My world was a small perfect place. Nothing existed outside our bed.

His eyes closed but mine stayed open. He kissed his way over the lips of my sex and then traced the divide with the tip of his tongue. That worked. Warmth suffused me inside. Hands wrapped around the underneath of my thighs, fingers rubbing small circles into my skin. His lips never left my sex. It was exactly as if he was kissing me there. Mouth open wide and tongue stroking, making me writhe. The grip on my thighs tightened, holding me to him. Even the brush of his hair and the prickle of his stubble against me were thrilling things. I don't know when I stopped watching. My eyes shut of their own accord as the pleasure took over. It was amazing. I didn't want it to end. But the pressure inside me built until I couldn't contain it any longer. I came with a shout, my body drawn tight from top to toe. Every part of me tingled. He didn't pull back until I lay perfectly still, concentrating on just breathing.

"Am I forgiven for laughing at you?" he asked, crawling up the bed to plant a kiss on my shoulder.

"Sure."

"How about the rough sex on the hardwood floor? Am I forgiven for that too?"

"Mmhmm."

The mattress shifted beneath me as he hovered above. His wet mouth lingered over the curve of my breast, the line of my collarbone.

"I really liked that," I said, my voice low and lazy. Gradually I opened my eyes.

"Fuck drunk suits you, Evelyn." A hand smoothed over my hip, and he smiled down at me. "I'll eat you out whenever you like. You only have to ask."

I smiled back at him. And the smile may have twitched a little at the edges. Talking about this kind of thing was still new to me.

"Tell me you liked me licking your gorgeous pussy."

"I said I liked it."

"You're embarrassed." David's brows drew together. There was mischief in his eyes. "You can talk rough sex on hardwood floors but not cunnilingus, hey? Say 'pussy.' "

I rolled my eyes. "Pussy."

"Again. Not as in 'cat.' "

"I'm not saying it as in 'cat.' Pussy. Pussy, pussy, pussy. Pussy not as in 'cat.' Happy?" I laughed, moving a hand to slide down his chest, heading for his groin. "Can I do something for you now?"

He stopped my hand, brought it to his mouth and kissed it. "I'm going to wait till tonight when we can make love again, if you're feeling okay."

"We're making love tonight, Mr. Smooth?"

"Sure." He smirked, climbing off the bed. "We'll make love again and then we'll fuck again. I think we should put some serious time into exploring the differences. It'll be fun."

"Okay," I quickly agreed. I wasn't stupid.

"That's my girl." He held a hand out for me, eyes intent. "You are so damn pretty. You know, I'm never going to be able to wait until tonight."

"No?"

"Nope. Look at you lying all naked on my bed. I've never seen anything I've liked more." He shook his head, mouth rueful as his eyes traveled over my body. My husband was incredibly good for my ego. But he made me feel humble at the same time, grateful. "I was a fucking idiot to suggest waiting," he said, taking a step back and crooking his finger at me. "And you know how I hate being away from you. Come help me in the shower? It'll give you some good hands-on experience."

I crawled off the bed after him. "That so?"

"Oh, yeah. And you know how seriously I take you and your education."

"You suck," said Lauren, her voice echoing down the line. Pam had warned me some parts of the coast could be iffy with cell coverage.

"I'm not saying I don't still love you," she said. "But, you know . . ."

"I know. I'm sorry," I said, settling into the corner of the lounge. The menfolk were busy downstairs making music. Pam had gone running errands in town. I had calls to make. Boxes to unpack. Dreams of blissful wedlock to work up to insane, impossible proportions inside my head.

"Never mind. Update me," she demanded.

"Well, we're still married. In a good way this time."

Lauren screamed in my ear. It took her a good couple of

minutes to calm down. "Oh, my God, I was hoping something would work out. He's so fucking hot."

"Yes, indeed he is. But he's more than that. He's wonderful."

"Keep going."

"I mean, really wonderful."

She huffed out a laugh. "You already used 'wonderful.' Try a new word, Cinderella. Give my inner fangirl something to work with here."

"Don't crush on my husband. That's not cool."

"You're six years too late with that warning. I was crushing on David Ferris long before you put a ring on him in Vegas."

"Actually, he doesn't have a ring."

"No? You should fix that."

"Hmm." I stared out the window at the ocean. Out in the distance a bird drifted in lazy circles high up in the sky. "We're at his place in Monterey. It's beautiful here."

"You left LA?"

"LA was not so great. What with the groupies and lawyers and business managers and everything, it was pretty shitty."

"Details, babe. Gimme."

I drew my knees up to my chest and fidgeted with the seam of my jeans, feeling conflicted. Discussing our personal details behind David's back didn't sit well with me. Not even with Lauren. Things had changed. Most noticeably, our marriage had changed. But there were still some things I could share. "The people there were like something from another planet. I did not fit in. Though you would have liked seeing the parties they threw. All the glamorous people packed into this mansion. It was impressive."

"You're making me insanely jealous. Who was there?"

I gave her a couple of names as she oohed and aahed.

"But I don't miss LA. Things are so good now, out here, Lauren. We've put the annulment on hold. We're going to see how things go."

"That's so romantic. Tell me you've jumped that fine-looking man's bones, please. Don't make me cry."

"Lauren." I sighed.

"Yes or no?"

I hesitated, and she got screamy at me, rather predictably. "YES OR NO?"

"Yes. All right? Yes."

This time, her shriek definitely did my cardrums permanent damage. All I could hear was ringing. When it ended, someone was mumbling in the background. Someone male.

"Who was that?" I asked.

"No one. Just a friend."

"A friend-friend or a friend?"

"Just a friend. Hang on, changing rooms. And we were talking about you, partner of David Ferris, world-famous lead guitarist for Stage Dive."

"A friend that I know?" I asked, curiosity now fully aroused.

"You are aware of the picture of your ass making the rounds, aren't you?"

Cue the squirming. "Uh, yeah. I am."

"Bummer. Haha! But seriously, you look good. Mine wouldn't have looked half as nice. Bet you're glad you walked to campus last semester instead of driving all the time like lazy ol' me. That sure was some night you had in Vegas, missy."

"Let's talk about your friend instead of my butt. Or Vegas."

"Or we could talk about your sex life. Because we've been talking about mine for a couple of years now, but we haven't much been able to talk about yours, girlfriend," she said in a glee-filled singsong voice.

"Evvie! Want a soda?" Mal shouted as he sailed past on his way to the kitchen, having emerged from below.

"Yes, please."

"Who is that?" asked Lauren.

"The drummer. They're doing some work in the studio downstairs."

Lauren gasped. "The whole band is there?"

"No, just Mal and another friend of David's."

"Malcolm is there? He's really hot, but a total man slut," she supplied helpfully. "You should see the number of women he gets photographed with."

"Here you go, child bride." Mal passed me an icy-cold bottle, the top already removed.

"Thanks, Mal," I said.

He winked and wandered off again.

"None of my business," I told Lauren.

She clucked her tongue. "You haven't been on the Internet to find anything out about them, have you? You're flying totally blind in this situation."

"It feels wrong checking up on them behind their backs."

"Naïveté is only sexy up to a point, chica."

"It's not naïveté, chica. It's respecting their personal lives."

"Which you're now a part of."

"Privacy matters. Why should they trust me if I'm stalking them online?"

"You and your excuses." Lauren sighed. "So you don't know that the band started touring when David was only sixteen? They got a gig supporting a band through Asia and have pretty much stayed on the road or in the recording studio from then onward. Hell of a life, huh?"

"Yeah. He said he's ready to slow down."

"I'm not surprised. Rumors about the band breaking up are

everywhere. Do try and stop that from happening if you can, please. And get your husbo to get his shit into gear and hurry up and write a new album. I'm counting on you."

"No problem," I said, not sharing that David was writing me songs. That was private. For now, at least. The list of things I didn't feel I could share with Lauren was growing exponentially.

"I wanted you to crush that boy's heart so we could have another album like *San Pedro*. But I can tell you're going to be difficult about that."

"Your powers of perception are uncanny."

She chuckled. "You know there's a song about the Monterey house on that album?"

"There is?"

"Oh, yeah. That's the famous 'House of Sand.' Epic love song. David's high school sweetheart cheated on him while he was touring in Europe at age twenty-one. He'd bought that house for them to live in."

"Stop, Lauren. This is . . . shit, this is personal." My heart and mind raced. "This house?"

"Yeah. They'd been together for years. David was gutted. Then some bitch he slept with sold her story to the tabloids. Also, his mother left when he was twelve. Expect there to be some issues all around where women are concerned."

"No, Lauren, stop. I'm serious," I said, nearly strangling the phone. "He'll tell me things like that when he's ready. This doesn't feel right."

"It's just being prepared. I don't see what the problem is."

"Lauren."

"Okay. No more. You did need to know those tidbits, though, seriously. Events like that leave a permanent scar."

She had a point. The information did explain his accusations regarding my leaving and the strength of his reactions to

that. Two of the most important women in his world had de-
serted him. Though finding out this way about his history still
felt wrong. When he trusted me enough to tell me, he would.
But I hadn't had enough of a chance yet to earn that sort of
trust from him. Personal information didn't just roll off the
tongue at the first meeting. How horrible to have it all set out
there on the Internet just waiting for people to look it up and
mull it over for their entertainment. So much for privacy. Little
wonder he'd been worried about my talking to the press.

I took a sip of the soda, then rested the cold bottle against
my cheek. "I really want this to work."

"I know you do. I can hear it in your voice when you talk
about him—you're in love with him."

My spine snapped to attention. "What? No. That's crazy
talk. Not yet, at least. It's only been a couple of days. Do I
sound in love? Really?"

"Time is irrelevant where the heart is concerned."

"Maybe," I said, concerned.

"Listen, Jimmy has been dating Liv Andrews. If you meet
her, I definitely want an autograph. Loved her last film."

"Jimmy is not the greatest. That could get uncomfortable."

She huffed. "Fine. But you are in love."

"Hush now."

"What? I think it's nice."

Mutterings from Lauren's mysterious friend interrupted my
rising fear.

"I've got to go," she said. "Keep in touch, okay? Call me."

"I will."

"Bye."

I said "bye," but she was already gone.

CHAPTER FOURTEEN

"You're frowning." David walked up behind me slowly. His head cocked to the side, making his dark hair fall over the side of his face. He tucked it behind an ear and moved closer. "Why are you doing that, hmm?"

I'd been putting together dinner. I'd found pizza crusts in the freezer, so I took them out to defrost and started cutting up toppings and grating cheese, while worrying about what Lauren had told me, of course. The house didn't seem so welcoming anymore. Armed with the knowledge that it had been bought with another woman in mind, my feelings toward the place had shifted. I was back to feeling like an interloper. Horrible but true. Insecurities sucked.

"Gimme." From behind me he snagged my wrist and brought my hand to his mouth, sucking a smear of tomato paste from my finger. "Mm. Yum."

My stomach squeezed tight in response. God, his mouth on me this morning. His plans for us tonight. It all felt like a dream, a crazy beautiful dream that I didn't want to wake from. Nor did I need to. All would be well. We'd work things out. We were married again now, committed. He snaked an arm around me and pressed himself against my back, leaving no room between us for doubt.

"How are things going downstairs?" I asked.

"Real good. We've got four songs shaping up nicely. Sorry we ran a bit over," he said, planting a kiss on the side of my neck, chasing the last of the bad thoughts far away. "But now it's our time."

"Good."

"Making pizza?"

"Yeah."

"Can I help?" he asked, still nuzzling the side of my neck. The stubble on his jaw scratched lightly at my skin, feeling strange and wonderful all at once. He made me shivery. Right up until he stopped. "You're putting broccoli on it?"

"I like vegetables on pizza."

"Zucchini too. Huh." His voice sounded slightly incredulous and he perched his chin on my shoulder. "How about that?"

"And bacon, sausage, mushrooms, peppers, tomatoes, and three different types of cheeses." I pointed the chopping knife at my excellent collection of ingredients. "Wait till you taste them. They're going to be the best pizzas ever."

"Course they are. Here, I'll put them together." He turned me to face him, rearing back when my chopping knife accidentally waved at him. His hands fastened onto my hips and he lifted me up onto the kitchen island. "Keep me company."

"Sure thing."

From the fridge he took a beer for him and a soda for me, since I was still avoiding alcohol. Tyler's and Mal's voices drifted through from the lounge room.

"We working again tomorrow?" Tyler called out.

"Sorry, man. We gotta head back to LA," said David, washing his hands at the sink. He had great hands, long, strong fingers. "Give me a couple of days to sort shit out down there then we'll be up again."

Tyler stuck his head around the corner, giving me a wave. "Sounds good. The new stuff is coming together well. Bringing Ben and Jimmy back with you next time?"

David's brow wrinkled, his eyes not so happy. "Yeah, I'll see what they're up to."

"Cool. Pammy's outside, so I gotta run. It's date night."

"Have fun." I waved back.

Tyler grinned. "Always do."

Chuckling quietly, Mal ambled in. "Date night, seriously . . . what the fuck is that about? Old people are the weirdest. Dude, you can't put broccoli on pizza."

"Yeah, you can." David kept busy, scattering peppers around the little trees of broccoli.

"No," said Mal. "That's just not right."

"Shut up. Ev wants broccoli on the pizza, then that's what she gets."

Ice-cold lovely sweet soda slid down my throat, feeling all sorts of good. "Don't stress, Mal. Vegetables are your friend."

"You lie, child bride." His mouth stretched wide in disgust and he retrieved a bottle of juice from the fridge. "Never mind. I'll just pick it off."

"No, you're going out," said David. "Me and Ev are having date night too."

"What? You're fucking kidding me. Where am I supposed to go?"

David just shrugged and scattered pepperoni atop his steadily growing creations.

"Oh, come on. Evvie, you'll stand up for me, won't you?" Mal gave me the most pitiful face in all of existence. It was sadness blended with misery with a touch of forlorn on top. He even bent over and laid his head on my knee. "If I stay in town they'll know we're here."

"You've got your car," said David.

"We're in the middle of nowhere," Mal complained. "Don't let him throw me out into the wild. I'll get eaten by fucking bears or something."

"I'm not sure they have bears around here," I said.

"Cut the shit, Mal," said David. "And get your head off my wife's leg."

With a growl, Mal straightened. "Your wife is my friend. She's not going to let you do this to me!"

"That so?" David looked at me and his face fell. "Fuck, baby. No. You cannot be falling for this shit. It's only one night."

I winced. "Maybe we could go up to our room. Or he could just stay downstairs or something."

David shoved his hands through his hair. The bruise on his poor cheek, I needed to kiss it better. His forehead did that James Dean wrinkling thing as he studied his friend. "Jesus. Stop making that pathetic face at her. Have some dignity."

He cuffed the back of Mal's head, making his long blond hair fly in his face. Skipping back, Mal retreated beyond the line of fire. "All right, I'll stay downstairs. I'll even eat your shitty broccoli pizza."

"David." I grabbed his T-shirt and tugged him toward me. And he came, abandoning his pursuit of Mal.

"This is supposed to be our time," he said.

"I know. It will be."

"Yes!" hissed Mal, getting gone while he was ahead. "I'll be downstairs. Yell when dinner's ready."

"He's got a girl in every city," said David, scowling after him. "No way was he sleeping in his car. You've been played."

"Maybe. But I would have worried about him." I tucked his dark hair behind his ears, then trailed my hands down to the back of his neck, drawing him closer. The studs in his ears were all small, silver. A skull, an X, and a super-tiny winking diamond. He pressed his earlobe between his thumb and a finger, blocking my view.

"Something wrong?" he asked.

"I was just looking at your earrings. Do they mean anything special?"

"Nope." He gave me a quick peck on the cheek. "Why were you frowning earlier?" He picked up a handful of mushrooms and started adding them to the pizzas. "You're doing it again now."

Crap. I kicked my heels, turned all the excuses over inside my head. I had no idea how he'd react to my knowing the things Lauren had told me. What would he think if I asked about them? Starting a fight did not appeal. But lying didn't either. Withholding was lying, deep down where it mattered. I knew that.

"I talked to my friend Lauren today."

"Mmhmm."

I pushed my hands down between my legs and squeezed them tight, delaying. "She's a really big fan."

"Yeah, you said." He gave me a smile. "Am I allowed to meet her, or is she off-limits like your dad?"

"You can meet my dad if you want."

"I want. We'll take a trip to Miami sometime soon and I'll introduce you to mine, okay?"

"I'd like that." I took a deep breath, let it out. "David, Lauren told me some things. And I don't want to keep secrets from you. But I don't know how happy you're going to be about these things that she told me."

He turned his head, narrowed his eyes. "Things?"

"About you."

"Ah. I see." He picked up two handfuls of grated cheese and sprinkled them across the pizzas. "So you hadn't looked me up on Wikipedia or some shit?"

"No," I said, horrified at the thought.

He grunted. "It's no big deal. What do you want to know, Ev?"

I didn't know what to say. So I picked up my soda and downed about half of it in one go. Bad idea—it didn't help. Instead, it gave me a mild case of brain freeze, stinging above the bridge of my nose.

"Go on. Ask me whatever you want," he said. He wasn't happy. The angry monobrow from drawing his eyebrows together clued me in to that. I didn't think I'd ever met anyone with such an expressive face as David. Or maybe he just fascinated me full stop.

"All right. What's your favorite color?"

He scoffed. "That's not one of the things your friend told you about."

"You said I could ask whatever I wanted, and I want to know what your favorite color is."

"Black. And I know it's not really a color. I did miss a lot of school, but I was there that day." His tongue played behind his cheek. "What's yours?"

"Blue." I watched as he opened the gargantuan oven door. The pizza trays clattered against the racks. "What's your favorite song?"

"We're covering all the basics, huh?"

"We are married. I thought it would be nice. We sort of skipped a lot of the getting-to-know-you stuff."

"All right." The side of his mouth kicked up and he gave me a look that said he was onto my game of avoidance. The faint smile set the world to rights.

"I got a lot of favorite music," he said. " 'Four Sticks' by Led Zeppelin, that's up there. Yours is 'Need You Now' by Lady Antebellum, as sung by an Elvis impersonator. Sadly."

"Come on, I was under the influence. That's not fair."

"But it is true."

"Maybe." I still wished I could remember it. "Favorite book?"

"I like graphic novels. Stuff like *Hellblazer, Preacher*."

I took another mouthful of soda, trying to think up a genius question. Only all the blatantly obvious ones appeared inside my head. I sucked at dating. It was probably just as well that we'd skipped that part.

"Wait," he said. "What's yours?"

"*Jane Eyre.* How about your favorite movie?"

"*Evil Dead 2.* Yours?"

"*Walk the Line.*"

"The one about the Man in Black? Nice. Okay." He clapped his hands together and rubbed them. "My turn. Tell me something terrible. Something you did that you've never confessed to another living soul."

"Ooh, good one." Scary, but good. Why couldn't I have thought of a question like that?

He grinned around the top of his bottle of beer, well pleased with himself.

"Let me think . . ."

"There's a time limit."

I screwed up my face at him. "There is not a time limit."

"There is," he said. "Because you can't try and think up something half-assed to tell me. You've gotta give me the first worst thing that comes into your head that you don't want anyone else ever knowing about. This is about honesty."

"Fine." I sniffed. "I kissed a girl named Amanda Harper when I was fifteen."

His chin rose. "You did?"

"Yes."

He sidled closer, eyes curious. "Did you like it?"

"No. Not really. I mean, it was okay." I gripped the edge of the bench, hunching forward. "She was the school lesbian and I wanted to see if I was one too."

"There was just the one lesbian at your school?"

"Oh, I suspected quite a few people, but only she was open about it. She gave herself the title."

"Good for her." His hands settled on my knees and pushed them apart, making room for him. "Why did you think you were a lesbian?"

"To be accurate, I was hoping I was bi," I said. "More options. Because, honestly, the guys at school were . . ."

"They were what?" He gripped my butt and pulled me across the bench, bringing me closer. No way did I resist.

"They didn't really interest me, I guess."

"But kissing your lesbian friend Amanda didn't do it for you either?" he asked.

"No."

He clicked his tongue. "Damn. That's a sad story. You're cheating, by the way."

"What? How?"

"You were meant to tell me something terrible." His smile left a mile way behind. "Telling me you tongue-kissed a girl isn't even remotely terrible."

"I never said there was tongue."

"Was there?"

"A little. The briefest of touches, maybe. But then I got weirded out and stopped it."

He took another swig of beer. "Your ear tips are doing the pink thing again."

"I bet they are." I laughed and ducked my head. "I didn't cheat. I never told anyone about that kiss. I was going to take it to my grave. You should feel honored by my trust in you."

"Yeah, but telling me something I'm likely to find a huge turn-on is cheating. You were meant to tell me something terrible. The rules were clear. Go again and give me something bad this time."

"It's a huge turn-on, huh?"

"Next time I hit the shower I'm definitely using that story."

I bit my tongue and looked away. Memories from this morning of David soaping up my hands and then putting them on him assailed my mind. The thought of him masturbating to my brief bout of teen sexual experimentation . . . "honored" wasn't quite the right word. But I couldn't say I wasn't pleased by the notion. "Well, remember to make me older. Fifteen is a bit skeevy."

"You only kissed her."

"You'll leave it at that in your head? You'll respect accuracy and legalities, and not take it any further between Amanda and me?"

"Fine, I'll make you older. And wildly fucking curious." He pulled me closer, using the hands-on-my-butt method again, and I put my arms around him.

"Now, go again, and do it right this time."

"Yeah, yeah."

He gave the side of my neck a lingering kiss. "You weren't lying about Amanda, were you?"

"No."

"Good. I like that story. You should tell it to me often. Now go again."

I ummed and ahhed, procrastinating my little heart out. David rested his forehead against mine with a heavy sigh. "Just fucking tell me something."

"I can't think of anything."

"Bullshit."

"I can't," I whined. Not anything I wanted to share, anyway.

"Tell me."

I groaned and bumped my forehead against his ever so lightly. "David, come on, you're the last person I want to make myself look bad in front of."

He drew back, inspecting me down the length of his nose. "You're worried about what I think of you?"

"Of course I am."

"You're honest and good, baby. Nothing you might have done is gonna be that bad."

"But honest isn't always good," I said, trying to explain. "I've opened my mouth plenty of times when I shouldn't have. Given people my opinion when I should have kept quiet. I react first and think later. Look at what happened in Vegas, between us. I didn't ask any of the right questions that morning. I'm always going to regret that."

"Vegas was a pretty extreme situation." His hand rubbed my back, reassuring me. "You got nothing to worry about."

"You asked me how I felt when you had that groupie hanging off you in LA. I dealt with it then. But the fact is, if that happened now and some woman tried to come on to you, I'd probably get stabby. I'm not always going to react well to the rock star hoopla that surrounds you. What happens then?"

He made a noise in his throat. "I dunno, I finally have to realize that you're human? That you fuck up sometimes just like everybody else?"

I didn't answer.

"We'll both screw up, Ev. That's a given. We just gotta be patient with each other." He put a finger beneath my chin, raising it up so he could kiss me. "Now tell me about what Lauren told you today."

I stared at him, caught and cornered. The contents of my stomach curdled for real. I had to tell him. There would be no getting around it. How he reacted was beyond my control. "She told me that your first girlfriend cheated on you."

He blinked. "Yeah. That happened. We'd been together a long time, but . . . I was always either recording or on the road," he said. "We'd been touring Europe for eight, nine months when it happened. Touring fucks up a lot of couples. The groupies and the whole lifestyle can really screw with you. Being left behind all the time is probably no picnic either."

I bet it wasn't. "When do you tour next?"

He shook his head. "There're none booked. Won't be until we get this new record down, and that hasn't been going so well until now."

"Okay. How does this work? I mean, do you believe what happens on the road, stays on the road?" I asked. The boundaries of our relationship had never really been established. Exactly what did our marriage mean? He wanted us to stick together, but I had school to consider, my job, my life. Maybe the good wives just dumped it all and went with the band. Or maybe wives weren't even invited. I didn't have a clue.

"You asking me if I'm planning on cheating on you?"

"I'm asking how we fit into each other's lives."

"Right." He pinched his lips between his thumb and finger. "Well, I think not fucking around on each other would be a good start. Let's just make that a rule for us, okay? As for the band and stuff, I guess we take it as it comes."

"Agreed."

Without a word he stepped back from me, crossing over to the staircase. "Mal?"

"What?"

"Close the door down there and lock it," David yelled. "Don't you come up here under any circumstances. Not till I tell you it's okay. Understood?"

There was a pause, then Mal yelled back, "What if there's a fire?"

"Burn."

"Fuck you." The door downstairs slammed shut.

"Lock it!"

Mal's reply was muffled, but the pissy tone carried just fine. These two were more akin to actual brothers than David and his biological sibling. Jimmy was a jerk and just one of the very good reasons we should never return to LA. Sadly, hiding out in Monterey wasn't a viable long-term solution.

School, band, family, friends, blah blah blah.

David reached for the back of his T-shirt and dragged it off over his head. "Rule number two, if I take my shirt off you have to take off yours. The shirt-off rule now applies to these sorts of conversations. I know we need to talk about stuff. But there's no reason we can't make it easier."

"This'll make it easier?" Highly doubtful. All that smooth, hot skin just waiting for my touch, and my fingers itching to do so. Keeping my tongue inside my mouth while his flat stomach and six-pack were revealed tested my moral fortitude no end. All that beautiful inked skin on display, driving any attempt at a coherent thought straight out of my mind. Good God, the man had some power over me. But wait up, we were married. Morally, I was obliged to ogle my husband. It would be unnatural and wrong to do otherwise.

"Get it off," he said, tipping his chin at my offending items of clothing.

The staircase sat calm and quiet. No signs of life.

"He ain't coming up here. I promise." David's hands gripped the bottom of my T-shirt and carefully pulled it off over my head, rescuing my ponytail when it got caught.

When he reached for my bra, I pressed my forearms to my chest, holding it in place. "Why don't I keep the bra, just in case . . ."

"It's against the rules. You really wanna go breaking rules already? That's not like you."

"David."

"Evelyn." The bra's band relaxed as he undid the clasp. "I need to see your bare breasts, baby. You have no idea how much I fucking love them. Let it go."

"Why do you get to make all the rules?"

"I only made that one. Oh, no two. We have the no-cheating rule as well." He tugged at my bra and I eased my grip, letting him take it. No way was I moving my arms, though.

"Go on, you make some rules," he said, running his fingers over my arms, making every little hair stand on end.

"Are you just trying to distract me from the conversation with the no-clothes thing?"

"Absolutely not. Now make a rule."

My hands stayed tucked beneath my chin, arms covering all the essentials, just in case. "No lies. Not about anything."

"Done."

I nodded, relieved. We could do this marriage thing. I knew it in my head, my heart. We were going to be okay. "I trust you."

He stopped, stared. "Thanks. That's big."

I waited, but he said no more.

"Do you trust me?" I asked, filling the silence. The minute the words left my lips I wanted them back. If I had to demand his faith and affection, it didn't mean a damn thing. Worse than that, it did damage. I could feel it, a sudden jagged wound between us. One that I'd made. Of all the stupid times for me to get impatient! I wished it was the middle of winter so I could go stick my head in a snowdrift.

His gaze wandered away, over my shoulder. There was my answer right there. Honesty had already shown me who was boss. How about that? I suddenly felt cold, and though it had nothing to do with losing my shirt, I really wanted to put it back on.

"I'm getting there, Ev. Just . . . give me time." Frustration lined his face. He pressed his lips together till they whitened. Then he looked me in the eye. Whatever he saw didn't help matters. "Shit."

"It's okay, really," I said, willing it to be true.

"You lying to me?"

"No. No. We'll be fine."

In lieu of an answer, he kissed me.

You couldn't beat a well-timed distraction. Heat rushed back into me. His regret and my hurt both took a backseat when I placed my hands on top of his. With fingers meshed, I moved our combined hands to cover my breasts. We both groaned. The heat of his palms felt sublime. The chill of disappointment couldn't combat it. Our chemistry won out every time. I had to believe more feelings would follow. My shoulders pushed forward, pressing me harder into his hands as if gravity had shifted toward him. But also, I wanted his mouth. Hell, I wanted to crawl around inside him and read his mind. I wanted everything. Each dark corner of him. Every stray thought.

Our lips met again and he groaned, hands kneading my breasts. His tongue slipped into my mouth, and that fast and easy I ached for him. Needed him. My insides squeezed tight and my legs wrapped around him, holding on. Let him try and get away now. I'd fight tooth and nail to keep him. Thumbs stroked over my nipples, teasing me. My hands slid up his arms, curved over his shoulders, holding steady. Hot kisses trailed over my face, my jaw, the side of my neck. Half naked or not, I don't think I'd have cared if my high school marching band paraded through the room. They could bring baton twirlers and all. Only this mattered.

No wonder people took sex so seriously, or not seriously enough at all. Sex addled your wits and stole your body. It was like being lost and found all at once. Frankly, it was a little frightening.

"We will be fine," he said, teasing my earlobe with his teeth. Rubbing his hardness against me. God bless whoever had thought to put a seam right there in jeans. Lights danced before my eyes. Did it feel as good for him? I wanted it to be the best and I wanted him to be right about us being fine.

"Sweet baby, just need time," he said, his warm breath skating over my skin.

"Because of her," I said, needing it to be out there in the open. No secrets.

"Yeah," he said, his voice faint. "Because of her."

The truth bit.

"Evelyn, there's just you and me in this. I swear." He returned to my mouth and kissed me as if I was delicate, giving me only the briefest taste of him. An awareness of warmth, the firmness of his lips.

"Wait," I said, making my legs give up their grip on him.

He blinked dark, hazy eyes at me.

"Move back. I want to hop down."

"You do?" His lovely mouth turned down at the edges. The front of his jeans was in a state of obvious distress. I'd done that to him. A victory lap around the kitchen counter would probably be taking it too far, but still, it felt good. That knowledge sat well within me. She didn't do that to him these days. I did.

I shuffled off the edge of the counter and he grabbed my hips, easing my descent to the floor. Just as well. My legs were liquid. He stared down at me, his brow wrinkled.

"There's something I want to do," I explained, fingers shaking from nerves and excitement. First I wrangled with the button of his jeans before moving on to the straining zipper.

His hands gripped my wrists. "Hey. Wait."

I hesitated, wanting to hear what he had to say. Surely he wouldn't try to tell me he didn't want this. Every guy liked this, or so I'd been told. He looked perplexed, as if I was a piece that refused to fit the puzzle. I honestly didn't know if he meant to stop me or hurry me onward.

"Is there a problem?" I asked, when he didn't speak.

Slowly he removed his hands from my wrists, setting me free. He held them up like I'd pointed a gun at him. "This is what you want?"

"Yes. David, why is this a big deal? Don't you want my mouth on you?"

A soft smile curved his lips. "You have no idea how much I want that. But this is another first for you, isn't it?"

I nodded, fingers fiddling with the waistband of his jeans, but going no further.

"That's why it's a big deal. I want all your firsts to be perfect. Even this. And I'm pretty fucking worked up here just at the thought of you sucking me."

"Oh."

"I've been thinking about you all damn day. I kept fucking things up, couldn't concentrate for shit. Amazing we got anything done." He pushed his fingers through his long hair, pulling it back from his face. His hands stayed on top of his head, stretching out his lean, muscular torso. The bruise on his ribs from the bar fight last night was a dark gray smudge, marring perfection. I leaned in, kissing it. His gaze never left me because my bare breasts were still most definitely a part of me. My eyes, my mouth, my breasts: he couldn't seem to decide what fascinated him the most.

Carefully, I lowered the zipper over his erection. No underwear. At least I didn't jump this time when his hard-on made its sudden appearance. With two hands I pushed down his jeans, freeing his cock. It stood tall and proud. Just like this morning, I pressed my hand against the underside, feeling the heat of the silken skin. Funny, the idea of the male appendage had never particularly moved me before. But now I felt moved, as my clenched thighs attested.

Moved and more than a little proprietary.

"You're mine," I whispered, my thumb rubbing around the edge of the head, feeling out the ridge and the dip in the middle. Learning him.

"Yeah."

The sweet spot sat below that little tuck. Over the years, I'd read enough magazines and listened to enough of Lauren's tales of sexcapades to know as much. She did love her details. I made a mental note to thank her, take her out to dinner somewhere nice.

I moved my hand around so that I gripped him and massaged the area with the pad of my thumb, waiting to see what happened. Much easier to see what was going on without the soap bubbles in the way. It didn't take long. Especially not once I tightened my hold on him a little and pumped slightly. His stomach muscles flinched and danced, the same as they had this morning in the shower. My fingers moved the soft, smooth skin, massaging the hard flesh beneath, pumping once, twice. A bead of milky fluid leaked from the small slit in the top.

"That means you're fucking killing me," my husband supplied helpfully, his voice guttural. "Just in case you were wondering."

I grinned.

He swore.

"I swear it gets bigger every time I see it."

His smile was lopsided. "You inspire me."

I stroked him again and his chest heaved. "Evelyn. Please."

Time to put him out of his misery. I knelt, the floor uncomfortably hard beneath me. If you were going to kneel in front of someone, some minor discomfort seemed an obvious part of the territory. It all added to the atmosphere, the experience. The musky scent of him was stronger later in the day. I took his cock in hand and nuzzled his hip bone, breathing him in deep.

He still watched. I checked to be sure. Hell, his eyes were huge and dark and focused solely on me. Beside him, his hands gripped the counter as if he expected a tremor to hit at any time, knuckles white.

When I took him into my mouth, he moaned. My inexperience and his size prevented me from taking him too deep. He didn't seem to mind. The salty taste of his skin and the bitterness of that liquid, the warm scent of him and the feel of his hardness merged into one unique experience. Pleasing David was a brilliant thing.

He groaned and his hips jerked, pushing him farther into my mouth. My throat tightened in surprise and I gagged slightly. His hand flew to my hair, patting, soothing. "Fuck, baby. Sorry."

I resumed my ministrations, rubbing my tongue against him, drawing on him. Figuring out the best way to fit him into my mouth. Doing everything I could to make him tremble and cuss. What a glorious thing giving head was. His hand tightened in my hair, pulling some, and I loved it. All of it. Anything with the ability to reduce my world-weary husband to a stammering mess while giving him such pleasure deserved a serious time investment. His hips shifted restlessly and his cock jerked against my tongue, filling my mouth with that salty, bitter taste faster than I could swallow.

So it was messy. Never mind. My jaw hurt a little. Big deal. And I could have done with a glass of water. But his reaction . . .

David dropped to his knees and gathered me up in his arms, all the better to squish me against him. My ribs creaked, and his dug into me over and over as he fought for breath. I pressed my face against his shoulder and waited till he'd calmed down some to seek my acclaim.

"Was it okay?" I asked, reasonably certain of a favorable response. Which is always the best time to ask, in my opinion.

He grunted.

That was it? I sat there feeling rather proud of myself and he gave me a grunt. No, I needed more validation than that. I both wanted and deserved it. "Are you sure?"

He sat back on his heels and stared at me. Then he looked around, searching for something. The T-shirt he'd left forgotten on the floor. And then he wiped beneath my chin, cleaning me up. Nice.

"There's some on your shoulder too." I pointed at the unfortunate spillage I'd obviously transferred onto him. He wiped it up as well.

"Sex can get messy," he said.

"Yes, it can."

"You on the pill?"

"You can't get pregnant that way, David."

The side of his mouth twitched. "Cute. Are you on the pill?"

"No, but I have the birth control thing implanted in my arm because my periods are erratic so—" His mouth slammed over the top of mine, kissing me hard and deep. Shutting me up really effectively. A hand cradled the back of my head as he took me down to the floor, stretching out on top of me. The cold, hard flooring beneath my bare back barely registered. It didn't matter so long as he kissed me. My hands clung to his shoulders, fingers sliding over slick skin.

"I care about your periods, Ev. Honest to fuck I do." He kissed my cheeks, my forehead.

"Thanks."

"But right now I wanna know how you feel about us going bare?"

"You mean more than losing the shirts, I take it?"

"I mean fucking without a condom." His hands framed my face as he stared down at me, eyes that intense shade of blue. "I'm clean. I've been tested. I don't do drugs and I always used protection, ever since I broke up with her. But it's your call."

The mention of "her" cooled me a bit, but not much or for long. Impossible with David sprawled all over me and the scent of sex so heavy in the air. Plus pizza. But mostly David. He made my mouth water, forget about the food. Thinking wasn't easy given the situation. I'd said I trusted him and I did.

"Baby, just think about it," he said. "There's no rush. Okay?"

"No, I think we should."

"Are you certain?"

I nodded.

He exhaled a deep breath and kissed me again.

"I fucking love your mouth." With the top of a finger he traced my lips, still swollen from what we'd been up to.

"You did like it? It was okay?"

"It was perfect. Nothing you do could be wrong. I almost lose it just knowing it's you. You could accidentally bite me and I'd probably think it was fucking hot." He gave a rough laugh, then hastened to add, "But don't do that."

"No." I arched my neck and pressed my lips to his, kissing him sweet and slow. Showing him what he meant to me. We were still rolling around on the kitchen floor when the buzzer on the oven screeched, startling us apart. Then the phone rang.

"Shit."

"I'll get the pizza," I said, wriggling out from beneath him.

"I'll grab the phone. No one should even have this damn number."

An oven mitt sat waiting on the counter and I slipped it over my hand. Hot air and the rich scent of melted cheese wafted out when I opened the oven door. My stomach rumbled. So maybe I was hungry after all. The pizzas were a touch burnt around the edges. Nothing too bad, though. The tips of my broccoli were toasted golden brown. We could concentrate on the middle. I transferred the pizzas onto the cool stovetop and turned off the heat.

David talked quietly in the background. He stood in front of the bank of windows, legs spread wide and shoulders set like he was bracing himself for an attack. Relaxed, happy people didn't strike that pose. Outside the sun was setting. The violet and gray of evening cast shadows on his skin.

"Yeah, yeah, Adrian. I know," he said.

Trepidation tightened me one muscle at a time. God, please, not now. We were doing so well. Couldn't they stay away just a little longer?

"What time's the flight?" he asked.

"Fuck," came next.

"No, we'll be there. Relax. Yeah, bye."

He turned to face me, phone dangling from his hand. "There's some stuff going on in LA that Mal and I need to be there for. Adrian's sending a chopper for us. We all need to get ready."

My smile strained my face, I could feel it. "Okay."

"Sorry we're getting cut short here. We'll come back soon, yeah?"

"Absolutely. It's fine."

That was a lie, because we were going back to LA.

CHAPTER FIFTEEN

David's knee jiggled all the way back to LA. When I put my hand on his leg, he took to toying with my wedding ring instead, turning it around on my finger. Seemed we were both fidgeters, given the right circumstances.

I'd never been in a helicopter before. The view was spectacular, but it was loud and uncomfortable—I could see why people preferred planes. A chain of lights, from streetlights to houses to the blazing high-rise towers in LA, lit the way. Everything about the situation had changed, but I was the same bundle of nervous energy in need of sleep that I had been leaving Portland not so many days back. Mal had thrown himself into the corner, closed his eyes, and gone to sleep. Nothing fazed him. Of course, there was no reason this should. He was part of the band, welded into David's life.

We landed a little before four in the morning, having left sometime after midnight. Bodyguard Sam stood waiting at the helicopter pad with a business face on.

"Mrs. Ferris. Gentlemen." He ushered us into a big black SUV waiting nearby.

"Straight back home, thanks, Sam," David said. His home, not mine. LA had no happy memories for me.

Then we were ensconced in luxury, locked away behind

dark windows. I sank back against the soft seating, closing my eyes. It kind of amazed me I could be so damn tired and worried all at once.

Back at the mansion, Martha waited, leaning against the front door, wrapped up in some expensive-looking red shawl. His PA gave me all the bad feelings. But I was determined to fit in this time. David and I were together. Screw her, she'd have to adapt. Her dark hair shone, flowing over her shoulders, not a strand out of place. No doubt I looked like someone who'd been awake for over twenty hours.

Sam opened the SUV door and offered me a hand. I could feel Martha's eyes zero in on the way David slung an arm around me, keeping me close. Her face hardened to stone. The look she gave me was poison. Whatever her issues, I was too damn tired to deal with them.

"Martie," Mal crowed, running up the steps to slip an arm around her waist. "Help me find breakfast, O gorgeous one."

"You know where the kitchen is, Mal."

The curt dismissal didn't stop Mal from sweeping her off with him. Martha's first few steps faltered, but then she strutted once more, ever on show. Mal had cleared the way. I could have kissed his feet.

David said nothing as we made our way up the stairs to the second floor, our footsteps echoing in the quiet. When I went to turn toward the white room, the one I'd stayed in last time, he steered me right instead. At a set of double doors we stopped and he fished a key out of his pocket. I gave him a curious look.

"So I have trust issues." He unlocked the door.

Inside, the room was simple, lacking the antiques and flashy décor of the rest of the house. A huge bed made up with dark gray linens. A comfortable sofa to match. Lots of guitars. An open wardrobe, full of clothes. Mostly, there was empty space.

Room for him to breathe, I think. This room felt different from the rest of the house, less showy, calmer.

"It's okay, you can look around." His hand slid down to the base of my spine, resting just above the curve of my ass. "It's our room now," he said.

God, I hoped he didn't want to live here permanently. I mean, I did have school to go back to eventually. We hadn't yet gotten around to discussing where we'd live. But the thought of Martha, Jimmy, and Adrian being around all the time sent me into a panic. Shit. I couldn't afford to think like that. Negativity would swallow me whole. What was important was being with David. Sticking together and making it work.

How horrible, being forced to live in the lap of luxury with my wonderful husband. Poor me. I needed a good slap and a cup of coffee. Or twelve hours' sleep. Either would work wonders.

He drew the curtains, blocking out the dawn's early light. "You look beat. Come lie down with me?"

"That's, umm . . . yeah, good idea. I'll just use the bathroom."

"Okay." David started stripping, dumping his leather jacket on the lounge chair, pulling off his T-shirt. The normal hoorah of my hormones was sorely missing in action. Drowned out by the nerves. I fled into the bathroom, needing a minute to pull myself together. I closed the door and switched on the lights. The room blazed to life, blinding me. Spots flickered before my eyes. I stabbed switches at random until finally it dimmed to a soft glow. Much better.

A giant white tub that looked like a bowl, gray stone walls, and clear glass partitions. Simply put, it was opulent. One day I'd probably become inured to all this, but I hoped not. Taking it for granted would be terrible.

A shower would soothe me. Sitting in the giant soup bowl

would have been nice. But I didn't totally trust myself to get into it without falling on my butt and breaking something. Not in the overtired, wound-up state I was in.

No, a long, hot shower would be perfect.

I stepped out of my flats and undid the zip on my jeans, getting undressed in record time. The shower could have fit me and ten close friends. Steaming hot water poured out from overhead and I stepped into it, grateful. It pounded down in the best way possible, making my muscles more pliable in minutes, relaxing me. I loved this shower. This shower and I needed to spend quality time together, often. Apart from David, and occasionally Mal, this shower was the best damn thing in the whole house.

David's arms slipped around me from behind, drawing me back against him. I hadn't even heard him come in.

"Hi." I leaned back against him, lifting my arms to thread them around his neck. "I think I'm in love with your shower."

"You're cheating on me with the shower? Damn, Evelyn. That's harsh." He picked up a bar of soap and started washing me, rubbing it over my belly, my breasts, softly between my legs. Once the soapsuds had reached critical mass, he helped the warm water chase the bubbles away. His big hands slid over my skin, bringing it to life and returning my hormones to me tenfold. One strong arm wrapped around my waist. The fingers of his other hand, however, lingered atop my sex, stroking lightly.

"I know you're worried about being here. But you don't need to be. Everything'll be fine." His lips brushed against my ear as the magic he was working on me grew. I could feel myself turning liquid hot like the water. My thighs trembled. I widened my stance, giving him more room.

"I—I know."

"It's you and me against the world."

I couldn't have kept the smile off my face if I tried.

"My lovely wife. Let's go this way." With careful steps he turned us, so that his back was to the water. I braced my hands on the glass wall. The tip of his finger teased between the lips of my sex, coaxing me open. God, he was good at this. "Your pussy is the sweetest fucking thing I've ever seen."

My insides fluttered with delight. "Whatever I did to deserve you, I need to do it much more often."

He chuckled, his mouth fixing to the side of my neck and sucking, making me groan. I swear the room spun. Or that might have been my blood rushing about. For certain, my hips bucked of their own volition. But he didn't let me go far. The hard length of him pressed against my butt and my lower back. My sex clenched unhappily, aching for more.

"David."

"Hmm?"

I tried to turn, but his splayed hand against my middle stopped me. "Let me."

"Let you what? What do you want, baby? Tell me and it's yours."

"I just want you."

"You've got me. I'm all over you. Feel." He pressed himself hard against me, holding me tight.

"But—"

"Now, let's see what happens when I strum your clit."

Feather-light strokes worked me higher and higher, all centered around that one magic spot. No great surprise he could play me to perfection. He'd already proved it several times over. And the way he rubbed himself against me drove me out of my mind. My body knew exactly what it wanted and it wasn't his damn clever fingers. I wanted to feel that connection with him again.

"Wait," I said, my voice high and needy.

"What, baby?"

"I want you inside of me."

He eased a finger into me, massaging an area behind my clit that made me see stars. Still, it was wrong, wildly insufficient. Not a bit funny. It would be a tragedy to have to kill him, but he was really pushing it.

"David. Please."

"No good?"

"I want you."

"And I want you. I'm crazy about you."

"But—"

"How about I get you off with a showerhead? Wouldn't that be nice?"

I actually stamped my foot, despite my wobbling knees. "No."

At which point my husband cracked up laughing and I hated him.

"I thought you were in love with the shower." He tittered away, highly amused with himself and all but begging for death.

Tears of frustration actually welled in my eyes. "No."

"You sure? I'm pretty certain I remember hearing you say it."

"David, for fuck's sake, I'm in love with you."

He stilled completely. Even the finger embedded within me stopped moving. There was only the sound of the water falling. You'd think those words would have lost their power. Weren't we already married? Hadn't we decided to stay married? Invoking the l-word should have lost its mystical punch, given our crazy situation. But it hadn't.

Everything changed.

Strong hands turned me and lifted me, leaving my feet dangling precariously in the air. It took me a second to figure out where I was and what had happened. I wrapped my legs and arms around him for safekeeping, holding on tight. His face . . . I'd never seen such a fierce, determined expression. It went well beyond lust and closer toward being what I needed from him.

His hands gripped my rear, taking my weight and holding me to him. Slowly, steadily, he lowered me onto him. There was none of the pain this time to rob me of pleasure. Nothing to distract me from the feel of him filling me. It was such a strange, wonderful sensation, having him inside of me. I squirmed, trying to get more comfortable. Instantly, his fingers dug into my butt cheeks.

"Fuck," he groaned.

"What?"

"Just . . . just stay still for a minute."

I scrunched up my nose, concentrated on catching my breath. This sex stuff was tricky. Also, I wanted to memorize every moment of this perfect experience. I didn't want to forget a thing.

He balanced my back against the shower wall and pushed more fully into me. A startled sound burst out of my mouth. Most closely it resembled "argh."

"Easy," he murmured. "You okay?"

I felt really full. Stretched. And it might have felt good. It was hard to tell. I needed him to do something so I could figure out where this new sensation was taking me. "Are you going to move now?"

"If you're okay now."

"I'm okay."

He did move then, watching my face all the while. The slide

out lit me up inside in a lovely rush, but the thrust back in got my immediate attention. Whoa. Good or bad, I still couldn't quite tell. I needed more. He gave it to me, his pelvis shifting against me, keeping the warmth and tension building. My blood felt fever hot, surging through me, burning beneath my skin. I fit my mouth to his, wanting more. Wanting it all. The wet of his mouth and the skill of his tongue. All of him. No one kissed like David. As though kissing me beat breathing, eating, sleeping, or anything else he might have otherwise planned to do with the rest of his life.

My back bumped hard against the glass wall and our teeth clinked together. He broke the kiss with a wary look, but he never stopped moving. Harder, faster, he rocked into me. It just got better and better. We needed to do this all the time. Constantly. Nothing else mattered when it was like this between us. Every worry disappeared.

It was so damn good. He was all that I needed.

Then he hit upon some spot inside of me and my whole body seized up, nerves tingling and running riot. My muscles squeezed him tight, and he thrust in deep several times in rapid succession. The world blacked out, or I closed my eyes. The pressure inside me shattered into a million amazing pieces. It went on and on. My mind left the stratosphere, I was sure of it. Everything sparkled. If it felt anything like that for David, I don't know how he stayed on his feet. But he did. He stood strong and whole with me clutched tight against him like he'd never let me go.

Eventually, about a decade later, he did set me down. His hands hovered by my waist, just in case. Once my limbs proved trustworthy, he turned me to face the water. With a gentle hand, he cleaned me between my legs. I didn't get what he was up to at first and tried to back away. Touching anything there right then didn't seem a smart idea.

"It's okay," he said, drawing me back into the spray of water. "Trust me."

I stood still, flinching out of instinct. He took nothing but care. The whole world seemed weird, everything too close and yet buffered at the same time. Weariness and the best orgasm of my life had undone me.

Next he reached over and turned off the water, stepped out, and grabbed two towels. One he tied around his waist, the other he patted me dry with.

"That was good, right?" I asked as he dried off my hair, tending to me. My body still shook and quivered. It seemed like a good sign. My world had been torn apart and remade into some sparkly surreal love-fest thing. If he said it was only okay, I might hit him.

"That was fucking incredible," he corrected, throwing my towel onto the bathroom counter.

Even my grin quivered. I saw it in the mirror. "Yes. It was."

"Us together, always is."

Hand in hand we walked back into the bedroom. Being naked in front of him didn't feel weird for once. There was no hesitation. He discarded his towel and we climbed onto his giant-size bed, gravitating naturally toward the middle and each other. We both lay on our sides, face-to-face. I could slip into a coma, I was so worn out. Such a pity to have to close my eyes when he lay right there in front of me. My husband.

"You swore at me," he said, eyes amused.

"Did I?"

His hand sat atop of my thigh, his thumb sliding back and

forth over my hip bone. "Gonna pretend you don't remember what you said? Really?"

"No. I remember." Though I hadn't meant to say it, neither the cuss word nor the declaration of love. But I had. Big-girl-panties time. "I said I was in love with you."

"Mm. People say stuff during sex. It happens."

He was giving me an out, but I couldn't take it. I wouldn't take it, no matter how tempting. I wasn't about to diminish the moment like that.

"I am in love with you," I said, feeling awkward. The same as when I'd said I trusted him, he was going to leave me hanging here too. I knew it.

His gaze lingered on my face, patient and kind. It hurt. Something inside me felt brittle and he brought it straight to the fore. Love made spelunking look sensible. BASE jumping and wrestling bears couldn't be far behind. But it was much, much too late to worry. The words were already out there. If love was for fools, then so be it. At least I'd be an honest one.

He stroked my face with the back of his fingers. "That was a beautiful thing to say."

"David, it's okay—"

"You're so fucking important to me," he said, stopping me short. "I want you to know that."

"Thank you." Ouch, not exactly the words I wanted to hear after I admitted I loved him.

Rising up on one elbow, he brought his lips to mine, kissing me silly. Stroking my tongue with his and taking me over. It left no room for worry.

"I need you again," he whispered, kneeling between my legs.

This time we did make love. There was no other word for it. He rocked into me at his own pace, pressing his cheek against mine, scratching me with his stubble. His voice went on and on, whispering secrets in my ear. How no one had ever been this right for him. How he wanted to stay just like this as long as could. Sweat dripped off his body, running over my skin before soaking into the bedsheet. He made himself a permanent part of me. It was bliss. Sweet, tender, and slow. Maddeningly slow near the end.

It felt like it went on for forever. I wish it had.

CHAPTER SIXTEEN

Adrian went ballistic over the bruises on David's face. He didn't seem too pleased to see me again, either. There was a brief flash of shark's teeth before I was hustled into a corner of the big dressing room out of harm's way. Security stood outside, letting only those invited into the inner sanctum.

The show was in a ballroom at one of the big, fancy hotels in town. Lots of twinkling chandeliers and red satin, big round tables crammed full of stars and the pretty-people posses that accompanied them. Luckily, I'd worn a blue dress, the only one that remotely covered everything, and a pair of the mile-high shoes Martha had ordered. Kaetrin, Bikini Girl, David's old friend, had been on the other side of the room, wearing a red frock and a scowl. She was going to get wrinkles if she kept that up. Happily, she got bored with pouting at me after a while and wandered away. I didn't blame her for being mad. If I'd lost David, I'd be pissed too. Women hovered near David, hoping for his attention. I could have high-fived someone over the way he ignored them.

There was no sign of Jimmy. Mal sat with a stunning Asian girl on one knee and a busty blond on the other, much too busy to talk to me. I still hadn't met the fourth member of the band, Ben.

"Hey," David said, exchanging my untouched glass of Cristal for a bottle of water. "Thought you might prefer this. Everything okay?"

"Thank you. Yes. Everything's great."

Wonderful man, he knew I still hadn't recovered enough from Vegas to risk the taste of alcohol. He nodded and passed the glass of champagne off to a waiter. Then he started slipping out of his leather jacket. Other people might put on tuxedos, but David stuck to his jeans and boots. His one concession to the occasion was a black button-down shirt. "Do me a favor and put this on."

"You don't like my dress?"

"Sure I do. But the air-conditioning's a bit cold in here," he said, wrapping the jacket around my shoulders.

"No, it's not."

He gave me a lopsided grin that would have melted the hardest of hearts. Mine didn't stand a chance. With an arm either side of my head, he leaned in, blocking out the rest of the room and everyone in it.

"Trust me, you're finding it a bit cool." His gaze fell to my chest and understanding dawned on me. The dress was made from some light, gauzy fabric. Gorgeous, but not so subtle in certain ways. And obviously my bra wasn't helping at all.

"Oh," I said.

"Mm. And I'm over there, trying to talk business with Adrian, but I can't. I'm totally fucking distracted because I love your rack."

"Excellent." I put an arm over my chest as subtly as possible.

"They're so pretty and they fill my hands just right. It's like we were made for one another, you know?"

"David." I grinned like the horny, lovesick fool I was.

"Sometimes there's this almost-smile on your face. And I wonder what you're thinking, standing over here watching everything."

"Nothing in particular, just taking it all in. Looking forward to seeing you play."

"Are you, now?"

"Of course I am. I can't wait."

He kissed me lightly on the lips. "After I'm finished we'll get out of here, yeah? Head off somewhere, just you and me. We can do whatever you feel like. Go for a drive or get something to eat, maybe."

"Just us?"

"Absolutely. Whatever you want."

"It all sounds good."

His graze dipped back to my chest. "You're still a little cold. I could warm you up. Where do you stand on me copping a feel in public?"

"That's a no." I turned my face to take a sip of the water. Arctic air or no, I needed cooling down.

"Yeah, that's what I thought. Come on. With great breasts come great responsibility." He took my hand and led me through the crowd of party people as I laughed. He didn't stop for anyone.

There was a small room attached to the back with a rack of garment bags and some makeup scattered around. Mirrors on the walls, a big bouquet of flowers, and a sofa that was very much occupied. Jimmy sat there in another dapper suit, legs spread with a woman kneeling between them. Her face was in his lap, head bobbing. No prizes for guessing what they were up to. The red of her dress clued me in to her identity, though I could have lived a long and happy life never knowing. Kaetrin's dark hair was wrapped tight around Jimmy's fist. In his other hand he held a bottle of whiskey. Two neat white lines of powder sat on the coffee table along with a small silver straw.

Holy crap. So this was the rock 'n' roll lifestyle. Suddenly my palms felt sweaty. But this wasn't what David was into. This wasn't him. I knew that.

"Ev," Jimmy said in a husky voice, a sleazy, slow smile spreading across his face. "Looking good, darlin'."

I snapped my mouth shut.

"Come on." David's hands clutched my shoulders, turning me away from the scene. He was livid, his mouth a bitter line.

"What, not going to say hi to Kaetrin, Dave? That's a bit harsh. Thought you two were good friends."

"Fuck off, Jimmy."

Behind us Jimmy groaned long and loud as the show on the couch reached its obvious conclusion. David slammed the door shut. The party continued on, music pumping out of the sound system, glasses clinking, and lots of loud conversation. We were out of there, but David stared off into the middle distance, oblivious of everything, it seemed. His face was lined with tension.

"David?"

"Five minutes," yelled Adrian, clapping his hands high in the air. "Showtime. Let's go."

David's eyelids blinked rapidly, as if he was waking up in the middle of a bad dream.

The atmosphere in the room was suddenly charged with excitement. The crowd cheered and Jimmy staggered on out with Kaetrin in tow. More cheering and shouts of encouragement for the band to take to the stage, along with some knowing laughter over Jimmy and the girl's reappearance.

"Let's do this!" shouted Jimmy, shaking hands and clapping people on the back as he moved through the room. "Come on, Davie."

My husband's shoulders hiked up. "Martha."

The woman sauntered over, her face a careful mask. "What can I do for you?"

"Look after Ev while I'm onstage."

"Sure."

"Look, I've got to go but I'll be right back," he said to me.

"Of course. Go."

With a final kiss to my forehead, he went, shoulders hunched in protectively. I had the maddest impulse to go after him. To stop him. To do something. Mal joined him at the door and slung an arm around his neck. David didn't look back. The bulk of the people followed them. I stood alone, watching the exodus. He'd been right, the room was cold. I clutched his jacket around me tighter, letting the scent of him soothe me. Everything was fine. If I kept telling myself that, sooner or later it would become true. Even the bits I didn't understand would work out. I had to have faith. And damn it, I did have faith. But my smile was long gone.

Martha watched me, her immaculate expression never altering.

After a moment, her red lips parted. "I've known David a very long time."

"That's nice," I said, refusing to be cowed by her cool gaze.

"Yes. He's enormously talented and driven. It makes him intense about things, passionate."

I said nothing.

"Sometimes he gets carried away. It doesn't mean anything." Martha stared at my ring. With an elegant motion she tucked her dark hair back behind her ear. Above a beautifully set cluster of dark red stones sat a single, small, winking diamond. Little more than a chip, it didn't really seem to fit Martha's expensive veneer. "When you're ready, I'll show you where you can watch the show from."

The sensation of spiraling that had started when David walked away from me became stronger. Beside me, Martha waited patiently, not saying a word, for which I was grateful. She'd said more than enough already. Only the clutter of red stones hung from her other ear. Paranoia wasn't pretty. Could this be the mate to the diamond earring David wore? No. That made no sense.

Lots of people wore tiny diamond solitaire earrings. Even millionaires.

I pushed my water aside, forcing a smile. "Shall we go?"

Watching the show was amazing. Martha took me to a spot to the side of the stage, behind the curtains, but it still felt like I was right in the thick of things. And things were loud and thrilling. Music thrummed through my chest, making my heart race. The music was a great distraction from my worries about the earring. David and I needed to talk. I'd been all for waiting until he felt comfortable enough to tell me things, but my questions were getting out of hand. I didn't want to be second-guessing him in this way. We needed honesty.

With a guitar in his hands, David was a god. Little wonder people worshiped him. His hands moved over the strings of his electric guitar with absolute precision, his concentration total. The muscles flexing in his forearms made his tattoos come to life. I stood in awe of him, mouth agape. There were other people onstage too, but David held me spellbound. I'd only seen the private side of him, who he was when he was with me. This seemed to be almost another entity. A stranger. My husband had taken a backseat to the performer. The rock star. It was actually a little daunting. But in that moment, his passion made perfect sense to me. His talent was such a gift.

They played five songs, then it was announced another big-name artist would take to the stage. All four of the band members exited by the other side. Martha had disappeared. Hard to be upset about that, despite backstage being a maze of hallways and dressing rooms. The woman was a monster. I was better off alone.

I made my way back on my own, taking tiny, delicate steps because my stupid shoes were killing me. Blisters lined my toes where the strap cut across, rubbing away at my skin. Didn't matter, my joy would not be dimmed. The memory of the music stayed with me. The way David had looked all caught up in the performance, both exciting and unknown. Talk about a rush.

I smiled and swore, quietly, ignoring my poor feet and wending my way through the mix of roadies, sound technicians, makeup artists, and general hangers-on.

"Child bride." Mal smacked a noisy kiss on my cheek. "I'm heading to a club. You guys coming or taking off back to your love nest?"

"I don't know. Just let me find David. That was amazing, by the way. You guys were brilliant."

"Glad you liked it. Don't tell David I carried the show, though. He's so precious about that sort of thing."

"My lips are sealed."

He laughed. "He's better with you, you know? Artistic types have a bad habit of disappearing up their own asses. He's smiled more in the last few days with you than I've seen him do in the last five years put together. You're good for him."

"Really?"

Mal grinned. "Really. You tell him I'm going to Charlotte's. See you there later, maybe."

"Okay."

Mal took off and I made my way toward the band's dressing room through the even bigger and better crush of people assembled. Inside the dressing room, however, things were quiet. Jimmy and Adrian had stood huddled out in the hallway, deep in conversation as I passed on by. Definitely not stopping. Sam and a second security person nodded to me as I passed.

The door to the back room where Jimmy had been busy earlier stood partly open. David's voice carried to me, clear as day, despite the noise outside. It was like I was becoming tuned in to him on some cosmic level. Scary but exhilarating at the same time. I couldn't wait to get out of here with him and do whatever. Go meet Mal or take off on our own. I didn't mind, so long as we were together.

I just wanted to be with him.

The sound of Martha's raised voice from within the same room decreased my happy.

"Don't," someone said from behind me, halting me at the door.

I turned to face the fourth member of the band: Ben. I remembered him now from some show Lauren had made me sit through years ago. He played bass, and he made Sam the bodyguard look like a cute, fluffy kitten. Short dark hair and the neck of a bull. Attractive in a strange, serial-killer kind of way. Though it might have just been the way he looked at me, eyes dead serious and jaw rigid. Another one on drugs, perhaps. To me, he felt nothing but bad.

"Let them sort it out," he said, voice low. His gaze darted to the partially open doorway. "You don't know what they were like when they were together."

"What?" I edged back a bit and he noticed, taking a step to the side to get closer to the door. Trying to maneuver me to the outer.

Ben just looked at me, his thick arm barring the way. "Mal said you're nice and I'm sure you are. But she's my sister. David and her have always been crazy about each other, ever since we were kids."

"I don't understand." I flinched, my head shaking.

"I know."

"Move, Ben."

"I'm sorry. Can't do that."

Fact was, he didn't need to. I held his gaze, making sure I had his full attention. Then I balanced my weight on one of my hooker heels, using the other to kick the door open. Since it had never been fully closed, it swung inward with ease.

David stood with his back partially turned toward us. Martha's hands were in his hair, holding him to her. Their mouths were mushed together. It was a hard, ugly kiss. Or maybe that was just the way it looked from the outside.

I didn't feel anything. Seeing that should have been big, but it wasn't. It made me small and it shut me down inside. If anything, it felt almost oddly inevitable. The pieces had all been there. I'd been so stupid, trying not to see this. Thinking everything would be fine.

A noise escaped my throat and David broke away from her. He looked over his shoulder at me.

"Ev," he said, face drawn and eyes bright.

My heart must have given up. Blood wasn't flowing. How bizarre. My hands and feet were ice-cold. I shook my head. I had nothing. I took a step back, and he flung out a hand to me.

"Don't," he said.

"David." Martha gave him a hazardous smile. No other

word for it. Her hand stroked over his arm as if she could sink her nails into him at any time. I guessed she could.

David came toward me. I took several hasty steps back, stumbling in my heels. He stopped and stared at me like I was a stranger.

"Baby, this is nothing," he said. He reached for me again. I held my arms tight to my chest, guarding myself from harm. Too late.

"It was her? She's the high school sweetheart?"

The familiar old muscle in his jaw went pop. "That was a long time ago. It doesn't matter."

"Jesus, David."

"It has nothing to do with us."

The more he spoke, the colder I felt. I did my best to ignore Ben and Martha hovering in the background.

David swore. "Come on, we're getting out of here."

I shook my head slowly. He grabbed my arms, stopping me from retreating any farther. "What the fuck are you doing, Evelyn?"

"What are *you* doing, David? What have you done?"

"Nothing," he said, teeth gritted. "I haven't done a damn thing. You said you trusted me."

"Why do you both still wear the earrings if it's nothing?"

His hand flew to his ear, covering the offending items. "It's not like that."

"Why does she still work for you?"

"You said you trusted me," he repeated.

"Why keep the house in Monterey all these years?"

"No," he said and then stopped.

I stared at him, incredulous. "No? That's it? That's not enough. Was I supposed to just not see all this? Ignore it?"

"You don't understand."

"Then explain it to me," I pleaded. His eyes looked right through me. I might as well not have spoken. My questions went unanswered, same as they ever had. "You can't do it, can you?"

I took another step back and his face hardened to fury. His hands fisted at his sides. "Don't you dare fucking leave me. You promised!"

I didn't know him at all. I stared at him, transfixed, letting his anger wash over me. It couldn't hope to pierce the hurt. Not a chance.

"You walk out of here and it's over. Don't you fucking think of coming back."

"Okay."

"I mean it. You'll be nothing to me."

Behind David, Ben's mouth opened but nothing came out. Just as well. Even numb had its limits.

"Evelyn!" David snarled.

I slipped off the stupid shoes and went barefoot for my grand exit. Might as well be comfortable. Normally I'd never wear heels like that. There was nothing wrong with normal. I was long overdue for a huge heaping dose of it. I'd wrap myself in normal like it was cotton wool, protecting me from everything. I had the café to get back to, school to start thinking about. I had a life waiting.

A door slammed shut behind me. Something thumped against it on the other side. The sound of shouting was muted.

Outside the dressing room door, Jimmy and Adrian were still deep in conversation. By which I mean Adrian spoke and Jimmy stared at the ceiling, grinning like a lunatic. I doubted a rocket ship could have reached Jimmy just then, he looked that high.

"Excuse me," I said, butting in.

Adrian turned and frowned, the flash of bright teeth coming a moment too late. "Evelyn. Honey, I'm just in the middle of something here—"

"I'd like to go back to Portland now."

"You would? Okay." He rubbed his hands together. Ah, I'd pleased him. His smile was huge, genuine for once and glaringly bright. Headlights had nothing on him. He'd apparently been holding back previously.

"Sam!" he yelled.

The bodyguard appeared, weaving through the crowd with ease. "Mrs. Ferris."

"Miss Thomas," Adrian corrected. "Would you mind seeing her safely returned to her home, thanks, Sam?"

The polite professional expression didn't falter for a second. "Yes, sir. Of course."

"Excellent."

Jimmy started laughing, big belly laughs that shook his whole body. Then he started cackling, the noise vaguely reminiscent of the Wicked Witch of the West in *The Wizard of Oz*. If she'd been on crack or cocaine or whatever Jimmy had been digging into, of course.

These people, they made no sense.

I didn't belong here. I'd never belonged here.

"This way." Sam pressed a hand lightly to the small of my back, which was sufficient to get me moving. Time to go home, wake up from the too-good-to-be-true dream that had twisted into this warped nightmare.

The laughter got louder and louder, ringing in my ears, until suddenly it cut off. I turned in time to watch Jimmy slump to the ground, his slick suit a mess. One woman gasped. Another chuckled and rolled her eyes.

"Fuck's sake," growled Adrian, kneeling beside the unconscious man. He slapped at his face. "Jimmy. Jimmy!"

More burly bodyguards appeared, crowding around the fallen singer, blocking him from view.

"Not again," Adrian ranted. "Get the doctor in here. God-damn it, Jimmy."

"Mrs. Ferris?" asked Sam.

"Is he all right?"

Sam scowled at the scene. "He's probably just passed out. It's been happening a lot lately. Shall we go?"

"Get me out of here, Sam. Please."

I was back in Portland before the sun rose. I didn't cry on the trip. It was as if my brain had diagnosed the emergency and cau-terized my emotions. I felt numb, as if Sam could swerve the car into the oncoming traffic and I wouldn't utter a peep. I was done, frozen solid. We went via the mansion so Sam could collect my bag before heading to the airport. He put me on the jet and we flew to Portland. He got me off the jet and drove me home.

Sam insisted on carrying my bag, just like he'd insisted on calling me by my married name. The man did the best subtle, concerned sidelong glance I'd ever seen. Never said much, though, which I appreciated immensely.

I sleepwalked my sorry self up the stairs to the apartment Lauren and I shared. Home was a garlic-scented hallway cour-tesy of Mrs. Lucia downstairs, constantly cooking. Peeling green wallpaper and worn wooden floorboards, scuffed and stained. Lucky I'd put the Converses on, or my feet would have been full of splinters. This floor was nothing like the gloss and gleam of David's house. You could see yourself in that sucker.

Shit. I didn't want to think of him. All of those memories belonged in a box buried in the back of my mind. Never again would they see the light of day.

My key still fit the lock. It comforted me. I might as well have been missing for years instead of days. It hadn't even been a week. I'd left early Thursday morning and now it was Tuesday. Less than six short days. That was insane. Everything felt different. I pushed open the door, being quiet because of the early hour. Lauren would be asleep. Or she might not be. I heard laughing.

She might, in fact, be spread out over our small breakfast table, giggling as some guy stuffed his head beneath one of the old oversized T-shirts she slept in. He buried his face in her cleavage and tickled her. Lauren squirmed, making all sorts of happy noises. Thankfully the guy's pants were still on, whoever he was. They were really into it, didn't notice our entry at all.

Sam stared at the far wall, avoiding the scene. Poor guy, the things he must have witnessed over the years.

"Hi," I said. "Um, Lauren?"

Lauren screeched and rolled, twisting the guy up in her shirt as he fought to get free. If she accidentally strangled him, at least he'd go happy, given the view.

"Ev," she panted. "You're back."

The guy finally liberated his face.

"Nathan?" I asked, stupefied. I cocked my head just to be sure, narrowed my eyes.

"Hi." My brother raised one hand while pulling down Lauren's shirt with the other. "How are you?"

"Fine, yeah," I said. "Sam, this is my friend Lauren and my brother, Nate. Guys, this is Sam."

Sam did his polite nod and set down my bag. "Can I do anything else for you, Mrs. Ferris?"

"No, Sam. Thank you for seeing me home."

"You're very welcome." He looked to the door then back at

me, a small wrinkle between his brows. I couldn't be certain, but I think it was as close as Sam got to an actual frown. His facial expressions seemed limited. Restrained was probably a better word. He reached out and gave me a stiff pat on the back. Then he left, closing the door behind him.

My eyes heated, threatening tears. I blinked like crazy, holding it in. His kindness nearly cracked the numb, damn it. I couldn't afford that yet.

"So, you two?" I asked.

"We're together. Yes," said Lauren, reaching behind her. Nate took her hand and held on tight. They actually looked good together. Though, seriously, how much stranger could things get? My world had changed. It felt different, though the small apartment looked the same. Things were pretty much where I'd left them. Lauren's collection of demented porcelain cats still sat on a shelf collecting dust. Our cheap or second-hand furniture and turquoise blue walls hadn't altered. Though I might never use the table again, considering what I'd seen. Lord knew what else they'd been up to on there.

I flexed my fingers, willing some life back into my limbs. "I thought you two hated each other?"

"We did," confirmed Lauren. "But, you know . . . now we don't. It's a surprisingly uncomplicated story, actually. It just kind of happened while you were away."

"Wow."

"Nice dress," said Lauren, looking me over.

"Thanks."

"Valentino?"

I smoothed the blue fabric over my stomach. "I don't know."

"That's a statement, matching it with the sneakers," Lauren said. Then she gave Nate a look. They apparently already had the silent communication thing down because he tippy-toed off toward her bedroom. Interesting . . .

My best friend and my brother. And she'd never said a word. But then, there were plenty of things I hadn't told her either. Maybe we were past the age of sharing every last little detail of our lives. How sad.

Loneliness and a healthy dose of self-pity cooled me right off and I wrapped my arms around myself.

Lauren came over and pried one of my hands loose. "Hon, what happened?"

I shook my head, warding off questions. "I can't. Not yet."

She joined me leaning against the wall. "I have ice cream."

"What kind?"

"Triple choc. I was thinking of torturing your brother with it later in a sexually explicit manner."

There went my vague interest in ice cream. I scrubbed my face with my hands. "Lauren, if you love me, you'll never say anything like that to me ever again."

"Sorry."

I almost smiled. My mouth definitely came close to it but faltered at the last. "Nate makes you happy, doesn't he?"

"Yeah, he really does. It just feels like . . . I don't know, it's like we're in tune or something. Ever since the night he picked me up from your folks' place we've pretty much been together. It feels right. He's not angry like he used to be in high school. He's given up his man-slut ways. He's calmed down and grown up. Shit, out of the two of us, he's the sensible one." She mock pouted. "But our days of sharing every last detail about our lives really are over, aren't they?"

"I guess they are."

"Ah, well. We'll always have middle school."

"Yeah." I managed a smile.

"Hon, I'm sorry things went bad. I mean, that's obviously why you're back looking like shit in that absolutely exquisite dress." She eyed up my gown with great lust.

"You can have it." Hell, she could have all of the other stuff as well. I never wanted to touch any of it ever again. His jacket I'd left with Sam, the ring stuffed into a pocket. Sam would take care of it. See that it got back to him. My hand seemed bare without it, lighter. Lighter and freer should have gone together, but they didn't. Inside me sat a great weight. I'd been dragging my sorry ass around for hours now. Onto the plane. Off the plane. Into the car. Up the stairs. Neither time nor distance had helped so far.

"I want to hug you but you're giving off that don't-touch-me vibe," she said, propping her hands on her slim hips. "Tell me what to do."

"Sorry." The smile I gave her was twisted and awful. I could feel it. "Later?"

"How much later? Because frankly, you look like you need it bad."

I couldn't stop the tears this time. They just started flowing, and once they started, they wouldn't stop. I wiped at them uselessly, then just gave up and covered my face with my hands. "Fuck."

Lauren threw her arms around me, held me tight. "Let it go."

I did.

CHAPTER SEVENTEEN

Twenty-eight days later . . .

The woman was taking forever to order. Her eyes kept shifting between me and the menu as she leaned across the counter. I knew that look. I dreaded that look. I loved being in the café, with the aroma of coffee beans and the soothing blend of music and chatter. I loved the camaraderie we had going on behind the counter and the fact that the work kept my hands and brain busy. Weirdly enough, being a barista relaxed me. I was good at it. With my studies a constant struggle, I reveled in that fact. If everything ever hit the wall, I'd always have coffee to fall back on. It was the modern-day Portland equivalent of typing. The city ran on coffee beans and cafés. Coffee and beer were in our blood.

Lately, however, some customers had been a pain in the ass to deal with.

"You seem really familiar," she started, much as they all did. "Weren't you all over the Internet a while back? Something to do with David Ferris?"

At least I didn't flinch at his name anymore. And it had been days since I'd felt the urge to actually vomit. Definitely not pregnant, just getting annulled.

After the first few days of hiding in bed, crying my eyes

out, I took every shift the café would give me to keep busy. I couldn't mourn him forever. Pity my heart remained unconvinced. He was in my dreams every night when I closed my eyes. I had to chase him out of my mind a thousand times a day.

By the time I surfaced, the few lingering paparazzi had cleared off back to LA. Apparently Jimmy had gone into rehab. Lauren switched channels every time I walked in, but I couldn't help but catch enough news to know what was going on. It seemed Stage Dive were being talked about everywhere. Someone had even asked me to sign a picture of David striding into the treatment facility, head hanging down and hands stuffed in his pockets. He'd looked so alone. Several times, I'd almost called him. Just to ask if he was okay. Just to hear his voice. How stupid was that? And what if I rang and Martha answered?

At any rate, Jimmy's meltdown was much more interesting than me. I barely rated a mention on the news these days.

But people, customers, they drove me nuts. Outside of work, I'd become a complete shut-in. That had its own issues on account of my brother basically living with us now. People in love were sickening. It was a proven medical fact. Customers with speculation shining bright in their beady little eyes weren't much better.

"You're mistaken," I told the nosy woman.

She gave me a coy look. "I don't think so."

Ten bucks said she was working her way up to asking me for his autograph. This would make the eighth attempt to obtain one today. Some of them wanted to take me home for intimate relations because, you know, rock star's ex. My vagina clearly had to be something special. I sometimes wondered if they thought there was a little plaque on my inner thigh saying David Ferris had been there.

This chick, however, wasn't checking me out. No, she wanted an autograph.

"Look," she said, speculation turning to wheedling. "I wouldn't ask, it's just that I'm such a huge fan of his."

"I can't help you, sorry. We're actually about to close. So would you like to order something before that happens?" I asked, pleasant smile firmly in place. Sam would have been proud of that smile, as fake as it was. But with my eyes I told the woman the truth. That I was all used up and I honestly had no fucks left to give. Especially when it came to David Ferris.

"Can you at least tell me if the band is really breaking up? Come on. Everyone's saying an announcement's going to be made any day now."

"I don't know anything about it. Would you liked to order something, or not?"

Further denial generally led to either anger or tears. She chose anger. A good choice, because tears annoyed the living hell out of me. I was sick of them, both on myself and others. Despite it being common knowledge that I'd been dumped, they still figured I had connections. Or so they hoped.

She did a fake little laugh. "There's no need to be a bitch about it. Would letting me know what's happening really have killed you?"

"Leave," said my lovely manager, Ruby. "Right now. Get out."

The woman switched to incredulous, mouth open wide. "What?"

"Amanda, call the cops." Ruby stood tall beside me.

"On it, boss." Amanda snapped open her cell and punched in the numbers, leveling the woman with her evil eye. Amanda, having moved on from being my high school's sole lesbian, was studying drama. These confrontations were her favorite part of the day. They might have sapped my strength, but Amanda sucked all of her power from them. A dark, malevolent force, to be sure, but it was all hers and she reveled in it. "Yes, we've got a fake blonde with a bad tan giving us trouble, Officer. I'm pretty certain I saw her at a frat party doing some serious underage drinking last week. I don't want to say what happened after that but the footage is available on YouTube for your viewing pleasure if you're over eighteen."

"No wonder he dropped you. I saw the picture, your ass is wide as fucking Texas," the woman sneered, and then sped out of the café.

"Do you really have to stir them up?" I asked.

Amanda clucked her tongue. "Please. She started it."

I'd heard worse than what she'd said. Way worse. Several times now I'd had to change my e-mail address to stop the hate mail from flooding in. I had closed my Facebook account early on.

Still, I checked my butt to be sure. It was a close call, but I was pretty sure Texas was, in fact, wider.

"As far as I can tell you're living on a diet of breath mints and lattes. Your ass is not a concern." Amanda had long since forgiven me for the bad kiss back in high school, bless her. I was beyond lucky to have the friends I did. I really don't know how I'd have made it through the last month without them.

"I eat."

"Really? Whose jeans are those?"

I started cleaning the coffee machine because it really was getting on closing time. That, and for reasons of subject avoidance. Fact was, getting cheated on and lied to by rock 'n' roll's favorite son did make for quite the diet. Definitely not one I'd recommend. My sleep was shot to shit and I was tired all the time. I was depression's bitch. Inside and out, I didn't feel like me. The time I'd spent with David, the way it had changed things, was a constant agitation, an itch I couldn't scratch. Partly because I lacked the power but also because I lacked the will. You could sing "I Will Survive" only so many times before the urge to throttle yourself took over.

"Lauren doesn't wear these. Said they were the wrong shade of dark wash and that the placement of the back pockets made her look hippy. Apparently pocket placement matters."

"And you started wearing that skinny cow's clothes when?"

"Don't call her that."

Amanda rolled her eyes. "Please, she takes it as a compliment."

True. "Well, I think the jeans are nice. Are you wiping down the tables, or would you like me to?"

Amanda just sighed. "Jo and I want to thank you for helping us move last weekend. So we're taking you out tonight. Drinking and dancing ahoy!"

"Oh." Alcohol and I already had a bad reputation. "I don't know."

"I do."

"I had plans to—"

"No you don't. This is why I left it to the last minute to tell you. I knew you'd try to make excuses." Amanda's dark eyes brooked no nonsense. "Ruby, I'm taking our girl out for a night on the town."

"Good idea," Ruby called out from the kitchen. "Get her out of here. I'll clean up."

My practiced pleasant smile fell off my face. "But—"

"It's the sad eyes," said Ruby, confiscating my cleaning cloth. "I can't bear them any longer. Please go out and have some fun."

"Am I that much of a killjoy?" I asked, suddenly worried. I honestly thought I'd been putting on a good front. Their faces told me otherwise.

"No. You're a normal twenty-one-year-old going through a breakup. You need to get back out there and reclaim your life." Ruby was in her early thirties and soon to be wed. "Trust me. I know best. Go."

"Or," said Amanda, waggling a finger at me, "you could sit at home watching *Walk the Line* for the eight hundredth time while listening to your brother and best friend going hard at it in the room next door."

When she put it like that . . . "Let's go."

"I want to be bi," I announced, because it was important. A girl had to have goals. I pushed back my chair and rose to my feet. "Let's dance. I love this song."

"You love any song that's not by the band who shall not be named." Amanda laughed, following me through the crowd. Her girlfriend, Jo, just shook her head, clinging to her hand. Vodka was doubtless as bad an idea as tequila, but I did feel somewhat unwound, looser. It was good to get out, and on an empty stomach three drinks went a long way, clearly. I did suspect Amanda had made at least one of them a double. It felt great to dance and laugh and let loose. Out of all of the getting-over-a-breakup tactics I'd attempted, keeping busy worked best. But going out dancing and drinking all dressed up shouldn't be mocked.

I tucked my hair behind my ears because my ponytail had started falling apart again. Perfect metaphor for my life. Nothing worked right since I'd gotten back from LA. Nothing lasted. Love was a lie, and rock 'n' roll sucked. Blah blah blah. Time for another drink.

And I'd been in the middle of making an important point.

"I'm serious," I said. "I'm going bi. It's my new plan."

"I think that's a great plan," yelled Jo, moving next to me. Jo also worked at the café, which was how the two had met. She had long blue hair that was the envy of all.

Amanda rolled her eyes at me. "You're not bi. Babe, don't encourage her."

Jo grinned, totally unrepentant. "Last week she wanted to be gay. Before that she talked monasteries. I think this is a constructive step toward her forgiving every penis-possessing human and moving on with her life."

"I am moving on with my life," I said.

"Which is why you two have been talking about him for the past four hours?" Amanda grinned, throwing her arms around Jo's shoulders.

"We weren't talking about him. We were insulting him. How do you say 'useless stinking sheep fornicator' in German again?" I asked, leaning in to be heard over the music. "That was my favorite."

Jo and Amanda got busy close dancing and I let them go, unperturbed. Because I wasn't afraid of being alone. I was action-packed, full of single-girl power. Fuck David Ferris. Fuck him good and hard.

The music all blended into one long time-bending beat, and so long as I kept moving it was all perfect. Sweat slicked my neck and I popped another button on my dress, widening the neckline. I ignored the other people dancing around me. I shut my eyes, staying safe in my own little world. The alcohol had given me a nice buzz.

For some reason, the hands sliding over my hips didn't bother me, even though they were uninvited. They went no farther, made no demands on me. Their owner danced behind me, keeping a small safe distance between us. It was nice. Maybe the music had hypnotized me. Or maybe I had been lonely, because I didn't fight it. Instead I relaxed against him. For all of the next song we stayed like that, melded together, moving. The beat slowed down and I raised my arms, linking my hands behind his neck. After a month of avoiding almost all human contact, my body woke. The short, soft hair at the back of his neck brushed over my fingers. Smooth, warm skin beneath.

God, it was so nice. I hadn't realized how touch starved I was.

I leaned my head back against him and he whispered something softly. Too soft for me to hear. The bristles on his cheek and jaw lightly prickled the side of my face. Hands slid over my ribs, up my arms. Calloused fingers lightly stroked the sensitive underside of my arms. His body was solid behind me, strong, but he kept his touch light, restrained. I wasn't in the market for a rebound. My heart was too bruised for that, my mind too wary. I couldn't bring myself to move away from him, however. It felt too good there.

"Evelyn," he said, his lips teasing my ear.

My breath caught, my eyelids shot open. I turned to find David staring back at me. The long hair was gone. It was still longish on top but cut short at the sides. He could probably do a neat Elvis pompadour if the fancy took him. A short, dark beard covered his lower face.

"Y-you're here," I stuttered out. My tongue felt thick and useless inside my dry mouth. Christ, it was really him. Here in Portland. In the flesh.

"Yeah." His blue eyes burned. He didn't say anything else. Music kept playing, people kept moving. The world only stopped turning for me.

"Why?"

"Ev?" Amanda put a hand to my arm and I jumped, the spell broken. She gave David a quick glance, and then her face screwed up in distaste. "What the fuck is he doing here?"

"It's okay," I said.

Her gaze moved between David and me. She didn't really seem convinced. Fair enough.

"Amanda. Please." I squeezed her fingers, nodded. After a moment she turned back to Jo, who stared at David with open disbelief. And a healthy dose of star-struck. His new look made for a brilliant disguise. Unless you knew who you were looking for, of course.

I pushed through the crowd, getting the hell out of there. I knew he'd follow. Of course he would. It was no accident he was there, though I had no damn idea how he'd found me. I needed to get away from the heat and the noise so I could think straight. Down the back hallway past the men's and women's toilets. There, that was what I wanted. A big black door opened onto a back alleyway. Open night air. A few brave stars twinkled high overhead. Otherwise it was dark back here, damp from earlier summer rain. It was horrible and dirty and hateful. An ideal setting.

I might have been feeling a bit dramatic.

The door slammed shut behind David. He faced me, hands on hips. He opened his mouth to start talking and no, not happening. I snapped.

"Why are you here, David?"

"We need to talk."

"No, we don't."

He rubbed at his mouth. "Please. There're things I have to tell you."

"Too late."

Looking at him revived the pain. As if I had wounds lingering just beneath the skin, waiting to resurface. I couldn't help staring at him, however. Parts of me were desperate for the sight of him, the sound of him. My head and heart were a wreck. David didn't appear so great himself. He looked tired. There were shadows beneath his eyes and he seemed a little pale, even in this crappy lighting. The earrings were missing, all of them gone. Not that I cared.

He rocked back on his heels, eyes watching me desperately. "Jimmy went into rehab and there were other things going on I had to deal with. We had to do therapy together as part of his treatment. That's why I couldn't come right away."

"I'm sorry to hear about Jimmy."

He nodded. "Thanks. He's doing a lot better."

"Good. That's good."

Another nod. "Ev, about Martha—"

"Whoa." I held up a hand, backing up. "Don't."

His mouth turned down at the edges. "We have to talk."

"Do we?"

"Yes."

"Because now you've decided you're ready? Fuck you, David. It's been a month. Twenty-eight days without a word. I'm sorry about your brother, but no."

"I wanted to make sure I was coming after you for the right reasons."

"I don't even know what that means."

"Ev—"

"No." I shook my head, hurt and fury pushing me hard. So I pushed at him even harder, sending him back a step. He hit the wall and I had nowhere else to go with him. But that didn't stop me.

I went to push at him again and he grabbed my hands. "Calm down."

"No!"

His hands encircled my wrists. He gritted his teeth, grinding his molars together. I heard it. Impressive that he didn't crack anything. "No what? No to talking now? What? What do you mean?"

"I mean no to everything and anything to do with you." My words echoed through the narrow alleyway, up the sides of the buildings until they emptied out into the uncaring night sky. "We're finished, remember? You're fucking done with me. I'm nothing to you. You said so yourself."

"I was wrong. Goddamn it, Ev. Calm down. Listen to me."

"Let me go."

"I'm sorry. But it's not what you think."

Out of options, I got in his face. "You don't get to come here now. You lied to me. You cheated on me."

"Baby—"

"Don't you dare call me that," I yelled.

"I'm sorry." His gaze roamed my face, searching for sense, maybe. He was shit out of luck. "I'm sorry."

"Stop."

"I'm sorry. I'm sorry." Over and over he said, chanting the most worthless words in all of time and space. I had to stop it. Shut him up before he drove me insane. I smashed my mouth to his, halting the useless litany. He groaned and kissed me back hard, bruising my lips, hurting me. But then I hurt him too. The pain helped. I pushed my tongue into his mouth, taking what was supposed to be mine. In that moment I hated him and I loved him. There didn't seem to be any difference.

My hands were freed and I wound them around his neck.

He turned us, setting my back to the rough brick wall. His touch burned through my skin and bones. It all happened so fast, there wasn't time to wonder about the wisdom of it. He pushed up my dress and tore at my panties. They didn't stand a chance. The cool of the night air and the heat of his palms smoothed over my thighs.

"I missed you so fucking much," he groaned.

"David."

He lowered his zipper and pushed down the front of his jeans. Then he lifted my leg, bringing it up to his hip. My hands dragged at his neck. I think I was trying to climb him. There wasn't much thought going into it. Just the drive to get as close to him as physically possible. He nipped at my lips, taking my mouth in another hard kiss. His cock pushed against me, easing into me. The feel of him filling me made my head spin. The slight ache as he stretched me. His other hand slid around beneath my butt, then he lifted me up, pushing in all the way, making me moan. I wrapped my legs around him and held on tight. He pounded himself into me with nil finesse. Rough suited both our moods. My fingernails clawed at his neck, my heels drumming his ass. His teeth pressed hard into the side of my neck. The pain was perfect.

"Harder," I panted.

"Fuck yes."

The rough brickwork abraded my back, pulling at the fabric of my dress. The hard drive of his cock took my breath away. I clung on tight, trying to savor the feel of him, the tension building inside me. It was all too much and still not enough. The thought that this could be our last time, a brutally angry joining like this . . . I wanted to cry but I didn't have the tears. His fingers dug into my ass cheeks, marking my flesh. The pressure inside me grew higher and higher. He changed his angle slightly, hitting my clit, and I came hard, my arms wrapped around his head, my cheek pressed against his. His beard brushed against up my face. My whole body shuddered and shook.

"Evelyn," he snarled, grinding himself into me, emptying himself inside me.

Every muscle in my body went liquid. It was all I could do to hang on to him.

"It's fine, baby." His mouth pressed against my damp face. "It'll be okay, I promise. I'll fix it."

"P-put me down."

His shoulders rose and fell on a harsh breath, and carefully he did so. Quickly I pulled down the skirt of my dress, set myself to rights. Like that was even possible. This situation was out of control. Without fuss he pulled up his jeans, made himself presentable. I looked everywhere but at him. An alleyway. Holy hell.

"Are you all right?" His fingers brushed over my face, tucked back my hair. Until I put a hand to his chest, forcing him back a step. Well, not forcing him. He chose to give me my space.

"I . . . um." I licked my lips and tried again. "I need to go home."

"Come on, I'll get us a cab."

"No. I'm sorry. I know I started this. But . . ." I shook my head.

David hung his.

"That was good-bye."

"Like fuck it was. Don't you even try to tell me that." His finger slid beneath my chin, making me look at him. "We are not finished, you hear me? Not even fucking remotely. New plan. I'm not leaving Portland until we've talked this out. I promise you that."

"Not tonight."

"No. Not tonight. Tomorrow, then?"

I opened my mouth but nothing came out. I had no idea what I wanted to say. My fingernails dug into my sides through my dress. What I wanted these days was a mystery even to me. To stop hurting would be nice. To remove all memory of him from my head and heart. To get my breathing back under control.

"Tomorrow," he repeated.

"I don't know." Now I felt tired, facing him. I could have slept for a year. My shoulders slumped and my brain stalled.

He just stared at me, eyes intense. "Okay."

Where that left us, I had no idea. But I nodded as if something had been decided.

"Good," he said, taking a deep breath.

My muscles still trembled. Semen slid down the inside of my leg. Shit. We'd had the talk, but things had been different back then.

"David, you practiced safe sex, right, the last month?"

"You have nothing to worry about."

"Good."

He took a step toward me. "As far as I'm concerned we're still married. So no, Evelyn, I haven't been fucking around on you."

I had nothing. My knees wavered. Probably due to the recent action they'd seen. Relief over him not taking to the groupies with a vengeance after our split couldn't be part of it, surely. I didn't even want to think about Martha, that tentacle-wielding sea monster from the deep.

Sex was so messy. Love was far and away worse.

One of us had to go. He made no move, so I left, hightailing it back toward the club to find Amanda and Jo. I needed new panties and a heart transplant. I needed to go home. He followed me, opening the door. The heavy bass of the music boomed out into the night.

I rushed into the ladies' room and locked myself into a stall to clean up. When I came out to wash my hands, looking in the mirror was hard. The harsh fluorescent lighting did me no favors. My long blond hair hung around my face a knotted mess thanks to David's hands. My eyes were wide and wounded. I looked terrified, but of what I didn't want to say. Also, there was the mother of all hickeys forming on my neck. Hell.

A couple of girls came in, giggling and casting longing looks back over their shoulders. Before the door swung shut, I caught a glance of David leaning against the wall opposite, waiting, staring at his boots. The girls' excited chatter was jarringly loud. But they made no mention of his name. David's disguise was holding up. Arms wrapped around myself, I went out to meet him.

"Ready to go?" he asked, pushing off from the wall.

"Yeah."

We made our way back through the club, dodging dancers and drunks, searching for Amanda and Jo. They were on the edge of the dance floor, talking. Amanda had her cranky face on.

She took me in and a brow arched. "Are you fucking kidding me?"

"Thanks for asking me out, guys. But I'm going to head home," I said, ignoring the pointed look.

"With him?" She jerked her chin at David, who lurked at my shoulder.

Jo stepped forward, wrapping me up in her arms. "Ignore her. You do what's right for you."

"Thanks."

Amanda rolled her eyes and followed suit, pulling me in for a hug. "He hurt you so bad."

"I know." My eyes welled with tears. Highly unhelpful. "Thanks for asking me out."

I'd bet all the money I had Amanda was roasting David over my shoulder with her eyes. I almost felt bad for him. Almost.

We left the club as one of his songs came over the speakers. There were numerous cries of "Divers!" Jimmy's voice purred out the lyrics, "Damn I hate these last days of love, cherry lips and long good-byes . . ."

David ducked his head and we rushed out. Outside in the open air, the song was no more than the faraway thumping of bass and drums. I kept sneaking sidelong glances, checking he was really there and not some figment of my imagination. So many times I'd dreamed he'd come to me. And every time I'd woken up alone, my face wet with tears. Now he was here and I couldn't risk it. If he broke me again, I wasn't convinced I'd manage to get back up a second time. My heart might not make it. So I did my best to keep my mouth and my mind shut.

It was still relatively early and there weren't many people milling about outside. I held out my hand to the passing traffic and a cab cruised to a stop soon after. David held the door open for me. I climbed in without a word.

"I'm seeing you home." He slid in after me and I scurried across the seat in surprise.

"You don't need—"

"I do. Okay. I do need to do that much, so just . . ."

"All right."

"Where to?" The cabdriver asked, giving us an uninterested look in the rearview mirror. Another feuding couple in his backseat. I'm sure he saw at least a dozen a night.

David rattled off my address without blinking. The taxi pulled out into the flow of traffic. He could have gotten my address from Sam, and as for the rest . . .

"Lauren," I sighed, sinking back against the seat. "Of course, that's how you knew where to find me."

He winced. "I talked to Lauren earlier. Listen, don't be mad at her. She took a lot of convincing."

"Right."

"I'm serious. She ripped me a new one for messing things up with you, yelled at me for half an hour. Please don't be mad at her."

I gritted my teeth and stared out the window. Until his fingers slid over mine. I snatched back my hand.

"You'll let me inside you but you won't let me hold your hand?" he whispered, his face sad in the dim glow of the passing cars and streetlights.

It was on the tip of my mouth to say that it had been an accident. That what had happened between us was wrong. But I couldn't do it. I knew how much it would hurt him. We stared at each other as my mouth hung open, my brain useless.

"I missed you so fucking much," he said. "You have no idea."

"Don't."

His lips shut but he didn't look away. I sat there caught by his gaze. He looked so different with his long hair gone, with the short beard. Familiar but unknown. It wasn't a long trip home, though it seemed to take forever. The cab stopped outside the old block of flats, and the driver gave us an impatient look over his shoulder.

I pushed open the car door, ready to be gone but hesitating just the same. My foot hovered in thin air above the curb. "I honestly didn't think I'd ever see you again."

"Hey," he said, his arm stretching out across the back of the seat. His fingers reached toward me but fell short of making contact. "You're going to see me again. Tomorrow."

I didn't know what to say.

"Tomorrow," he repeated, voice determined.

"I don't know if it'll make any difference."

He lifted his chin, inhaling sharply. "I know I fucked us up, but I'm going to fix it. Just don't make up your mind yet, all right? Give me that much."

I gave him a brief nod and hurried inside on unsteady legs. Once I'd locked myself inside, the cab pulled away, its taillights fading to black through the frosted glass of the downstairs door.

What the hell was I supposed to do now?

CHAPTER EIGHTEEN

I was running late for work. Rushing about like a mad thing trying to get ready. I ran into the bathroom, jumped in the shower. Gave my face a good scrub to get rid of the remnants of last night's makeup. Gruesome, crusty stuff. It would serve me right if I got the pimple from hell. Last night had all been some bizarre dream. But this was real life. Work and school and friends. My plans for the future. Those were the things that were important. And if I just kept telling myself that, everything would be fine and dandy. Someday.

Ruby didn't much mind what we wore at work beyond the official café T-shirt. Her roots were strongly alternative. She'd planned to be a poet but wound up inheriting her aunt's coffee shop in the Pearl District. Urban development had upped property prices and Ruby became quite the well-to-do businesswoman. Now she wrote her poetry on the walls in the café. I don't think you could find a better boss. But late was still late. Not good.

I'd stayed up worrying about what had happened with David in that alleyway. Reliving the moment where he told me he considered us still married. Sleep would have been far more beneficial. Pity my brain wouldn't switch off.

I pulled on a black pencil skirt, the official café T-shirt, and a pair of flats. Done. Nothing was going to help the bruises beneath my eyes. People had pretty much gotten used to them on me lately. It took about half a stick of concealer to cover the bruise on my neck.

I roared out of the bathroom in a cloud of steam, just in time to see Lauren waltz out of the kitchen, broad smile on her face. "You're late for work."

"That I am."

I looped my handbag over my shoulder, grabbed my keys off the table, and got going. There wasn't time for this. Not now. Quite possibly not ever. I couldn't imagine her ever having a good enough reason for siding with David. Over the last month she'd spent many nights by my side, letting me talk myself hoarse about him when I needed to. Because eventually, it all had to come out. Daily I told her that I didn't deserve her, and she'd smack a kiss on my cheek. Why betray me now? I thumped down the stairs with extra oomph.

"Ev, wait." Lauren ran after me as I stormed down the front steps.

I turned on her, house keys held before me like a weapon. "You told him where I was."

"What was I supposed to do?"

"Oh, I don't know. Not tell him? You knew I didn't want to see him." I looked her over, noticing all sorts of things I didn't want to. "Full hair and makeup at this hour? Really, Lauren? Were you expecting him to be here, perhaps?"

Her chin dipped as she had the good grace to look embarrassed at last. "I'm sorry. You're right, I got carried away. But he's here to make amends. I thought you might at least want to hear what he has to say."

I shook my head, fury bubbling away inside me. "Not your call."

"You've been miserable. What was I supposed to do?" She threw her arms sky-high. "He said that he'd come to make things right with you. I believe him."

"Of course you do. He's David Ferris, your very own teen idol."

"No. If he wasn't here to kiss your feet I'd have killed him. No matter who he is, he hurt you." She seemed sincere, her mouth pinched and eyes huge. "I'm sorry about dressing up this morning. It won't happen again."

"You look great. But you're wasting your time. He's not going to be here. That isn't going to happen."

"No? So who gave you that monster on your neck?"

I didn't even need to answer that. Damn it. The sun beat down overhead, warming up the day.

"If there's a chance you think he might be the one," she said, making my stomach twist. "If you think you two can sort this out somehow . . . He's the only one that ever got to you. The way you talk about him . . ."

"We were only together a few days."

"You really think that matters?"

"Yes. No. I don't know," I flailed. It wasn't pretty. "We never made sense, Lauren. Not from day one."

"Gah," she said, making a strangled noise to accompany it. "This is about your fucking plan, isn't it? Let me clue you in on something. You don't have to make sense. You just have to want to be together and be willing to do whatever it takes to make that happen. It's amazingly simple. That's love, Ev, putting each other first. Not worrying about if you fit into some fucktard plan that your dad brainwashed you into believing was what you wanted out of life."

"It's not about the plan." I scrubbed at my face with my hands, holding back tears of frustration and fear. "He broke me. It feels like he broke me. Why would anyone willingly take that chance again?"

Lauren looked at me, her own eyes bright. "I know he hurt you. So punish the bastard, keep him waiting. The fucker, he deserves it. But if you love him, then think about hearing what he has to say."

Maybe I was coming down with a cold, tight chest and itchy eyes. Having your heart broken should come with some positives, some perspective to balance out the bad. I should have been wiser, tougher, but I didn't feel it just then. I jangled my house keys. Ruby was going to kill me. I'd have to forgo my usual walk and catch a streetcar to have even a hope in hell of not getting my Texas-size ass fired. "I have to go."

Lauren nodded, face set. "You know, I love you so much more than I ever loved him. Without question."

I snorted. "Thanks."

"But has it occurred to you that you wouldn't be this upset if you didn't still love him at least a little bit?"

"I don't like you making sense at this hour of the morning. Stop it."

She took a step back, giving me a smile. "You were always there talking sense at me when I needed it. So I'm not going to stop nagging you just because you don't like what you're hearing. Deal with it."

"I love you, Lauren."

"I know, you Thomas kids are crazy for me. Why, just last night, your brother did this thing . . ."

I fled from the sound of her evil laughter.

Work was fine. Two guys came in to ask me to a frat party that was coming up. I'd never received such invites pre-David. I therefore declined them post-David. If I was indeed post-David. Who knew? Various people tried for autographs or information, and I sold them coffee and cake instead. We closed up at dusk.

All day I'd been on edge, wondering if he'd put in an appearance. Tomorrow was today, but I hadn't seen any sign of him. Maybe he'd changed his mind. Mine changed from one minute to the next. My promise to him not to decide yet was safe and sound.

We were just locking up when Ruby jabbed me in the ribs with her elbow. Probably a bit harder than she meant to because I'm pretty sure I sustained a kidney injury.

"He's really here," she hissed, nodding at David who did indeed lurk nearby, waiting. He was here, just like he'd said he'd be. Nervous excitement bubbled up inside of me. With a ball cap on and the beard, he blended well. Especially with the haircut. My heart sobbed a little at the loss of his long dark hair. But I'd never admit to it. Amanda had told Ruby about his reappearance last night. Given the lack of paparazzi and screaming fans in the vicinity, it must still be a secret from the rest of the city.

I stared at him, unsure how to feel. Last night at the club had been surreal. Here and now, this was me living my normal life. Seeing him in it, I didn't know how I felt. Discombobulated was a good word.

"Do you want to meet him?" I asked.

"No, I'm reserving judgment. I think actually meeting him might render me partial. He's very attractive, isn't he?" Ruby gave him a slow look-over, lingering on his jeans-clad legs longer than necessary. She had a thing for men's thighs. Soccer players sent her into a frenzy. Odd for a poet, but then I'd found no one ever really fit a certain type. Everyone had their quirks.

Ruby continued looking him over like he was meat at market. "Maybe don't divorce him."

"You sound very impartial. See you later."

Her hand hooked my arm. "Wait. If you stay with him will you still work for me?"

"Yes. I'll even try to be on time more often. Night, Ruby."

He stood on the sidewalk, hands stuffed into the pockets of his jeans. Seeing him felt similar to standing at a cliff's edge. The little voice in the back of my head whispered damn the consequences, you know you can probably fly. If you can't, imagine the thrill of the fall. Reason, on the other hand, screamed bloody murder at me.

At what point exactly could you decide you were going insane?

"Evelyn."

Everything stopped. If he ever figured out what it did to me when he said my name like that, I was done for. God, I'd missed him. It'd been like having a piece of me missing. But now that he was back, I didn't know how we fit together anymore. I didn't even know if we could.

"Hi," I said.

"You look tired," he said, mouth turning downward. "I mean, you look good, of course. But . . ."

"It's fine." I studied the sidewalk, took a deep breath. "It was a busy day."

"So this is where you work?"

"Yeah."

Ruby's café sat quiet and empty. Fairy lights twinkled in the windows alongside a host of flyers taped to the glass advertising this and that. Streetlights flickered on around us.

"Looks nice. Listen, we don't have to talk right now," he said. "I just wanna walk you home."

I crossed my arms over my chest. "You don't have to do that."

"It's not like it's a chore. Let me walk you home, Ev. Please."

I nodded and after a moment started a hesitant stride down

the city street. David fell into step beside me. What to talk about? Every topic seemed loaded. An open pit full of sharp stakes lay waiting around every corner. He kept shooting me wary sidelong glances. Opening his mouth and then shutting it. Apparently the situation sucked for both of us. I couldn't bring myself to talk about LA. Last night seemed safer territory. Wait. No, it wasn't. Bringing up alley sex was never going to pass for smart.

"How was your day?" he asked. "Apart from busy."

Why couldn't I have thought of something innocuous like that?

"Ah, fine. A couple of girls came in with stuff for you to sign. Some guys wanted me to give you a demo tape of their garage-reggae-blues band. One of the big-name jocks from school came in just to give me his number. He thinks we could have fun sometime," I babbled, trying to lighten the mood.

His face became thunderous, dark brows drawn tight together. "Shit. That been happening often?"

And I was an idiot to have opened my mouth. "It's no big deal, David. I told him I was busy and he went away."

"So he fucking should." He tipped his chin, giving me a long look. "You trying to make me jealous?"

"No, my mouth just ran away without my head. Sorry. Things are complicated enough."

"I am jealous."

I stared at him in surprise. I don't know why. He'd made it clear last night he was here for me. But the knowledge that maybe I wasn't alone out on the lovelorn precipice, thinking of throwing myself off . . . there was a lot of comfort in that.

"Come on," he said, resuming the walking. At the corner we stopped, waiting for the traffic to clear.

"I might get Sam up here to keep an eye on you," he said. "I don't want people bothering you at work."

"As much as I like Sam, he can stay where he is. Normal people don't take bodyguards to work."

His forehead scrunched up, but he said nothing. We crossed the road, continuing on. A streetcar rumbled past, all lit up. I preferred walking, getting in some outside time after being shut inside all day. Plus, Portland's beautiful: cafés and breweries and a weird heart. Take that, LA.

"So what did you do today?" I asked, proving myself a total winner in the creative conversation stakes.

"Just had a look around town, checking things out. I don't get to play the tourist too often. We're going left here," he said, turning me off the normal path toward home.

"Where are we going?"

"Just bear with me. I need to pick something up." He escorted me into a pizza place I went to occasionally with Lauren. "Pizza's the only thing I know you definitely eat. They were willing to stick on every fucking vegetable I could think of, so I hope you'll like it."

The place was only about a quarter full due to the early hour. Bare brick walls and black tables. A jukebox blared out something by the Beatles. I stood in the doorway, hesitant to go farther with him. The man nodded to David and fetched an order from the warmer behind him. David thanked him and headed back toward me.

"You didn't have to do that." I stepped back out onto the street, giving the pizza box suspicious glances.

"It's just pizza, Ev," he said. "Relax. You don't even have to ask me to share it with you if you don't want. Which way is it to your place from here?"

"Left."

We walked another block in silence with David carrying the pizza box up high on one hand.

"Stop frowning," he said. "When I picked you up last night you were lighter than in Monterey. You've lost weight."

I shrugged. Not going there. Definitely not remembering him lifting me and my legs going around him and how badly I'd missed him and the sound of his voice as he—

"Yeah, well, I liked you the way you were," he said. "I love your curves. So I came up with another plan. You're getting pizza with fifteen cheeses on it until you've got them back.

"My first instinct here is to say something snarky about how my body is no longer any of your business."

"Lucky you thought twice about saying that, huh? Especially since you let me back into your body last night." He met my scowl with one of his own. "Look, I just don't want you losing weight and getting sick, especially not on my account. It's that simple. Forget the rest and stop giving the pizza dirty looks or you'll hurt its feelings."

"You're not the boss of me," I muttered.

He barked out a laugh. "You feel better for saying that?"

"Yes."

I gave him a wary smile. Having him beside me again felt too easy. I shouldn't get comfortable, who knew when it would once again blow up in my face? But the truth was, I wanted him there so bad it hurt.

"Ba—" He cleared his throat and tried again, without the sentiment that would have earned him an automatic smack-down. "Friend. Are we friends again?"

"I don't know."

He shook his head. "We're friends. Ev, you're sad, you're tired, and you've lost weight, and I fucking hate that I'm the cause of it. I'm going to make this right with you one step at a time. Just . . . give me a little room to maneuver here. I promise I won't step on your toes too badly."

"I don't trust you anymore, David."

His teasing smile fell. "I know you don't. And when you're ready we're gonna talk about that."

I swallowed hard against the lump in my throat.

"When you're ready," he reiterated. "Come on. Let's get you home so you can eat this while it's still hot."

We walked the rest of the way home in silence. I think it was companionable. David gave me occasional small smiles. They seemed genuine.

He tramped up the stairs behind me, not really bothering to look around. I'd forgotten he'd been here last night when he got my whereabouts from Lauren. I unlocked the door and took a peek inside, still scarred from catching Lauren and my brother on the couch last week. Living with them wasn't going to work long term. I think everyone was getting to the point of needing their own space.

The last month, though, had been beneficial for Nate and me. It had given us a chance to talk. We were closer than we'd ever been. He loved his job at the mechanic shop. He was happy and settled. Lauren was right, he'd changed. My brother had figured out what he wanted and where he belonged. Now if I could just get my shit together and do the same.

Rock music played softly and Nate and Lauren danced in the middle of the room. An impromptu thing, obviously, given my brother's still-greasy work clothes. Lauren didn't seem to care, holding on to him tight, staring into his eyes.

I cleared my throat to announce our arrival and stepped into the room.

Nate looked over and gave me a welcoming smile. But then he saw David. Blood suffused his face and his eyes changed. The temperature in the room seemed to rocket.

"Nate," I said, making a grab for him as he charged David.

"Shit." Lauren ran after him. "No!"

Nate's fist connected with David's face. The pizza went flying. David stumbled back, blood gushing from his nose.

"You fucking asshole," my brother yelled.

I jumped on Nate's back, trying to wrestle him back. Lauren grabbed at his arm. David did nothing. He covered his bloody face but made no move to protect himself from further damage.

"I'm going to fucking kill you for hurting her," Nate roared. David just looked at him, eyes accepting.

"Stop, Nate!" My feet dragged at the floor, my arms wrapped around my brother's windpipe.

"You want him here?" Nate asked me, incredulous. "Are you fucking serious?" Then he looked at Lauren tugging at his arm. "What are you doing?"

"This is between them, Nate."

"What? No! You saw what he did to her. What she's been like for the last month."

"You need to calm down. She doesn't want this." Lauren's hands patted over his face. "Please, babe. This isn't you."

Slowly, Nate pulled back. His shoulders dropped back to normal levels, his muscles relaxing. I gave up my choke hold on him, not that it had done much good. My brother did the raging bull thing scarily well. Blood leaked out from between David's fingers, dripped onto the floor. "Crap. Come on." I grabbed his arm and led him into our bathroom.

He leaned over the sink, swearing quietly but profusely. I bundled up some toilet paper and handed it to him. He stuffed it beneath his bloody nostrils.

"Is it broken?"

"I dunno." His voice was muffled, thick.

"I'm so sorry."

"S'okay." From his back jeans pocket came a ringing noise.

"I'll get it." Carefully, I extracted his phone. The name flash-ing on screen stopped me cold. The universe had to be playing a prank. Surely. Except it wasn't. It was just the same old heart-break playing out all over again inside of me. I could already feel the ice-cold numbness spreading through my veins.

"It's her." I held the phone out to him.

Above the ball of bloody toilet paper his nose looked wounded but intact. Violence wasn't going to help. No matter the anger working through me, winding me up just then.

His gaze jumped from the screen to me. "Ev."

"You should go. I want you to go."

"I haven't talked to Martha since that night. I've had nothing to do with her."

I shook my head, out of words. The phone rang shrilly, the noise piercing my eardrums. It echoed on and on inside the small bathroom. It vibrated in my hand and my whole body trembled. "Take it before I break it."

Bloodstained fingers took it from my hand.

"You gotta let me explain," he said. "I promise, she's gone."

"Then why is she calling you?"

"I don't know and I'm not answering. I haven't spoken to her once since I fired her. You gotta believe me."

"But I don't. I mean, how can I?"

He blinked pained eyes at me. We just stared at one another as realization dawned. This wasn't going to work. This had never been going to work. He was always secrets and lies, and I was always on the outside looking in. Nothing had changed. My heart was breaking all over again. Surprising, really, that there was enough of it left to worry over.

"Just go," I said, my stupid eyes welling up.

Without another word, he walked out.

CHAPTER NINETEEN

David and I didn't speak after that. But every afternoon after work he was there, waiting across the street. He'd be watching me from beneath the brim of his baseball cap. All ready to stalk me home safely. It pissed me off, but in no way did I feel threatened. I'd ignored him for three days as he trailed me. Today was day number four. He'd traded his usual black jeans for blue, boots for sneakers. Even from a distance, his upper lip and nose looked bruised. The paparazzi were still missing in action, though today someone had asked me if he was in town. His days of moving around Portland unknown were probably coming to an end. I wondered if he knew.

When I didn't just ignore him as per my usual modus operandi, he took a step forward. Then stopped. A truck passed between us among a steady stream of city traffic. This was crazy. Why was he still here? Why hadn't he just gone back to Martha? Moving on was impossible with him here.

Decision half made, I rushed across during the next break in traffic, meeting him on the opposite sidewalk.

"Hi," I said, not fussing with the strap on my bag at all. "What are you doing here, David?"

He stuffed his hands in his pockets, looked around. "I'm walking you home. Same as I do every day."

"This is your life now?"

"Guess so."

"Huh," I said, summing up the situation perfectly. "Why don't you go back to LA?"

Blue eyes watched me warily and he didn't answer at first. "My wife lives in Portland."

My heart stuttered. The simplicity of the statement and the sincerity in his eyes caught me off guard. I wasn't nearly as immune to him as I should have been. "We can't keep doing this."

He studied the street, not me, his shoulders hunched over. "Will you walk with me, Ev?"

I nodded. We walked. Neither of us rushed, instead strolling past shop fronts and restaurants, peering into bars just getting going for the evening. I had a bad feeling that once we stopped walking we'd have to start talking, so dawdling suited me fine. Summer nights meant there were a fair number of people around.

An Irish bar sat on a street corner about halfway home. Music blared out, some old song by the White Stripes. Hands still stuffed into his pockets, David gestured toward the bar with an elbow. "Wanna get a drink?"

It took me a moment to find my voice. "Sure."

He led me straight to a table at the back, away from the growing crowd of after-work drinkers. He ordered two pints of Guinness. Once they arrived, we sat in silence, sipping. After a moment, David took off his cap and set it on the table. Shit, his poor face. I could see it more clearly now, and he looked like he had two black eyes.

We sat there staring at one another in some bizarre sort of standoff. Neither of us spoke. The way he looked at me, like he'd been hurt too, like he was hurting . . . I couldn't take it. Waiting to drag this whole sorry mess of a relationship out into the light wasn't helping either of us. Time for a new plan. We'd clear the air, then get on with our respective lives. No more hurt and heartache. "You wanted to tell me about her?" I prompted, sitting up straighter, preparing myself for the worst.

"Yeah. Martha and I were together a long time. You probably already know, she was the one who cheated on me. The one we talked about."

I nodded.

We started the band when I was fourteen, Mal and Jimmy and me. Ben joined a year later and she'd hang around too. They were like family," he said, brow puckered. "They are family. Even when things went bad I couldn't just turn my back on her . . ."

"You kissed her."

He sighed. "No, she kissed me. Martha and I are finished."

"I'm guessing she doesn't know that, since she's still calling you and all."

"She's moved to New York, no longer working for the band. I don't know what the phone call was about. I didn't return it."

I nodded, only slightly appeased. Our problems weren't that clear-cut. "Does your heart understand you're finished with her? I guess I mean your head, don't I? The heart's just another muscle, really. Silly to say it decides anything."

"Martha and I are finished. We have been for a long time. I promise."

"Even if that's true, doesn't that just make me the consolation prize? Your attempt at a normal life?"

"Ev, no. That's not the way it is."

"Are you sure about that?" I asked, disbelief thick in my voice. I picked up my beer, gulping down the bitter dark ale and creamy foam. Something to calm the nerves. "I was getting over you," I said, my voice a pitiful, small thing. My shoulders were right back where they belonged, way down. "A month. I didn't really give up on you until day seven, though. Then I knew you weren't coming. I knew it was over then. Because if I'd been so important to you, you'd have said something by then, right? I mean, you knew I was in love with you. So you'd have put me out of my misery by then, wouldn't you?"

He said nothing.

"You're all secrets and lies, David. I asked you about the earring, remember?"

He nodded.

"You lied."

"Yeah. I'm sorry."

"Did you do that before or after our honesty rule? I can't remember. It was definitely after the cheating rule, though, right?" Talking was a mistake. All of the jagged thoughts and emotions he inspired caught up with me too fast.

He didn't deign to reply.

"What's the story behind the earrings, anyway?"

"I brought them with my first paycheck after the record company signed us."

"Wow. And you both wore them all this time. Even after she cheated on you and everything."

"It was Jimmy," he said. "She cheated on me with Jimmy."

Holy shit, his own brother. So many things fell into place with that piece of information. "That's why you got so upset about finding him and that groupie together. And when you saw Jimmy talking to me at that party."

"Yeah. It was all a long time ago, but . . . Jimmy flew back for an appearance on a TV show. We were in the middle of a big tour, playing Spain at the time. The second album had just hit the top ten. We were finally really pulling in the crowds."

"So you forgave them to keep the band together?"

"No. Not exactly. I just got on with things. Even back then Jimmy was drinking too much. He'd changed." He licked his lips, studied the table. "I'm sorry about that night. More fucking sorry than I can say. What you walked in on . . . I know how it must have looked. And I hated myself for lying to you about the earring, for still wearing it in Monterey."

He flicked at his ear in annoyance. There was a visible wound there with shiny, pink, nearly healed skin around it. It didn't look like a fading earring hole at all.

"What did you do there?" I asked.

"Cut across it with a knife." He shrugged. "An earring hole takes years to grow over. Made a new cut when you left so it could heal properly."

"Oh."

"I waited to come talk to you because I needed some time. You walking out on me after you'd promised you wouldn't . . . that was hard to take."

"I didn't have any choice."

He leaned toward me, his eyes hard. "You had a choice."

"I'd just seen my husband kissing another woman. And then you refused to even discuss it with me. You just started yelling at me about leaving. Again." My hands gripped the edge of the table so tight I could feel my fingernails pressing into the wood. "What the fuck should I have done, David? Tell me. Because I've played that scene over in my head so many times and it always works out the same way, with you slamming the door shut behind me."

"Shit." He slumped back in his seat. "You knew you leaving was a problem for me. You should have stuck with me, given me a chance to calm down. We worked it out in Monterey after that bar fight. We could have done it again."

"Rough sex doesn't fix everything. Sometimes you actually have to talk."

"I tried to talk to you the other night at that club. Wasn't what was on your mind."

I could feel my face heat up. It just pissed me off even more.

"Fuck. Look," he said, rubbing at the back of his neck. "The thing is, I needed to get us straight in my head, okay? I needed to figure out if us being together was the right thing. Honestly, Ev, I didn't want to hurt you again."

A month he'd left me to stew in my misery. It was on the tip of my tongue to give him a flippant thank-you. Or even to flip him off. But this was too serious.

"You got us straight in your head? That's great. I wish I could get us straight in my head." I stopped babbling long enough to drink more beer. My throat was giving sandpaper serious competition.

He held himself perfectly still, watching me crash and burn with an eerie calm.

"So, I'm kind of beat." I looked everywhere but at him. "Does that cover everything you wanted to talk about?"

"No."

"No? There's more?" Please, God, don't let there be more.

"Yeah."

"Have at it." Time to drink.

"I love you."

I spat beer across the table, all over our combined hands. "Shit."

"I'll get some napkins," he said, releasing my hand and rising out of his chair. A moment later he was back. I sat there like a useless doll while he cleaned my arm and then the table, trembling was all I was good for. Carefully, he pulled back my seat, helped me to my feet, and ushered me out of the bar. The hum of traffic and rush of city air cleared my senses. I had room to think out on the street.

Immediately my feet got moving. They knew what was up. My boots stomped across the pavement, putting serious distance between me and there. Getting the hell away from him and what he'd said. David stayed right on my heels, however.

We stopped at a street corner and I punched the button, waiting for the Walk light. "Don't say that again."

"Is it such a surprise, really? Why the fuck else would I be doing this, huh? Of course I love you."

"Don't." I turned on him, face furious.

His lips formed a tight line. "All right. I won't say that again. For now. But we should talk some more."

I growled, gnashed my teeth.

"Ev."

Crap. Negotiation wasn't my strong suit. Not with him. I wanted him gone. Or at least I was pretty certain I wanted him gone. Gone so I could resume my mourning for him and us and everything we might have been. Gone so I didn't have to think about the fact that he now thought he loved me. What utter emotional bullshit. My tear ducts went crazy right on cue. I took huge deep breaths trying to get myself back under control.

"Later, not today," he said, in an affable, reasonable voice. I didn't trust it or him at all.

"Fine."

I strode another block with him hanging at my side until again a red light stopped us cold, leaving room for conversation. He had better not speak. At least not until I got my shit together and figured all this out. I straightened my pencil skirt, tucked back my hair, fidgeted. The light took forever. Since when did Portland turn against me? This wasn't fair.

"We're not finished," he said. It sounded like both a threat and a promise.

The first text arrived at midnight while I was lying on my bed, reading. Or trying to read. Because trying to sleep had been a bust. School started back soon, but I was finding it hard to raise my usual enthusiasm for my studies. I had the worst feeling that the seed of doubt David had planted regarding my career choices had taken root inside my brain. I liked architecture, but I didn't love it. Did that matter? Sadly, I had no answers. Lots of excuses—some bullshit and some valid—but no answers.

David would probably say I could do whatever the fuck I wanted to. I knew all too well what my father would say. It wouldn't be pretty.

I'd been avoiding seeing my parents since I got back. Easy enough to do considering I'd hung up on the lecture my father had attempted to give me the second day after my return. Relations had been frosty since then. The real surprise was that I wasn't surprised. They had never encouraged anything that didn't directly support the plan. There was a reason I'd never returned their calls when I was in Monterey. Because I couldn't tell them the things they wanted to hear anymore, it had seemed safer to stay mute.

Nathan had been running interference with the folks, which I appreciated, but my time was up. We'd all been summoned to dinner tomorrow night. I figured the text was my mother ensuring I wasn't going to try and weasel out of it. Sometimes she sat up late watching old black-and-white movies when her sleeping pills didn't kick in.

I was wrong.

David: She surprised me when she kissed me. That's
why I didn't stop her right away. But I didn't want it.

I stared at my cell, frowning.

David: You there?
Me: Yeah.
David: I need to know if you believe me about Martha.

Did I? I took a breath, searched deep. There was frustration,
plenty of confusion, but my anger had apparently burned itself
out at long last. Because I didn't doubt he'd told me the truth.

Me: I believe you.
David: Thank you. I keep thinking of more. Will you lis-
ten?
Me: Yes.
David: My folks got married because of Jimmy. Mom left
when I was 12. She drank. Jimmy's been paying her to
keep quiet. She's been hustling him for years.
Me: Holy hell!
David: Yeah. I got lawyers onto it now.
Me: Glad to hear it.
David: We retired Dad to Florida. I told him about you.
He wants to meet.
Me: Really? I don't know what to say . . .
David: Can I come up?
Me: You're here??

I didn't wait for a reply. Forget my pajama shorts and ragged
old T-shirt, washed so many times its original color was a faded
memory. He'd just have to take me as he found me. I unlocked the

front door of our apartment and padded down the stairs on bare feet, my cell still in my hand. Sure enough, a tall shadow loomed through the frosted glass of the building's front door. I pushed it open to find him sitting on the step. Outside, the night was still, peaceful. A fancy silver SUV was pulled up at the curb.

"Hey," he said, a finger busy on the screen of his cell. Mine beeped again.

David: Wanted to say good night.

"Okay," I said, looking up from the screen. "Come in."

The side of his mouth lifted and he looked up at me. I met his gaze, refusing to feel self-conscious. He didn't seem put off by my slacker bedtime style. If anything, his smile increased, his eyes warming. "You about to go to bed?"

"I was just reading. Couldn't sleep."

"Is your brother here?" He stood and followed me back up the stairs, his sneakers loud on the old wooden floors. I half expected Mrs. Lucia from downstairs to come out and yell. It was a hobby of hers.

"No," I said, closing the door behind us. "He and Lauren went out."

He looked around the apartment with interest. As usual he took up all the space. I don't know how he did that. It was like a magician's trick. He was somehow so much bigger than he actually seemed. And the man didn't seem small to begin with. In no rush at all, his gaze wandered around the room, taking in bright turquoise walls (Lauren's doing) and the shelves of neatly stacked books (my doing).

"Is this yours?" he asked, poking his head into my bedroom.

"Ah, yes. It's a bit of a mess right now, though." I squeezed past him and started speed-cleaning, picking up the books and other assorted debris scattered across the floor. I should have asked him to give me five minutes before coming up. My mother would be horrified. Since returning from LA I'd let my world descend into chaos. It suited my frazzled state of mind. Didn't mean David needed to see it. I needed to make a plan to clean up my act and actually stick to it this time.

"I used to be organized," I said, flailing, my fallback position for everything lately.

"It doesn't matter."

"This won't take a minute."

"Ev," he said, catching hold of my wrist in much the same manner that his gaze caught me. "I don't care. I just need to talk to you."

A sudden horrible thought entered my mind. "Are you leaving?" I asked, today's dirty work shirt clutched in my suddenly shaking hand.

His grip tightened around my wrist. "You want me to leave?"

"No. I mean, are you leaving Portland? Is that why you're here, to say good-bye?"

"No."

"Oh." The pincer grip my ribs had gotten on my heart and lungs eased back a little. "Okay."

"Where did that come from?" When I didn't answer, he tugged me gently toward him. "Hey."

I took a reluctant step in his direction, dropping the dirty laundry. He pressed for more, sitting on my bed and pulling me down alongside him. I sort of stumbled my butt onto the double mattress as opposed to doing it with any grace. Story of my life. Object achieved, he gave up his grip on me. My hands clenched the edge of the bed.

"So, you got a weird look on your face and then you asked me if I was leaving," he said, blue eyes concerned. "Care to explain?"

"You haven't turned up at midnight before. I guess I wondered if there was more to it than just dropping by."

"I drove by your apartment and I saw your light was on. Figured I'd send you a text, see what mood you were in after our talk today." He rubbed at his bearded chin with the palm of his hand. "Plus, like I said, I keep thinking of stuff I need to tell you."

"You drive by my apartment often?"

He gave me a wry smile. "Only a couple of times. It's my way of saying good night to you."

"How did you know which window was mine?"

"Ah, well, that time I talked to Lauren when I was first came to town? She had the light on in the other room. Figured this one must be yours." He didn't look at me, choosing instead to check out the photos of me and my friends on the walls. "You mad that I've been around?"

"No," I answered honestly. "I think I might be running out of mad."

"You are?"

"Yeah."

He let out a slow breath and stared back at me, saying nothing. Dark bruises lingered beneath his eyes, though his swollen nose had gone back to normal size.

"I really am sorry Nate hit you."

"If I was your brother, I'd have done the exact same fucking thing." He braced his elbows on his knees but kept his face turned toward me.

"Would you?"

"Without question."

Males and their penchant for beating on things, it knew no end.

The silence dragged out. It wasn't uncomfortable, exactly. At least we weren't fighting or rehashing our breakup one more time. Being broken and angry got old.

"Can we just hang out?" I asked.

"Absolutely. Lemme see this." He picked up my iPhone and started flicking through the music files. "Where are the earbuds?"

I hopped up and retrieved them from among the crap on my desk. David plugged them in, then handed me an earbud. I sat at his side, curious what he'd choose out of my music. When the rocking, jumpy beat of "Jackson" by Johnny Cash and June Carter started, I looked at him in amusement. He smirked and mouthed the lyrics. We had indeed gotten married in a fever.

"You making fun of me?" I asked.

Light danced in his eyes. "I'm making fun of us."

"Fair enough."

"What else have you got here?"

Cash and Carter finished and he continued his search for songs. I watched his face, waiting for a reaction to my musical tastes. All I got was a smothered yawn.

"They're not that bad," I protested.

"Sorry. Big day."

"David, if you're tired, we don't have to—"

"No. I'm fine. But do you mind if I lie down?"

David on my bed. Well, he was already on my bed but . . . "Sure."

He gave me a cagey look but started tugging off his sneakers. "You just being polite?"

"No, it's fine. And, I mean, legally the bed is still half yours,"

I joked, pulling out the earbud before his movements did it for me. "So, what did you do today?"

"Been working on the new album and sorting out some stuff." Hands behind his head, he stretched out across my bed. "You lying down too? We can't share the music if you don't."

I crawled on and lay down next to him, wriggling around a bit, making myself comfortable. It was, after all, my bed. And he would be the only male who'd ever lain on it. The slight scent of his soap came to me, clean and warm and David. All too well, I remembered. For once, hurt didn't seem to come attached to the memory. I poked around inside my head, double-checking. When I'd said I was out of mad, it had apparently been nothing more than the truth. We had our issues, but him cheating on me wasn't one of them. I knew that now and it meant a lot.

"Here." He handed me back the earbud and started playing with my cell again.

"How's Jimmy?" I rolled onto my side, needing to see him. The strong line of his nose and jaw was in profile, the curve of his lips. How many times had I kissed him? Not nearly enough to last me if it never happened again.

"He's doing a lot better. Seems to have really gotten himself right. I think he's going to be okay."

"That's great news."

"At least he comes by his problems honestly," he said, his tone turning bitter. "Our mother is a fucking disaster from what I hear. But then, she always was. She used to take us to the park because she needed to score. She'd turn up to school plays and parent-teacher nights high as a kite."

I kept my mouth shut, letting him get it out. The best thing I could do for him was to be there and listen. The pain and anger in his voice were heartbreaking. My parents had their overbearing issues, certainly, but nothing like this. David's childhood had been terrible. If I could have bitch-slapped his mother right then for putting that pain in his voice, I would have. Twice over.

"Dad ignored her using for years. He could. He was a long-haul truck driver, away most of the time. Jimmy and me were the ones that had to put up with her shit. The number of times we'd come home to find her babbling all sorts of stuff or passed out on the couch. There'd be no food in the house 'cause she'd spent the grocery money on pills. Then one day we came home from school and she and the TV were gone. That was it." He stared up at nothing, his face drawn. "She didn't even leave a note. Now she's back and she's been hurting Jimmy. It drives me nuts."

"That must have been hard for you," I said. "Hearing about her from Jimmy."

One of his shoulders did a little lift. "He shouldn't have had to deal with her on his own. Said he wanted to protect me. Seems my big brother isn't a completely selfish prick."

"Thank you for texting me."

"S'okay. What do you feel like listening to?" The sudden change in topic told me he didn't want to talk about his family anymore. He yawned again, his jaw cracking. "Sorry."

"The Saint Johns."

He nodded, flicking through to find the only song I had of theirs. The strum of the guitar started softly, filling my head. He put the cell on his chest and his eyelids drifted down. A man and a woman took turns singing about their head and their heart. Throughout it, his face remained calm, relaxed. I started to wonder if he'd fallen asleep. But when the song finished, he turned to look at me.

"Nice. A bit sad," he said.

"You don't think they'll be together in the end?"

He rolled onto his side too. There was no more than a hand's width between us. With a curious look, he handed me the cell. "Play me another song you like."

I scrolled through the screens, trying to decide what to play for him. "I forgot to tell you, someone was in saying she'd seen you today. Your anonymity might be about to run out."

He sighed. "Bound to happen sooner or later. They'll just have to get used to me being around."

"You're really not leaving?" I tried to keep my voice light, but it didn't work.

"No. I'm really not." He looked at me and I just knew he saw everything. All of my fears and dreams and the hopes I did my best to keep hidden, even from myself. But I couldn't hide from him if I tried. "Okay?"

"Okay," I said.

"You asked me if you were my attempt at normal. I need you to understand, that's not it at all. Being with you, the way I feel about you, it does ground me. But that's because it makes me question fucking everything. It makes me want to make things better. Makes me want to be better. I can't hide from shit or make excuses when it comes to you, because that won't work. Neither of us is happy when things are that way, and I want you to be happy . . ." His forehead furrowed and his dark brows drew tight. "Do you understand?"

"I think so," I whispered, feeling so much for him right then I didn't know which way was up.

He yawned again, his jaw cracking. "Sorry. Fuck, I'm beat. You mind if I close my eyes for five minutes?"

"No."

He did so. "Play me another song?"

"On it."

I played him "Revelator" by Gillian Welch, the longest, most soothing song I could find. I'd guess he fell asleep about half-way through. His features relaxed and his breathing deepened. Carefully, I pulled out the earbuds and put the cell away. I switched on the bedside lamp and turned off the main one, shut the door so Lauren and Nate's eventual return didn't wake him. Then I lay back down and just stared at him. I don't know for how long. The compulsion to stroke his face or trace his tattoos made my fingers itch, but I didn't want to wake him. He obviously needed the sleep.

When I woke up in the morning, he was gone. Disappointment was a bitter taste. I'd just had the best night's sleep I'd had in weeks, devoid of the usual tense and angsty dreams I seemed to specialize in of late. When had he left? I rolled onto my back and something crinkled, complaining loudly. With a hand, I fished out a piece of paper. It had obviously been torn from one of my notepads. The message was brief but beautiful:

I'm still not leaving Portland.

CHAPTER TWENTY

I think I'd have preferred to find Genghis Khan staring back at me from across the café counter than Martha. I don't know—a Mongol horde versus Martha, tough call. Both were horrible in their own unique ways.

The lunchtime crowd had eased to a few determined patrons, settling in for the afternoon with their lattes and friands. It had been a busy day and Ruby had been distracted, messing up orders. Not like her usual self at all. I'd sat her at a corner table with a pot of tea for a while. Then we'd gotten busy again. When I'd asked what was wrong, she'd just waved me away. Eventually, I'd corner her.

And now here was Martha.

"We need to talk," she said. Her dark hair was tied back and her makeup minimal. There was none of the LA flashiness to her now. If anything, she seemed somber, subdued. Still just a touch smarmy, but hey, this was Martha, after all. And what the hell was she doing here?

"Ruby, is it okay if I take my break?" Jo was out back stocking shelves. She'd just come back from her break, making me due for mine. Ruby nodded, giving Martha a covert evil eye. No matter what was going on with her, Ruby was good people. She recognized a man-stealing sea monster when she saw one.

Martha headed back outside with her nose in the air, and I followed. The usual flow of city traffic cruised by. Overhead, the sky was clear blue, a perfect summer's day. I'd have felt more comfortable if nature had been about to dump a bucket-load of rain on top of her perfect head, but it was not to be.

After a brief inspection of the surface, Martha perched on the edge of a bench. "Jimmy called me."

I sat down a little way away from her.

"Apparently he has to apologize to people as part of his re-hab process." Perfectly manicured nails tapped at the wooden seat. "It wasn't much of an apology, actually. He told me I needed to come to Portland and clean up the shit I'd caused between you and David."

She stared determinedly ahead. "Things aren't great between Ben and him. I love my brother. I don't want him on the outs with Dave because of me."

"What do you expect me to do here, Martha?"

"I don't expect you to do anything for me. I just want you to listen." She ducked her chin, shut her eyes for a second. "I always figured I could get him back whenever I wanted. After he'd had a few years to calm down, of course. He never got to screw around, we were each other's first. So I just bided my time, let him sow all the wild oats. I was his one true love, right, no matter what I'd done? He was still out there playing those songs about me night after night, wearing our earring even after all those years . . ."

Traffic roared past, people chatted, but Martha and I were apart from it. I wasn't sure I wanted to hear this, but I soaked up every word anyway, desperate to understand.

"Turns out artists can be very sentimental." Her laughter sounded self-mocking. "It doesn't necessarily mean anything." She turned to me, eyes hard, hateful. "I think I was just a habit for him back then. He never gave up a damn thing for me. He sure as hell never moved cities to fit in with what I wanted."

"What do you mean?"

"He's got the album written, Ev. Apparently the new songs are brilliant. The best he's ever done. There's no reason he couldn't be in whatever studio he wanted putting it together, doing what he loves. Instead he's here, recording in some setup a few streets over. Because being close to you means more to him." She rocked forward, her smile harsh. "He's sold the Monterey house, bought a place here. I waited years for him to come back, to have time for me. For you he reorganizes everything in the blink of a fucking eye."

"I didn't know," I said, stunned.

"The band is all here. They're recording at a place called the Bent Basement."

"I've heard of it."

"If you're stupid enough to let him go, then you deserve to be miserable for a very long time." The woman looked at me like she had firsthand experience with that situation. She stood, brushed off her hands. "That's me done."

Martha walked away. She disappeared among the crowds of midafternoon shoppers like she'd never been.

David was recording in Portland. He'd said he was working on the new album. I hadn't imagined that meant actually recording here. Let alone buying a place.

Holy shit.

I stood and moved in the opposite direction from the one Martha had taken. First I walked, trying to figure out what I was doing, giving my brain a chance to catch up with me. Then I gave it up as a lost cause and ran, dodging pedestrians and café tables, parked cars and whatever. Faster and faster my Doc Martens boots carried me. I found the Bent Basement two blocks over, situated down a flight of stairs, between a micro-brewery and an upmarket dress shop. I slapped my hands against the wood, pushed it open. The unassuming green door was unlocked. Speakers carried the strains of an almighty electric guitar solo through the dark-painted rooms. Sam sat on a sofa, reading a magazine. For once his standard black suit was missing, and he wore slacks and a short-sleeved Hawaiian shirt.

"Mrs. Ferris," He smiled.

"Hi, Sam," I panted, trying to catch my breath. "You look very cool."

He winked at me. "Mr. Ferris is in one of the sound booths at the moment, but if you go through that door there you'll be able to observe."

"Thanks, Sam. Good to see you again."

The thick door led to the soundboard setup. A man I didn't know sat behind it with headphones on. This setup left the small studio at Monterey in the dust. Through the window I could see David playing, his eyes closed, enmeshed with the music. He too wore headphones.

"Hey," Jimmy said quietly. I hadn't realized the rest of them were behind me, lounging, waiting to take their turn.

"Hi, Jimmy."

He gave me a strained smile. His suit was gone. So were the pinprick eyes. "It's good to see you here."

"Thanks." I didn't know what the etiquette was regarding rehab. Should I ask after his health, or sweep the situation under the rug? "And thank you for calling Martha."

"She came to talk to you, huh? Good. I'm glad." He slid his hands into the pockets of his black jeans. "Least I could do. I'm sorry about our previous meetings, Ev. I was . . . not where I should have been. I hope we can move on from that."

Off the drugs, the similarities between him and David were

more pronounced. But his blue eyes and his smile didn't do to me the things David's did. No one else's ever could. Not in five years, not in fifty. For the first time in a long time, I could accept that. I was good with it, even. The epiphanies seemed to be coming thick and fast today.

Jimmy waited patiently for me to come back from wherever I was and say something. When I didn't, he continued on. "I've never had a sister-in-law before."

"I've never had a brother-in-law."

"No? We're useful for all sorts of shit. Just you wait and see."

I smiled and he smiled back at me, far more relaxed this time.

Ben sat on the corner of a black leather lounge, talking with Mal. Mal tipped his chin at me, and I did the same back. All Ben gave me was a worried look. He was still every bit as big and imposing, but he seemed more afraid of me than I was of him today. I nodded hello to him and he returned it, with a tight smile. After talking to Martha, I could understand a little better where he'd been coming from that night. We'd never be besties, but there would be peace for David's sake.

The guitar solo cut off. I turned back to see David watching me, pulling off his headphones. Then he lifted his guitar strap off over his head and headed for the connecting door.

"Hey," he said, coming toward me. "Everything okay?"

"Yes. Can we talk?"

"Sure." He ushered me back into the booth. "Won't be long, Jack."

The man at the board nodded and fiddled with some buttons, turning off the microphones, I assume. He didn't seem overly irritated with the interruption. Instruments and microphones were everywhere. The place was organized chaos. We stood in the corner, out of view of the rest.

"Martha came to see me," I said once he'd closed the door. He stood tall in front of me, blocking out everything else. I rested my back against the wall and looked up at him, still trying to catch my breath. My heart had been calming down after the sprint. Had been. But now he was here and he was so damn close. I put my hands behind my back before they started grabbing at him.

David did the wrinkly brow thing. "Martha?"

"It's okay," I rushed on. "Well, you know, she was her usual self. But we talked."

"About what?"

"You two, mostly. She gave me some things to think about. Are you busy tonight?"

His eyes widened slightly. "No. Would you like to do something?"

"Yeah." I nodded. "I missed you this morning when I woke up, when I realized you'd gone. I've missed you a lot, the last month. I don't think I ever told you that."

He exhaled hard. "No . . . no, you haven't. I missed you too. I'm sorry I couldn't stay this morning."

"Another time."

"Definitely." He took a step closer till the toes of his boots touched mine. No one had ever been more welcome in my personal space. "I'd promised we'd start here early or I would have been there when you woke."

"You didn't tell me about the band recording here."

"We've had other things to deal with. I thought it could wait."

"Right. That makes sense." I stared at the wall beside me, trying to get my thoughts in order. After a whole lot of slow and painful, everything seemed to be happening at once.

". . . About tonight, Ev?"

"Oh, I'm going to dinner at my parents'."

"Am I invited?"

"Yes," I said. "Yes, you are."

"Okay. Great."

"Did you actually buy a house here?"

"A three-bedroom condo a couple of blocks up. I figured it was close to your work and not too far from your school . . . you know, just in case." He studied my face. "Would you like to see it?"

"Wow." I changed the subject to buy some time. "Uh, Jimmy's looking well."

He smiled and put his hands either side of my head, closing the distance between us. "Yeah. He's doing good. Relocating up here is working out well for pretty much everyone. Seems I wasn't the only one ready for a break from all the fuckwittery in LA. Our playing's sharper than it's been in years. We're focusing on the important stuff again."

"That's great."

"Now, what did Martha say to you, baby?"

The endearment came accompanied by the warm old familiar feeling. I almost swayed, I was so grateful. "Well, we talked about you."

"I get that."

"I guess I'm still making sense of everything."

He nodded slowly, leaning in until our noses almost brushed. The perfect intimacy of it, the faint feel of his breath against my face. My need to get close to him had never disappeared. No matter how I'd tried to shut it down. Love and heartbreak made you breathtakingly stupid, desperate, even. The things you'd try to tell yourself to make it through, hoping one day you'd believe it.

"All right," he said. "Anything I can help you with?"

"No. I just wanted to check you were really here, I think."

"I'm here."

"Yes."

"That's not changing, Evelyn."

"No. I think I get that now. I guess I can be a little slow sometimes picking up on these things. I just wasn't sure, you know, with everything that's happened. But I still love you." Apparently I was back to blurting crap out whenever it occurred to me. With David, though, it was okay. I was safe. "I do."

"I know, baby. The question is, when are you going to come back to me?"

"It's really big, you know? It hurt so much when it fell apart last time."

He nodded sadly. "You left me. I think that's about the worst fucking thing I've ever experienced."

"I had to go, but also . . . part of it was me wanting to hurt you like you'd hurt me, I think." I needed to hold his hand again, but I didn't feel like I could. "I don't want to be vindictive like that, not with you, not ever again."

"I said some horrible shit to you that night. Both of us were hurting. We're just going to have to forgive each other and let it go."

"You didn't write a song about it, did you?"

He looked away.

"No! David," I said, aghast. "You can't. That was such a terrible night."

"On a scale of one to ten, how pissed would you be exactly?"

"Where one is divorce?"

He moved his lower body closer, placing his feet between mine. There was no more than a hair's breadth between us. I'd never catch my breath at this rate. Never.

"No," he said, his voice soft. "You don't even remember us getting married, so divorce or annulment or what-the-fuck-ever is not on. It never was. I just told the lawyers to keep looking busy for the last month while I figured things out. Did I forget to mention that?"

"Yeah, you did." I couldn't help but smile at that. "So what's one?"

"One is now. It's this, us living apart and being fucking miserable without each other."

"That is pretty horrible."

"It is," he agreed.

"Is the song a headliner, or are you just going to shove it in somewhere and hope no one notices? It's just a B-side or something, right? Unlisted and hidden at the end?"

"Let's pretend we'd been talking about making one of the songs the name of the album."

"One of them? How much of this brilliant album I've been hearing about is going to be about us?"

"I love you."

"David." I tried to maintain the mock angry, but it didn't work. I didn't have the strength for it.

"Can you trust me?" He asked, his face suddenly serious. "I need you to trust me again. About more than just the songs. Seeing that worry in your eyes all the time is fucking killing me."

"I know." I frowned, knitting my fingers together behind my back. "I'm getting there. And I'll learn to deal with the songs. Really. Music is a big part of who you are, and it's a huge compliment that you feel that strongly for me. I was mostly just teasing."

"I know. And they're not all about us splitting up."

"No?"

"No."

"That's good. I'm glad."

"Mm."

I licked my lips and his eyes tracked the movement. I waited for him to close the distance between us and kiss me. But he didn't and I didn't either. For some reason, it wasn't right to rush this. It should be perfect. Everything between us settled. No people waiting in the next room. Us being this close together, however, hearing the low rumble of his voice, I could have stayed there all day. But Ruby would be wondering what the hell had happened to me. I also had a small errand to run before I returned.

"I'd better get back to work," I said.

"Right." He drew back, slowly. "What time would you like me to pick you up tonight?"

"Ah, seven?"

"Sounds good." A shadow passed over his face. "Do you think your parents will like me?"

I took a deep breath and let it go. "I don't know. It doesn't matter. I like you."

"You do?"

I nodded.

The light in his eyes was like the sun rising. My knees trembled and my heart quaked. It was powerful and beautiful and perfect.

"That's all that matters, then," he said.

CHAPTER TWENTY-ONE

My parents hadn't liked him. For the better part of the meal they'd ignored David's presence. Every time they blatantly passed him over, I'd opened my mouth to object and David's foot would nudge mine beneath the table. He'd given me a small shake of the head. I'd sat and steamed, my anger growing by the moment. Things had long since moved beyond awkward, though Lauren had done her best to cover the silences.

David, for his part, had gone all out, wearing a gray button-down shirt with the sleeves secured to his wrists. It covered the bulk of his tattoos. Black jeans and plain black boots completed his meet-the-parents wardrobe. Considering he'd refused to dress up for a ballroom full of Hollywood royalty, I was impressed. He'd even poofed up his hair into a vaguely James Dean do. On most men I would not have liked it. David was not most men. Frankly, he looked gosh-almighty awesome, even with the fading bruises beneath his eyes. And the gracious manner with which he dealt with my parents' abysmal behavior only reinforced my belief in him. My pride that he'd chosen to be with me. But back to the dinner conversation.

Lauren was giving a detailed synopsis of her plans for classes for the upcoming semester. My dad nodded and listened intently, asking all the appropriate questions. Nate's falling for her was beyond my parents' wildest dreams. She'd been a de facto part of the family for a long time now. They couldn't have been more delighted. But more than that, she seemed to make them take a look at their son anew, noticing the changes in him. When Lauren talked about Nate's work and his responsibilities, they listened.

Meanwhile, David was only on the other side of the table, but I missed him. There was so much to talk about that I didn't know where to start. And hadn't we already talked over the bulk of it? So what was the problem? I had the strangest sensation that something was wrong, something was slipping away from me. David had moved to Portland. All would be well. But it wasn't. Classes started back soon. The threat of the plan still hung over my head because I allowed it to.

"Ev? Is something wrong?" Dad sat at one end of the table, his face drawn with concern.

"No, Dad," I said, my smile full of gritted teeth. There'd been no mention of my hanging up on him. I suspected it had been chalked up to brokenhearted girl rage or something similar.

Dad frowned, first at me and then at David. "My daughter goes back to school next week."

"Ah, yes," said David. "She did mention that, Mr. Thomas."

My father studied David from over the top of his glasses. "Her studies are very important."

A cold kind of panic gripped me as the horror unrolled right before my eyes. "Dad. Stop."

"Yes, Mr. Thomas," said David. "I have no intention of interrupting them."

"Good." Dad steepled his hands in front of him, settling in to give a lecture. "But the fact is, young women imagining themselves in love have a terrible tendency to not think."

"Dad—"

My dad held up a hand to stop me. "Ever since she was a little girl, she's planned to become an architect."

"Okay. No."

"What if you go on tour, David?" my father asked, continuing despite my commotion. "As you inevitably will. Do you expect her to drop everything and just follow you?"

"That would be up to your daughter, sir. But I don't plan on doing anything to make her have to choose between me and school. Whatever she wants to do, she's got my support."

"She wants to be an architect," Dad said, his tone absolute. "This relationship has already cost her dearly. She had an important internship canceled when all of this nonsense happened. It's set her back considerably."

I pushed back, rising from my chair. "That's enough."

Dad gave me the same glare he'd first dealt David, hostile and unwelcome. He looked at me like he no longer recognized me.

"I won't have you throwing away your future for him," he thundered.

"Him?" I asked, horrified at his tone. Anger had been pooling inside of me all night, filling me up. No wonder I'd barely touched my dinner. "The person you've both been unconscionably rude to for the past hour? David is the last person who would expect me to throw away anything that mattered to me."

"If he cared for you, he would walk away. Look at the damage he's done." A vein bulged on the side of my father's forehead as he stood too. Everyone else watched in stunned silence. It could be said I'd gone the bulk of my life backing down. But those had all been about things that didn't matter, not really. This was different.

"You're wrong."

"You're out of control," my father snarled, pointing his finger at me.

"No," I said to my father. Then I turned and said what I should have said a long time ago to my husband. "No, I'm not. What I am is the luckiest fucking girl in the entire world."

A smile lit David's eyes. He sucked in his bottom lip, trying to keep the happy contained in the face of my parents' fury.

"I am," I said, tearing up and not even minding for once.

He pushed back his chair and rose to his feet, facing me across the table. The promise of unconditional love and support in his eyes was all the answer I needed. And in that one perfect moment, I knew everything was fine. We were fine. We always would be if we stuck together. There wasn't a single doubt inside of me. In silence, he walked around the table and stood at my side.

The look on my parents' faces . . . whoa. They always said it was best to rip the Band-Aid off all at once, though, get it over and done with. So I did.

"I don't want to be an architect." The relief in finally saying it was staggering. I'm almost certain my knees knocked. There'd be no backing down, however. David took my hand in his, gave it a squeeze.

My father just blinked at me. "You don't mean that."

"I'm afraid I do. It was your dream, Dad. Not mine. I should never have gone along with this. That was my mistake and I'm sorry."

"What will you do?" asked my mother, her voice rising. "Make coffee?"

"Yes."

"That's ridiculous. All that money we spent—" Mom's eyes flashed in anger.

"I'll pay it back."

"This is insane," Dad said, his face going pale. "This is about him."

"No. This is about me, actually. David just made me start questioning what I really wanted. He made me want to be a better person. Lying about this, trying to fit in with your plan for so long . . . I was wrong to do that."

My father glared at me. "I think you should leave now, Evelyn. Think this over carefully. We'll talk about it later."

I guessed we would, but it wouldn't change anything. My good-girl status had well and truly taken a dive.

"You forgot to tell her that whatever she decides, you still love her." Nathan got to his feet, pulling out Lauren's chair for her. He faced my father with his jaw set. "We'd better go too."

"She knows that." Face screwed up in confusion, Dad stood at the head of the table.

Nate grunted. "No, she doesn't. Why do you think she fell into line for so many years?"

Mom knotted her hands.

"That's ridiculous," sputtered Dad.

"No, he's right," I said. "But I guess everyone has to grow up sometime."

Dad's eyes turned even colder. "Being an adult is not about turning your back on your responsibilities."

"Following in your footsteps is not my responsibility," I said, refusing to back down. The days of my doing that were gone. "I can't be you. I'm sorry I wasted so many years and so much of your money figuring that out."

"We only want what's best for you," said Mom, voice thick with emotion.

"I know you do. But that's for me to decide now." I turned

back to my husband, keeping a firm hold on his hand. "And my husband isn't going anywhere. You need to accept that."

Nate walked around the table, gave Mom a kiss. "Thanks for dinner."

"One day," she said, looking between the both of us, "when you have your own children, then you'll understand how hard it is."

Her words pretty much wrapped things up. My dad just kept shaking his head and huffing out breaths. I felt guilty for disappointing them. But not bad enough to return to my former ways. I'd finally reached an age where I understood that my parents were people too. They weren't perfect or omnipotent. They were every bit as fallible as me. It was my job to judge what was right.

I picked up my handbag. It was time to go.

David nodded to both my parents and escorted me out. A sleek new silver Lexus Hybrid sat waiting by the curb. It wasn't a big SUV like the ones Sam and the other bodyguards used. This one came in a more user-friendly size. Behind us, Nate and Lauren climbed into his car. Nothing much was said. Mom and Dad stood in the house's open doorway, dark silhouettes from the light behind them. David opened the door for me and I climbed into the passenger seat.

"I'm sorry about my father. Are you upset?" I asked.

"No." He shut my door and walked around to the driver's side.

"No? That's it?"

He shrugged. "He's your dad. Of course he's going to be concerned."

"I thought you might have been running for the hills by now with all the drama."

He flicked on the indicator and pulled out onto the road. "Did you really?"

"No. Sorry, that was a stupid thing to say." I watched my old neighborhood passing by, the park I'd played in and the path I'd taken to school. "So I'm a college dropout."

He gave me curious glance. "How does that feel?"

"God, I don't know." I shook my hands, rubbed them together. "Tingly. My toes and hands feel tingly. I don't know what I'm doing."

"Do you know what you want to do?"

"No. Not really."

"But you know what you don't want to do?"

"Yes," I answered definitely.

"Then there's your starting point."

A full moon hung heavy in the sky. The stars twinkled on. And I'd just upended my entire existence. Again. "You're now officially married to a college dropout who makes coffee for a living. Does that bother you?"

With a sigh, David flicked on the indicator and pulled over in front of a neat row of suburban houses. He picked up one of my hands, pressing it gently between both of his. "If I wanted to quit the band, would that bother you?"

"Of course not. That's your decision."

"If I wanted to give all the money away, what would you say?"

I shrugged. "You made the money, it's your choice. I guess you'd have to come live with me then. And I'm telling you now, the apartment we'd have on my salary alone would be small. Minuscule. Just so you know."

"But you'd still take me in?"

"Without question." I covered one of his hands with my

own, needing to borrow a bit of his strength just then. "Thank you for being there tonight."

Little creases lined his perfect dark blue eyes. "I didn't even say anything."

"You didn't have to."

"You called me your husband."

I nodded, my heart stuck in my throat.

"I didn't kiss you at the studio today because it felt like there was still too much up in the air between us. It didn't feel right. But I want to kiss you now."

"Please," I said.

He leaned into me and I met him halfway. His mouth covered mine, lips warm and firm and familiar. The only ones I wanted or needed. His hands cupped my face, holding me to him. The kiss was so sweet and perfect. It was a promise, one that wouldn't be broken this time. We'd both learned from our mistakes and we'd keep learning all our lives. That was marriage.

His fingers eased into my hair and I stroked my tongue against his. The taste of him was as necessary to me as air. The feel of his hands on me was the promise of everything to come. What started out as an affirmation turned into more at light speed. The groan that came out of him. Holy hell. I wanted to hear that noise for the rest of my life. My hands dragged at his shirt, trying to pull him closer. We had some serious time to make up for.

"We have to stop," he whispered.

"We do?" I asked, in between panting breaths.

"Sadly." He chuckled, nudged the tip of my nose with his. "Soon, my luckiest fucking girl in the world. Soon. Did you really have to throw the 'fucking' in there?"

"I really did."

"Your parents looked about ready to have kittens."

"I'm so sorry about the way they treated you." I ran my fingers over the spiky short dark hair on the side of his head, feeling the bristles.

"I can deal."

"You shouldn't have to. You won't have to. I'm not sitting by and—"

He shut down my rant by kissing me. Of course, it worked. His tongue played over my teeth, teasing me. I undid my seat belt and crawled into his lap, needing to get closer. Nobody kissed like David. His hands slipped beneath my top, molding to the curves of my breasts. Thumbs stroked my nipples. The poor things were so damn hard it hurt. Talking of which, I could feel David's erection pressing into my hip. We kept our lips locked until a car full of kids went by, horn blaring. Apparently our makeout session was somewhat visible from the street despite the fogged-up windows. Classy.

"Soon," he promised, his breathing harsh against my neck. "Fuck, it's good to get you alone. That was intense. But I'm proud of you for standing up for yourself. You did good."

"Thank you. You think we'll understand when we have kids, like my mom said?"

He looked up at me, his beautiful face and serious eyes so wonderfully familiar I could cry.

"We've never talked about kids," he said. "Do you want them?"

"One day. Do you?"

"One day, yeah. After we've had a few years' worth of alone time."

"Sounds good," I said. "You going to show me this condo of yours?"

"Of ours. Absolutely."

"I think you're going to need to take your hands out of my top if you're planning on driving us there."

"Mm. Pity." He gave my breasts a final squeeze before slipping his hands free of my clothing. "And you're going to have to hop back into your seat."

"Okeydokey."

His hands wrapped around my hips, helping me climb back over to my side of the vehicle. I refastened my seat belt while he took a deep breath. With a wince he adjusted himself, obviously trying to get more comfortable. "You're a terror."

"Me? What did I do?"

"You know what you did," he grouched, pulling back out onto the road.

"I don't know what you're talking about."

"Don't you give me that," he said, giving me a narrow-eyed look. "You did it in Vegas and then you did it in Monterey and LA too. Now you're doing it in Portland. I can't take you anywhere."

"Are you talking about the state of your fly? Because I'm not the one in control of your reactions to me, buddy. You are."

He barked out a laugh. "I've never been in control of my reactions to you. Not once."

"Is that why you married me? Because you were helpless against me?"

"You make me tremble in fear, rest assured." The smile he gave me made me tremble, and fear had nothing to do with it. "But I married you, Evelyn, because you made sense to me. We make sense. We're a whole lot better together than apart. You notice that?"

"Yeah, I really did."

"Good." His fingers stroked over my cheekbone. "We need to get home. Now."

I'm pretty sure he broke several speed limits on the drive. The condo was only a couple of blocks back from Ruby's café. It was located in a big old brown-brick building with Art Deco stonework surrounding the glass double doors. David punched in a code and led me into a white marble lobby. A statue of what looked like driftwood stood tall in the corner. Security cameras hid in the ceiling corners. He didn't give me time to look, rushing me through. I practically had to run to keep up with him.

"Come on," he said, tugging on my hand, drawing me into the elevator.

"This is all very impressive."

He pushed the button for the top floor. "Wait till you see our place. You're moving in with me now, right?"

"Right."

"Ah, we've got some visitors at the moment, by the way. Just while we record the album and all that. A few more weeks, probably." The elevator doors slid open and we stepped into the hall. At which point David took my handbag from me. Then he bent and set his shoulder to my stomach, lifting me high. "Here we are."

"Hey," I squeaked.

"I got you. Time to get carried over the threshold again."

"David, I'm wearing a skirt." It nearly went to my knees, but still. I'd rather not flash his guests and band members if I could avoid it.

"I know you are. Have I thanked you for that yet? I really appreciate having that easy access." His black boots thumped along the marble flooring. I took the opportunity to grope his ass because I was allowed to. My life was fucking fantastic like that.

"You're not wearing any underwear," I informed him.

"That so?"

A hand felt up my rear. Over my clothing, thankfully.

"You are," he said, voice low and growly in the best way possible. "Which ones you wearing, baby? Boy shorts by the feel."

"I don't think you've seen these."

"Yeah, well we're gonna change that real soon. Trust me."

"I do."

I heard the sound of a door opening, and the marble beneath me turned to a glossy, black-painted wooden floor. The walls were a pristine white. And I could hear male voices, laughing and trash-talking nearby. Music played in the background, Nine Inch Nails, I think. Nate had been playing his music at the apartment and they were a favorite of his. Of course the condo looked amazing. There were dark wooden dining room chairs and green couches. Plenty of space. Guitar cases were strewn about the place. From what I could see, it looked beautiful and lived in. It looked like a home.

Our home.

"You kidnapped a girl. That's awesome but illegal, Davie. You're probably going to have to give her back." My hair was lifted and Mal appeared, crouched beside me. "Hey there, child bride. Where's my hello kiss?"

"Leave my wife alone, you dickwad." David lifted one booted foot and negligently pushed him aside. "Go get your own."

"Why the fuck would I want to get married? That's for crazy folk like you two fine people. And while I applaud your insanity, no goddamn way am I following in your footsteps."

"Who the fuck would have him?" Jimmy's smoother voice moved up alongside me. "Hey, Ev."

"Hi, Jimmy." I took a hand off the seat of my husband's jeans and waved at him. "David, do I have to stay upside down?"

"Ah, right. It's date night," my husband announced.

"Got it," Mal said. "Come on, Jimmy. We'll go find Benny-boy. He was going to that Japanese place for a bite."

"Right." Jimmy's sneakers headed for the door. "Later, guys."

"Bye!" I gave him another wave.

"Night, Evvie." Mal left too, and the door slammed shut behind them.

"Alone at last." David sighed and started moving again, down a long hallway. With me still over his shoulder. "You like the place?"

"What I can see of it is lovely."

"That's good. I'll show you the rest later. First things first, I really need to get into those panties of yours."

"I don't think they'd fit you." I giggled. He slapped me on the ass. White-hot lightning, though it was more of a shock than anything. "Christ, David."

"Just warming you up, funny girl." He turned into the last room at the end of the hallway, kicked the door shut. My handbag was thrown into a chair. Without a word of warning, he upended me onto a king-size bed. My body bounced on the mattress. The blood was rushing around in my head, making it spin. I pushed my hair out of my face and rose up onto my elbows.

"Don't move," he said, voice guttural.

He stood at the end of the bed, undressing. The most amazing sight in existence. I could watch him do this always. He reached back and pulled off his shirt and I knew bone deep I wasn't the luckiest fucking girl in the world. I was the luckiest fucking girl in the entire universe. That was the truth. Not just because he was beyond beautiful and I was the only one that got to see him do this, but the way he watched me through hooded eyes the entire time. Lust was there, but also a whole lot of love.

"You have no idea how often I've imagined you lying on that bed in the last week." He pulled off his boots and socks, tossing them aside. "How many times I nearly called you in the last month."

"Why didn't you?"

"Why didn't you?" he asked, undoing the top button on his jeans

"Let's not do that again."

"No. Never." He crawled onto the bed, smoothing his hands down my calf muscles. My shoes went flying and his fingers slipped beneath my skirt, easing it up, higher and higher. Without breaking eye contact, he dragged down my boy shorts. He obviously wasn't interested in checking out my panties after all. The man had priorities. "Tell me you love me."

"I love you."

"Again."

"I love you."

"I missed the taste of you so fucking much." Big hands parted my legs, exposing me to his gaze. "I might just spend a few days with my head between your legs, all right?"

Oh, God. He rubbed his beard against my inner thigh, making my skin prickle with awareness. I couldn't speak if I tried.

"Say it again."

I swallowed hard, trying to get myself back under control.

"I'm waiting."

"I l-love you," I stuttered, my voice sounded barely there, breathy. My pelvis almost shot off the bed at the first touch of his mouth. Every bit of me was wound tight and trembling.

"Keep going." His tongue parted the lips of my sex, sliding between before delving within. The sweet, firm feel of his mouth and the ticklish sensation of his beard.

"I love you."

Strong hands slid beneath my ass, holding me to his mouth. "More."

I groaned out something. It must have been enough. He didn't stop or speak again. David attacked me. There was nothing easy about it. His mouth worked me hard, driving me sky-high in a matter of moments. The knot inside me tightened and grew as his tongue laved me. Electricity streaked up my spine. I don't know when I started shaking. But the strength went out of me and my back hit the mattress once again. I fisted my hands in his hair, fingers gripping at the short, gelled strands.

It was almost too much. I didn't know if I needed to get closer or get away. Either way, his hands held me to him. Every muscle in me tensed and my mouth opened on a soundless cry. Fireworks filled my mind. I came and came.

When my heart eased up on the hammering, I opened my eyes. David knelt between my legs. His jeans had been pushed down and his erection grazed his flat stomach. Dark blue eyes stared down at me.

"I can't wait."

"No. Don't." I tightened my legs around his hips. One of his hands remained beneath my ass, holding me high. With the other, he guided himself into me. He didn't rush. We were both still at least half dressed, him on the bottom and me on the top. There was no time to waste. We were too needy to wait and do this skin to skin. Next time.

He entered me so slowly I couldn't breathe. The only thing that mattered was feeling. And God, the feel of him thick and hard pushing inside of me. The perspiration on his bare chest gleamed in the low lighting. The muscles in his shoulders stood out in stark relief as he began to move.

"Mine," he said.

I could only nod.

He looked down on me, watching my breasts jiggle beneath my top with each thrust. Fingers gripped my hips hard. Mine clutched at the bedding, trying to find purchase so I could push back against him. His expression was wild, mouth swollen and wet. Only this was real, me and him together. Everything else could come and go. I'd found what was worth fighting for.

"I love you."

"C'mere." He picked me up off the mattress, holding me tight again him. My legs were braced around his waist, muscles burning from how hard I'd been holding on. I wound my arms around his neck as he sat me on his cock.

"I love you too." His hands slid beneath the back of my top. We moved harshly together. Our furious breaths mingled into one. Sweat slicked both our skins, the fabric of my shirt sticking to me. The heat gathered low inside me again. It didn't take long in this position. Not with the way he ground himself against me. His mouth sucked at the section of skin where my neck met my body, and I shuddered in his arms, coming again. The noises he made and the way he said my name . . . I never wanted to forget. Not a moment of it.

Eventually, he laid us both back on the bed. I wasn't willing to let him go, so he covered my body with his. The weight of him pressing me down into the bed, the feel of his mouth on the side of my face. We should never move. In the best-case scenario, we'd just stay like this forever.

But actually, I did have something I had to do.

"I need my bag," I said, squirming beneath him.

"What for?" He rose up on his elbows.

"I have to do something."

"What could be more important than this?"

"Roll over," I said, already urging him in that direction.

"All right. But this had better be good." He relaxed and let me roll him. I scampered across the mattress, trying to tug my skirt back down at the same time. David must have liked what he saw, because he came after me with snapping teeth.

"Get back here, wife," he ordered.

"Give me a second."

"My name looks good on your ass," he said. "The tattoo has healed very nicely."

"Well, thank you." I finally got off the mattress and set my pencil skirt to rights. In the month we'd been apart, I'd ignored my ink. But now, I was glad it was there.

"That skirt's coming off."

"Just wait."

"And that top. We have a lot more making up to do."

"Yes, in a minute. I've missed my topless cuddles."

He'd dumped my bag on a blue velvet wing-back chair by the door. Whoever had decorated the condo had done a hell of a job. It was beautiful. But I'd check it out later. Right now I had something important to do.

"I bought you a present today, after we talked at the studio."

"Did you, now?"

I nodded, searching my bag for the treasure. Bingo. The fancy little box was right where I'd left it. With it hidden in my hand, I walked back to him, a wide smile on my face. "Yes, I did."

"What have you got in your hand?" He climbed off the bed. Unlike me, he stripped off his jeans. My husband stood before me naked and perfectly disheveled. He looked at me like I was everything. As long as I lived, I knew I wouldn't want anyone else.

"Evelyn?"

For some reason I felt suddenly shy, awkward. Any money, the tips of my ears glowed bright pink.

"Give me your left hand." I reached for his hand and he

gave it to me. Carefully I slid on the thick platinum band I'd blown my savings on that afternoon, working it past his big knuckle. Perfect. I'd walk all winter and freeze my ass off, happily. David meant more to me than replacing my crappy old car. Given the money I now owed my parents, the timing wasn't brilliant. But this was more important.

Except the ring covered half of the second-to-last *E* on his *Live Free* tattoo. Shit, I hadn't thought of that. He probably wasn't going to want to wear it.

"Thank you."

My gaze darted to his face, trying to judge his sincerity. "You like it?"

"I fucking love it."

"Really? Because I forgot about your ink, but— "

He shut me up by kissing me. I kind of liked his new habit of doing that. His tongue stroked into my mouth and my eyes slid shut, every worry forgotten. He kissed me until not a single doubt remained as to how taken with his ring he was. Fingers fussed with the buttons on my top, slipping it off my shoulders. Next the band on my bra loosened.

"I love my ring," he said, his lips traveling over my jaw and down my neck. My bra straps slid down my arms and my breasts were free. Next he started in on my skirt, wrestling with the zip and pushing it down over my hips. He didn't stop until I was every bit as bare as him. "I'm never taking it off."

"I'm glad you like it."

"I do. And I need to get you naked right now and show you how much I like it. But then I'll give you back your ring. I promise."

"No rush," I murmured, arching my neck to give him better access. "We've got forever."

CHAPTER TWENTY-TWO

We'd planned to meet Amanda, Jo, and a few other friends at one of the local bars the next night. My insides were in a permanent state of upheaval. Excited and nervous and a hundred other emotions I couldn't begin to process. But not doubtful. Never that. I'd talked to Ruby about continuing on with the extra shifts at the café and she'd been delighted. It turned out her distraction the previous day had been on account of her finding out she was pregnant. My dropping out of college couldn't come at a better time as far as she was concerned. Eventually I'd go back to school. I liked the idea of teaching, maybe. I don't know. There was time.

The bar was one of the smaller ones, not far from our new home. A four-piece rock band on the small corner stage played grunge classics interspersed with a few new songs. Jo waved us over to a table out of the way. Meeting David was obviously big for her. Puppies jumped less.

"David. It's so great," she said over and over. That was about it. If she started to hump his leg, I was stepping in.

Amanda, on the other hand, needed to turn that frown upside down. At least, unlike my parents', her protest was silent. I appreciated her concern, but she'd just have to get used to David being around.

David ordered drinks for us and settled into a seat pulled up beside me. The music was really too loud for conversation. Soon afterward, Nate and Lauren arrived. A fragile peace had emerged between my brother and my husband, for which I was profoundly grateful.

David shuffled closer. "I wanna ask you something."

"What?"

He slipped a hand around my waist, drawing me closer. I did the job better by simply planting myself in his lap. With a warm smile, his arms wound around me, holding me tight. "Hey."

"Hey," I said. "What did you want to ask me?"

"I was wondering . . . would you like to hear one of the songs I wrote for you?"

"Really? I'd love to."

"Excellent," he said, his hand smoothing over the back of my simple black dress. Worn because it was his favorite color, of course. Also, I'd strongly suspected the V-neck would appeal to him. Tonight, I was all about pleasing my husband. There'd no doubt be times in the future when we needed to kick each other's asses, but not tonight. We were here to celebrate.

Lauren led Nate out onto the dance floor and Amanda and Jo followed, abandoning us to our private talk. I honest to God had the best brother and friends in the whole wide world. All of them had taken the news of the plan going boom with calm faces. They had hugged me, and not one word of doubt over my sudden change in direction had been voiced. When Lauren recounted her version of how David stood beside me at dinner, I'd caught Amanda giving him a nod of approval. It gave me great hope.

I'd even called my mother earlier. The conversation had been brief, but I was glad I had. We were still family.

David had eventually given me my ring back the night before. Turned out his list of things to do to me was long. He fed me ice cream in bed for breakfast while the sun rose. Best night ever.

It felt right having the ring back on my hand. The weight and fit of it were perfect. As promised, his own had stayed put. He'd been proudly showing it to his brother when I'd stumbled out in search of coffee at midday. Once I'd been caffeinated, David and Jimmy had moved me into the condo. Mal and Ben had been busy at the studio. Nate and Lauren had helped move me too, once David and Jimmy finished signing everything Divers-related she could find. Despite her protestations that she'd miss me, I think she was also looking forward to having the apartment for her and Nate alone. They were good together.

"I've got something else I want to ask you too," he said.

"The answer is yes to everything and anything with you."

"Good, because I want you to come work for me as my assistant. When you're not working at the café, I mean." His hand rubbed down my back. "'Cause I know you wanna do that."

"David . . ."

"Or you could just let me pay the college money back to your parents so that's not hanging over your head."

"No," I said, my voice determined. "Thank you. But I need to do that. And I think my parents are going to need to see me doing that."

"That's what I figured you'd say. But that's a lot of money for you to make, baby. If you take a second job we're never going to see each other."

"You're right. But do you think that's a wise idea, us working together?"

"Yeah," he told me, blue eyes serious. "You like organizing and that's what I need. It's a real job and I want you for it. If we find it starts to interfere with us, then we'll make a new plan. But I think mostly it'll just mean we spend more time together and have sex at work."

I laughed. "You promising to sexually harass me, Mr. Ferris?"

"Absolutely, Mrs. Ferris."

I kissed him soundly on the cheek. "Thank you for thinking of it. I'd love to work for you."

"If you decide to go back to college, then I'll get Adrian to find me a replacement. Not a big deal." He pulled me in against his chest. "But in the meantime, we're good."

"Best plan ever."

"Why, thank you. Coming from you, that means a lot."

David's gaze wandered over to the bar where Mal, Jimmy, and Ben were hanging out, keeping a low profile. I hadn't known they were joining us tonight. Jimmy had been steering clear of clubs and bars. "About time they got here," he murmured.

Next David turned to the band, rocking out in the corner. They were just in the process of winding up a solid rendition of a Pearl Jam classic.

"Wait here." David rose, taking me with him. He placed me back on the chair and signaled to his bandmates. Then he made his way toward the stage. His tall figure moved through the crowd with ease and the guys fell in behind him. En masse, they were pretty damn impressive. No matter how low-key they were trying to be. But I got the distinct feeling they were about to make their presence known. Once the band finished the song, David called the singer over. Holy shit. This was it. I bounced in my chair from excitement.

They talked for a moment, then the singer brought the

guitarist into it. Sure enough, the man gave his six-string over to David's waiting hands. I could see the look of surprise on both their faces as David's identity finally sank in. Jimmy gave the singer a nod and stepped up onto the platform. Behind him, Mal was already high-fiving the drummer and stealing his sticks. Even grim Ben smiled as he accepted the bass guitar from its original owner. The Divers took to the stage. Few in the bar seemed to realize quite what was going on yet.

"Hi. Sorry to interrupt, folks. My name's David Ferris and I'd like to play a song for my wife, Evelyn. Hope you don't mind."

Stunned silence broke out into thunderous applause. David stared at me across the sea of people as everyone swamped the dance floor to get closer.

"She's a Portland girl. So I guess that makes us in-laws. Be gentle with me, yeah?"

The crowd went batshit crazy in response. His hands moved over the strings, making the sweetest mix of rock and country music possible. Then he started to sing. Jimmy joined him for the chorus, their voices melding beautifully.

I thought I could let you go
I thought that you could leave and know
The time we took would fade
But I'm colder than the bed where we lay

You let go if you like, I'll hold on
Say no all you want, I'm not done
Baby, I promise you

Did you think I'd let you go?
That's never happening and now you know

Take your time, I'll wait
Regretting every last thing I said

The song was simple, sweet, and perfect. And the noise when they finished was deafening. People shouted and stamped their feet. It sounded like the roof was coming down on us. Security helped David and the guys move through the crush of people. More had arrived as they performed, alerted to the show by texts and calls and each and every sort of social media. A tidal wave of fans swamped them as they pressed through. A hand wrapped around my arm. I looked up to find Sam beside me with a grin on his face. We got our asses out of there pronto.

Sam and the security men cleared a path for us to the door and the waiting limousine outside. They were well prepared. We all bundled into the back of the limo. Immediately, David pulled me onto his lap. "Sam's going to make sure your friends are okay."

"Thank you. I think Portland knows you're here now."

"Yeah, I think you're right."

"Davie, you are a fucking show pony," Mal said, shaking his head. "I knew you were going to pull something like this. Guitarists are such a bunch of posers. If you had an ounce of sense, young lady, you'd have married a drummer."

I laughed and wiped the tears from my face.

"Why the fuck is she crying, what did you say to her?" David pulled me in closer. Outside people banged on the windows as the car slowly started moving forward.

"Are you okay?"

"I told her the truth, that she should have married a drummer. Impromptu fucking performances!" said Mal.

"Shut up."

"Like you've never gone all out to impress a girl," scoffed Ben.

"What happened in Tokyo?" asked Jimmy, reclining in the corner. "Remind me again about, ah . . . what was her name?"

"Oh shit, yeah. The chick from the restaurant," said Ben. "How much did they charge you for the damages, again?"

"I don't even know what you're talking about. Davie said to shut up," shouted Mal above the pair's raucous laughter. "Have some respect for his touching moment with Evelyn, you assholes."

"Ignore them." David cupped my face in the palm of his hand. "Why were you crying, hmm?"

"Because this is ten. If one was us being miserable and apart, then ten is your song. It's beautiful."

"You really liked it? 'Cause I can take it if you didn't, you don't have—"

I grabbed his face and kissed him, ignoring the noise and heckling around us. And I didn't stop kissing him until my lips were numb and swollen and so were his.

"Baby." He smiled, wiping away the last of my tears. "You say the best fucking things."